"Let me show you how to dance."

"I should not stay." Her eyes told him a far different story, however. She had an untamed nature that called to him on the most primal level.

"Wait." His fingertips reached out to curl lightly over hers. Gently, he steered her forward to begin their steps, the song wrapping them in the moment. When at last she looked up at him, a smile lit her face.

Heartbeats passed before he realized the song had faded. They stood frozen in the moonlight, their breathing evenly matched. "Shall I deliver you back to the keep?"

"Only if you promise to safeguard our encounter as a secret. I would not have my princess think that I am a wayward lady."

"If I protect your secret, you must agree to keep mine."

"I know nothing of you to keep quiet about."

"You must never tell anyone about this...."

Lowering his mouth to hers, he brushed a kiss across her lips.

* * *

A Knight Most Wicked
Harlequin® Historical #890—March 2008

✤ A Knight Most Wicked ✤

Joanne Rock

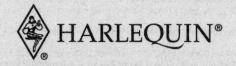

HARLEQUIN®

TORONTO • NEW YORK • LONDON
AMSTERDAM • PARIS • SYDNEY • HAMBURG
STOCKHOLM • ATHENS • TOKYO • MILAN • MADRID
PRAGUE • WARSAW • BUDAPEST • AUCKLAND

ISBN-13: 978-0-373-29490-9
ISBN-10:   0-373-29490-5

A KNIGHT MOST WICKED

DON'T MISS THESE OTHER
NOVELS AVAILABLE NOW:

#887 TAMING THE TEXAN—Charlene Sands

Clint Hayworth wants revenge—and he'll be damned if he'll allow his father's conniving, gold-digging widow to take over the family ranch! But something about her is getting under his skin....
This is one Texan in real need of taming—
and Tess is just the woman for the job!

#888 HIGH SEAS TO HIGH SOCIETY—Sophia James

Her ill-fitting, threadbare clothes concealed the body of an angel, but what kind of woman truly lay behind her refined mask? Highborn lady or artful courtesan, she intrigued him— and Asher wanted to possess both!
Let Sophia James sweep you away to adventure
and high-society romance.

#889 PICKPOCKET COUNTESS—Bronwyn Scott

Robbing from the rich to give to the poor, Nora may have taken more than she expected when she stole the earl's heart!
Sexy and intriguing, Bronwyn Scott's debut book heralds
an author to watch.

This book is dedicated with love to Katie Sue Morgan, my friend and mentor who guided me into a writers' group when I found myself alone and new in town upon arrival in Shreveport, Louisiana. Thank you, Sue, not only for finding me a romance writers' chapter to join, but for your immediate invitation to lunch two days after my first phone call. I've never been so grateful for a reprieve from unpacking boxes! Your generous spirit, your nurturing strength and your creative eye helped me take my work seriously as a writer and nudged me down a path that has given me so much joy.

Prologue

Bohemia
Autumn 1381

Arabella Rowan darted into the safety of the woods and forced herself to be still, eyes fixed on her mother's cottage in the open meadow beyond. Five horses bearing the king's standard were tethered near the door, stomping and snorting in the late afternoon air.

Men.

Arabella knew better than to approach her home if there were men within the walls. The rule had been clear all her life, though it had been stressed more since the arrival of her monthly courses some seven summers ago. Whether peasant or noble, men could pose a threat to a household of women living alone.

When the planked door swung open, five massive knights garbed in silks and velvets trooped out to their impatient mounts.

Arabella waited in the forest as the king's men tore out of sight in a cloud of dust. After she dared to breathe a sigh of relief, curiosity consumed her. Barefoot despite the chill of the earth, she ran up the grassy hill to the stone cottage. She burst through the front door, almost tripping on the top step.

"What happened? What did those men—"

Her voice trailed off as she noted the mood in the cottage. Her mother and grandmother huddled together in hushed conversation. Lines of worry added somber age to their expressions.

"What is it?" Sinking onto a wooden chair in the cool open area that served as both kitchen and hall, Arabella set her herb-gathering basket at her feet and pushed tangled locks from her forehead. Anxiety gnawed at her belly far more than a hunger for supper.

Zaharia walked toward her granddaughter. "You are to make a journey, Arabella. The king wishes to send you with the princess."

It could not be true. Her vision swam as her eyesight blurred, her mind reeling. Even in the farthermost outskirts of the Bohemian highlands, everyone knew the princess had agreed to wed a foreign king in a far-off land. Wordlessly, Arabella looked to her mother for confirmation, despite knowing her grandmother's dictate would be final in this as in so many things.

Arabella's mother buried her face in her hands, but not before a muffled sob escaped. Arabella's heart skipped a frightened beat.

"You know your duty, Bella." Grandmother Zaharia looked at her with stern green eyes, her long white hair tamed in a heavy knot at her nape, and sat down on the bench beside Arabella. "When the king sends Princess Anne to marry the young English king, you will join her as a lady-in-waiting."

She knew little of the world, yet she'd heard talk of the constraints placed on women on the remote island. It sounded so different from the wild freedom of her Bohemian hills.

"I do not understand. I thought women abounded at court in Prague. My place should be at your side as it has always been, learning the healing arts." Surely if she battled her grandmother's decision with dedication to the wise woman's craft, Zaharia would bend. Hadn't her grandmother always told her that a healer's blood ran in her veins?

"Apparently, King Wenceslas is gathering an unusually large retinue to accompany Anne. He wants her arrival to appear impressive to the English people, as her husband is accepting her without a dowry."

"But I am no lady-in-waiting. I am not capable of making anyone look impressive." She extended her bare foot as proof, while desperation knotted her stomach. If she left the country, would she ever see her family again? She might never complete her work as Grandmother's apprentice, never gather herbs again nor thrill to the discovery of a new healing tincture. "We have never lived as nobility. I might shame us all."

"Nevertheless, you are as noble as anyone at court, despite our lack of wealth." Grandmother Zaharia lifted a parchment scroll hidden in the folds of her gown and read from it. "'The presence of Lady Arabella Rowan, daughter of Sir Charles Vallia and Lady Luria Rowan, is requested in Prague next week.'"

"But my father has never acknowledged me." The fact had never bothered her overmuch. Her life was happier than that of many other people she knew. Still, if her estrangement from her father would aid her in her cause, she had to remark upon it.

"Do not mention your father in your travels, my dear." Zaharia's voice was unusually sharp. "Your heritage is far more important than you think, but it is a family matter."

Even Arabella's mother peered up at her through her tears to echo the sentiment. "Say nothing of your past, Arabella. The royal family knows who you are and there is no need to defend yourself against anyone else's whispered rumor."

Confused, Arabella wondered about her father for the first time in a long time. She had never met the nobleman rumored to have broken her mother's heart, but she suspected he sometimes met with her mother in secret. Perhaps that was one of the reasons the Rowan women remained wary of men. But Zaharia had already moved on to speak of other things.

"You must pack tomorrow so that you will arrive in Prague with enough time to prepare for the journey, my sweet girl. You have no choice but to leave us."

Arabella did not believe her ears. She felt as if the wind had been knocked out of her. Stricken. Aching.

She gasped for breath in the close air of the cottage. She needed to escape. To race the autumn winds and feel the earth beneath her feet.

Zaharia reached to embrace her. "Be strong, Arabella. Show your countrymen that Rowan blood runs as fierce as any knight's."

"How can I leave everything I've ever known to become someone I am not? How will I fulfill the legacy you have foretold would be mine?" She admired her grandmother's stature as a healer and had imagined her own arts might warrant such respect one day.

"You cannot be a wise woman without seeing something of the world, Bella. I have always known a day would come that would call you to your fate and give you the wisdom you need added to what I have taught you." Her words were soft and soothing, yet somehow rock solid at the same time. It was the tone she'd used to teach Arabella everything she knew about healing. "Think of your honor. Think of your family's honor. You will fulfill this obligation and return home. It is not as if you will have to remain in England forever."

Something about Zaharia's mention of "England" and "forever" in the same breath filled Arabella with hot frustration, forcing her feet toward the door. It was all too much, too fast, and she feared she would shame herself by shouting her fury to the heavens in front of her family. She needed to flee before that happened.

"I will be strong," she assured her grandmother, spine straight though her eyes burned at the thought of her fate slipping from her hands. "Somehow."

"Arabella." Luria rose to keep her daughter from bolting, but Zaharia held her back.

Zaharia's words of reassurance echoed in Arabella's

ears as her feet flew down the dusty path, each step of this lonely last run reminding her that her moments as a free woman were quickly disappearing.

Chapter One

"We'll stop here," Tristan Carlisle called as he reined in his horse and flung himself from the black destrier so his company might rest for the night.

He cursed his trip, even as he savored this last stop before he reached Prague and the squawking women awaiting him—the largest retinue ever to accompany a princess for her nuptials. A bloody dubious honor for a warrior.

"Escort," he muttered, disgusted by the very sound of the word. Fifteen years in service to kings of England, and this was the mission his hard work had earned?

England's war with France raged while he was sent on a courtier's assignment. Did they think his sword arm grew weak? He could fight better than half of Richard's hasty-witted front line with his dagger alone, since most of the young king's men were naught but beslubbering babes who'd seen little combat.

Richard had made excuses about the importance of his bride's protection and a recent threat to the Bohemian court. But the quest—and the king's concern—sounded a bit hollow to Tristan, despite Richard's promise of long-overdue lands in exchange for Tristan's success.

The black horse snorted as it slaked its thirst, echoing Tristan's opinion.

"I couldn't agree more, friend. No warrior in his right mind should accept a courtier's job, and yet here we are. Roaming our tired arses across this fair land with naught but a bastard's lot in life by way of royal appreciation. If Richard fails to come through with lands this time…" Snort, indeed. Tristan would be looking into a mercenary's life if the king did not recognize his efforts after this.

"Tris?" His friend Simon Percival called to him from a few feet away. The presence of Simon on the journey—a knight almost as ancient as Tristan at thirty summers—was one of the few circumstances that made the endless journey bearable. "Should we stop here for the night, or do you wish to ride farther? We can arrive in Prague tomorrow if we pick up speed."

"I am in no hurry. Tell the men to unload and I'll search the area." Needing to clear his resentful head so he might fulfill his duty, he vaulted back onto his horse.

Tristan worked with slow caution to secure the encampment as twilight approached. The solitude of the land suited his mood. The dark woods gave way to rolling hills, providing plenty of cover for foreign knights on strange terrain.

As the sounds of his men quieted in the last purple light of day, he heard a distinct cry from deeper in the forest.

He paused, reasonably sure the noise came from an

animal but waiting to be certain. Although he seemed to be in the middle of remote country, perhaps a road wound nearby and some hapless traveler had met with thieves. When the cry came again, Tristan still questioned whether it was animal or human, but it sounded too tortured to ignore.

Sliding from his horse, he stalked toward the sound. When it became continuous, he hastened his step until he reached a clearing with a perfect circle of aged oaks in the middle. The noise emanated from within that ring, but in the falling twilight he could not clearly make out a form. He was fairly certain there were no animals fighting here, nor could he see any horses or thieves.

Moving forward, he gained ground until he touched one of the old oaks.

The cries stopped.

A figure stirred within the ring of trees.

Squinting, Tristan recognized the shape of a young woman…or was it?

Half-reclining on the ground, the woman wore garments that belonged to neither a peasant nor a lady. Her long dress had a full skirt—he could see it floating all about her legs on the ground—but it was not long enough to hide her bare feet. She was covered from head to toe with small twigs and pine needles.

And her hair…

It called to mind a fey witch or fairy in a child's tale. Thick waves cloaked her upper body in the same way her long dress covered the lower half. The dark tresses reached her waist and looked unaccustomed to the rigors of a comb.

Surely he dreamed.

No woman would be in the middle of the wilderness like this. Yet, she appeared to belong in the woods—wild and uncivilized. An unearthly beauty about her made him wonder if he'd been bewitched.

Her strange appearance in the ancient circle of trees where no superstitious mortal would dare tread supported that conclusion. And before her abrupt silence, she had wailed with pagan fury to the unyielding oaks.

Tristan yearned to satisfy himself that she was real. Softly he approached her, spellbound by the strangeness of the vision.

For a moment, the woman did not move. She seemed frozen, peering into Tristan's eyes and searching his face. Tristan was so close that he caught a vague scent of her, could see the heavy rise and fall of her breasts, discern the damp trail of tears down dirt-smudged cheeks. Still not convinced she could possibly be real, Tristan lifted his hand to touch her. In one swift, soundless movement, the green-eyed wench sprang to her feet and ran.

"Sit still, Arabella."

By now the gentlewoman's command sounded like a threat, and Arabella forced herself to cease her restless wriggling on the velvet-covered bench inside the Prague home of the king. She had been sitting still—mostly still—for the last hour while the matron of the royal retinue pinched, pulled and poked in an effort to fit her with an appropriate traveling gown for the journey to England. Five other young women stood or sat quietly for their maids in the upstairs chamber that had served as home to Arabella and several other noblewomen from far-flung parts of Bohemia for the past few nights.

Yet Lady Hilda grumbled as she worked.

"Merciful heaven help us, you look as fit to join a royal entourage as a wildcat."

"Pay her no heed, Lady Arabella," a girlish voice whispered at Arabella's elbow. "You are a wonderful addition to our company."

Mary Natansia, Arabella's lone friend since she had arrived in Prague, squeezed her hand as the two of them suffered the none-too-gentle hands of Tryant Hilda, a distant relative of the princess with enough titles to give her freedom to speak her mind.

Arabella's brief education in the noble world had already taught her that much. Titles made women invincible here. Their power did not come from herbs and knowledge, or even saving lives.

"Thank you." She smiled back at the delicate blonde with skin so fair Hilda remarked glowingly upon it.

A quiet girl of eighteen summers, Mary was King Wenceslas IV's ward, a position of great prestige since the Bohemian king also served as the Holy Roman Emperor. Although Arabella gathered the younger woman was wealthy enough to rule the glittering court life of Prague, Mary shied away from it. After arriving in the city three days ago, Arabella had been consumed with preparations for the upcoming journey to England. She had worked on a few of her own surcoats under the careful tutelage of the princess's maids. She had been advised what was expected of her on the journey. But she had not ventured out of the women's apartments for long, and tonight would be her first formal supper at Prague Castle.

She was nervous since her old formal surcoat had appeared like peasant's garb next to the rich attire of the women who greeted her politely, then dismissed her with their gazes. It did not help that she had arrived at the castle's gate with her grandmother. Zaharia was a wise and gifted woman, but the superstitious called her a sorceress.

Mary Natansia, however, did not hold Arabella's family or less exalted appearance against her.

"There," Hilda announced, smiling with satisfaction at having finished her work. "I will render you present-able whether you like it or not." Pointing a long pin as if it were a sword, she threatened her wayward charge while she waved over a younger maid. "Now, Millie will assist you with your hair for the celebration this eve."

Submitting to the dressing and the brushing provided to ladies-in-waiting without their own maids, Arabella allowed her mind to wander with the rhythmic strokes of the silken brush.

The visage of the knight appeared in her mind's eye, the way it had so many other times during the past sennight since she had first seen him.

The knight had been brazen to walk so close to the circle of trees some called enchanted. No one of Arabella's acquaintance, aside from her family, would stray near such a place.

And no man had ever dared to look upon her so boldly. For that matter, she had hardly ever met a man's eyes directly until that day. Her mother worried about the motives of strange men after Luria's experience with Arabella's father, who could not be forced to wed the mother of his only heir.

The men of her homeland feared and respected Zaharia, so they avoided her granddaughter out of deference to the wise woman. But the knightly stranger had not only stared at her, he had shamelessly extended his hand to touch her.

His reaching out to her had been compelling…in those moments before her sense had returned. His presence had been impressive. Large and looming with gray eyes. His whole countenance had a rather fearsome element about it, with the predatory eye of a wolf.

She had run her fastest to elude that gaze and the touch that went with it. When she finally paused to discern his whereabouts, the forest remained silent as death. No one followed her. The stranger had vanished as quickly as he had appeared. Yet the moon had trekked halfway across the sky before Arabella stopped trembling. She realized she had grown up too isolated by half, if a stranger could frighten her thus. Who would ever call Arabella wise, like her grandmother, when she fled life like a craven minnow?

"All finished, my lady," Millie proclaimed finally, drawing Arabella to her feet. She and Hilda stood side by side, wreathed in smiles, until Hilda tugged Arabella's arm.

"Come and look in the glass, Arabella, and try to appreciate what magic we have wrought."

Hilda prodded her to a looking glass mounted inside a trunk that had been carted into the room for the day.

Curious, Arabella glanced into it. The startled figure who stared back at her bore little resemblance to the young woman she'd seen reflected in the stream that pooled near her home.

Gone were the unruly tresses that her mother once snipped off in frustration. They were replaced by silken waves that shone even in the dull glass. She reached to touch them until Hilda and Millie both lurched forward as if to intervene.

Dutifully returning her hands to her sides, she took in the crisp white linen kirtle topped with a cotehardie of royal-blue velvet, a color so deep and expensive none wore it but those of an exalted station. Tonight, that would be her. Her flat slippers were barely noticeable beneath her long skirts, but when they peeped out from underneath, they matched her velvet skirts.

Arabella wondered where her former untamed self had gone, now that this refined creature had taken her place.

As if sensing her thoughts, Hilda winked and gently turned her toward the door.

"I trust your manners will be inspired by the beauty of your appearance. Pray, do not disrupt our hard work too soon."

Turned loose to find her way to the great hall, Arabella felt every bit as lost here tonight as she had imagined she might in those final nights on her bed at home. But before she could become fully confused in the maze of corridors leading to the hall, Mary caught up with her, her pale hair tied with a sky-blue ribbon like an angel in one of the castle's religious paintings.

"This way," she called, gesturing in the opposite direction and then steering them down corridors growing more populated. The swell of music reached their ears as they neared the great hall. "Do not be nervous, Arabella. The feeling dissipates once you get through the door."

Arabella halted in her pretty slippers, adrift in this world that had hurt her mother deeply with false faces and false promises. Would Arabella be as susceptible to its beautiful cunning?

"Mary." She turned toward her new friend, trusting this one woman if no one else. "Perhaps you can guide me on one more matter, since I know nothing of men. I have no father. No brother. I have scarcely conversed with any male. Are we expected to…talk to them at an event such as this?"

Staring back at her with intent eyes, Mary said nothing for a long moment, but Arabella was only too glad to delay her entry into the hall as long as possible. Finally, Mary blinked.

"You're serious."

"Yes." Reflexively, she reached for a little knife she normally kept at her waist, only to remember she had lost it that day in the woods she'd met the strange knight. It had been a talisman from her grandmother. Arabella sorely missed the small charm that was the tool of a wise woman's herbal craft, especially when she needed the comfort of something familiar.

"You really did grow up in the forest, didn't you?" Mary's voice possessed a childlike wonder that made Arabella feel a bit stronger for having been raised by the region's most revered wise woman.

"I have never denied it. I do not look at it as a defect, the way the court does."

"Nor do I, Arabella, I promise you. Your life sounds wonderful to me. But truly, men are not so ill behaved, at least not around me." She laughed and her eyes took on a mischievous light. "There are advantages to being the emperor's ward. Remain at my side, and we will face the men you meet together."

"Together." It sounded simple enough. And, although her mother always talked about men as if they were dangerous creatures, Arabella had often wondered if Lady Luria had merely had the misfortune of meeting a poor example.

Arabella's father.

The lilting strains of the music drifted through the corridor, reminding them of their duty while other ladies-in-waiting passed by them in soft *swishes* of velvet and linen.

"You will be fine," Mary assured her, tugging her through the huge doors and into the extravagant hall.

Vaulted ceilings and narrow wooden arches supported the cavernous stone chamber, which vibrated with the din of humanity. Bright silks dazzled her, while torches lit walls filled with colorful tapestries and paintings etched with a metallic sheen that looked like gold.

A woman greeted Mary, who was well-known because of her position, despite her usual lack of presence at court. Arabella smiled, but used the time to study the vast chamber and the people within the walls.

Her attention moved slowly over each individual, fascinated by every detail of the lavish gathering. She admired the precious gems decorating the women's garments, the fur-lined cloaks of the men, the more austere dress of one man in particular….

Her heart caught in her throat.

There could be no mistaking the knight who had seen her crying in the woods. If crying it could be called, given how she had howled out her frustration.

The sight of him had a peculiar effect on her. She had experienced the same strange sensation the first time she had spied the man. This rush of blood through her veins hinted of a nervousness midway between fear and…anticipation?

She swallowed the uncomfortable thought and attempted to study the knight without him seeing her in return—a feat that did not prove difficult, since the man seemed engrossed in conversation with another dressed in similarly dark garb.

Foreigners.

The realization surprised her, for she had not understood as much the first time she'd encountered him. Unlike most of the men in the great hall, his hair was long, just beyond his shoulders, and dark as a new moon night. His large frame cleared a path through the crowded room as celebrants scurried out of his way. Arabella could not see his face now, but she remembered those piercing gray eyes all too well.

What was he doing here?

As if suddenly sensing her scrutiny, he turned and met her stare.

She held her breath, praying he would not ruin her already dubious reputation by revealing their encounter in the forest. Arabella knew now that most young gentlewomen did not wander about the woods by themselves. While she did not deny her untraditional heritage, neither did she wish to draw undue attention to herself as the granddaughter of a famed healer. Zaharia had urged her to remain on the fringes of the court.

His eyes narrowed and her chest constricted in answer. He betrayed no sign that he knew her, but abruptly turned and headed in her direction.

"Excuse me," Arabella mumbled, uncertain of her next move as she hurried away from the approaching knight, away from being anyone's center of attention.

People peered at her strangely as she hastened through the crowd, searching for safety from him, from recognition as a wild child of the forest. Her mother had warned her that court life could be merciless in its judgment of anyone different.

Reaching the back of the room, she turned to be sure he was gone. Unfortunately, he strode only a few steps behind her, yet he did not seem to see her at that precise moment.

A short corridor led from the back of the hall toward a series of doors. Arabella tested one of the handles, checking that he did not see her, and entered the room.

Safe.

Closing the door softly, she perceived the outline of furnishings in a small chamber, a masculine domain with a sturdy horn pitcher and heavy bone cups atop a sideboard. Wondering how long she could hide from the festivities, she wandered about to see a small stack of leather-bound books and a high window of Bohemia's famed colored glass. Her heartbeat had just returned to normal when a noise across the chamber caused her to jump.

The latch lifted behind her.

Chapter Two

"Can this wait? Our host is calling us to sup, Tris."

Tristan shook his head and led Simon into the small study. The din of the hall had grown tiresome, with arrogant nobles working too hard to impress their English guests and beautiful women disappearing into thin air. One beautiful woman, anyhow. Tristan could not stand the company much longer—especially when the lone female to capture his interest this eve obviously wanted no part of him.

Why had she looked familiar? He knew no one in this land. Yet she had escaped before he could speak to her.

"No, it cannot wait." He shut the door behind them, sealing out the minstrels' music and the noise. "We need to discover the extent of the threat against the royal retinue before we leave Prague Castle. If the nobles or the princess are at risk in any way, the situation has my immediate attention."

Turning to take a seat on the wooden table in the center of the room, Tristan swore he caught a woman's scent in the air. An odd thought in a dark haven that surely belonged to a man. A tapestry depicting a hunting party and a fleeing stag adorned the lone wall that did not contain stacks of books.

"While we remain in Bohemia, is it not the king's problem? Or the emperor's?" Simon sank onto a small bench. "Surely Prague has knights to protect their people while we are on their soil."

"But apparently two noblewomen have disappeared in the last fortnight and the king has done naught to discover what happened to them. Aside from all the ways that is disturbing, do you know how many women we will have to protect on our journey back home?" Tristan needed Simon's support in this, as their duty grew more demanding each day.

Tristan might be in charge, but they were more kin than fellow knights. Mutual orphans left in the hands of an abusive guardian, they'd forged a friendship in shared pain. They'd deserted their guardian to join Edward the Black Prince's army when they'd been scarcely old enough to swing a sword. That knight had found places for them, restored their sense of honor.

For that, Tristan owed the royal family everything, even though Edward had been dead these last four years. His son, King Richard, was but a boy and his reign had encountered enough trouble that his counselors thought a wife was in order.

"You really think this problem will follow us?" Simon steepled his fingers and leaned his chin onto the point.

"I wish to be prepared for anything. Let us relate the

incidents to the men and ask them to learn all they can about the missing women."

"Mayhap they merely ran off and left their husbands." Simon leaned back onto the stone wall behind him and plucked up an empty inkwell.

"Faithless though they might be, women rarely leave the security of respected court positions for lovers with little to offer them." Tristan knew well the potential treachery of the fair sex.

"Still, I will at least find out if that is why the Bohemian nobles are not searching more actively."

Musical feminine laughter floated through the closed door and Tristan wondered how he would manage the long journey back to England in a retinue where women far outnumbered men. He had seen women execute more cunning schemes of entrapment than he had ever witnessed on the battlefield. Long ago, he had been foolish enough to be lured in by a great beauty. The perfume had gone straight to his head.

"Good. We will see our troop safely home with every last woman intact." Tristan moved to the door, ready to rejoin the Bohemian court now that he'd given orders to heighten security. "I will not allow anyone's disappearance to besmirch our standing in London."

"Aye." Simon nodded, rising from his bench. "But what do you think of Prague after our long lament over having to make the journey? That the city is beautiful cannot be denied and the women have turned out in force to greet us. Have you seen anything that catches your eye?"

"Not this time, friend." He could hardly count the

fleeing beauty, since he'd barely had time to glimpse her before she made a quick escape.

The real woman who'd captured his thoughts of late was the waif from the forest he'd encountered the previous week. He'd made a halfhearted attempt to follow her that day, thinking mayhap she wanted him to.

He could almost believe he'd dreamed the whole thing. Except…

Reaching into the pouch at his waist, Tristan felt the small knife he'd found within the oak ring. The handle and blade were both short and flat. Smooth and well-worn, the knife appeared more primitive than a traditional dagger, but also more practical. Both handle and blade of this instrument were formed from one continuous piece of metal. Tristan felt certain this knife belonged to the woman. It suited her— smooth and perfectly formed, yet completely uncivilized.

"Gone moral on me, Tristan?"

"Nay. But I have the king's orders to consider and a threat to his bride on the loose. No doubt I should stick to my duty. As should you, perhaps?"

Simon laughed, his lighter perspective often a welcome counterpoint to Tristan's darker view of the world. "Seducing one would bring no harm, or maybe two…"

"Stick to the widows, friend, lest you care to find yourself with a bride. I want no whisper of dishonor on my watch."

As the men departed the study, Arabella peeked over the high chest she had been hiding behind.

The door closed once again. They were gone.

Her face burned from the overheard discussion. They spoke in English, but she understood their language well enough thanks to her grandmother's lessons.

It seemed her mother had not misled her after all. Noblemen were obviously creatures of lust with little regard for those weaker than they. The very idea that they would idly select a target for their lustful games made her blood chill.

No doubt her mother had been wounded by such a scheme at Charles Vallia's hands. Her mother had been at court when it happened, too. Arabella's father might have stood in this very room and plotted to steal Luria Rowan's innocence.

Arabella shivered at the thought. And yet, at least the dark-haired knight had suggested he wished to seek answers about the disappearances of women no one else seemed to care about. That was to his credit, even if he did it to preserve his reputation with his king. She wondered why the Bohemian nobility cared so little for the loss of their wives, sisters and daughters.

But there was no time for sad thoughts now. Someone might have missed her during her absence and she did not wish to become the subject of undue scrutiny. Quietly, she opened the door and peered out. When no one seemed to be looking in her direction, she slipped back into the party with a heavier heart. The English knights might protect the Bohemian retinue, but who would protect the group from the English knights?

Darting among the clusters of people, Arabella searched for Mary. When she finally caught a glimpse of the vibrant pink surcoat her friend wore, the fabric brushed alongside the austere black garb of the man called Tristan.

Backing away from the scene while wondering how to save Mary from the wicked purpose of her companion, Arabella bumped into someone.

"Excuse me, I—"

She looked up into the face of the most exalted woman present at court this evening. A golden tiara graced the head of the princess, who nodded in greeting.

"Lady Arabella, are you enjoying yourself?" Princess Anne of Bohemia asked, steadying Arabella.

How awkward.

"I am so sorry, Your Highness, really I—"

"Lady Mary has been searching for you. I will bring you to her."

Arabella sucked in a breath, her mind hunting feverishly for a reason to excuse herself. But before she could protest, Princess Anne was escorting her toward Mary and the strange knight, leading her to certain condemnation once he realized who she was and where he had seen her.

"Arabella," Mary called, drawing her friend in between herself and the knight from the magic circle. "I am sorry I lost you."

The princess greeted Tristan warmly, apparently well acquainted with him, though Arabella could not hear their words over Mary's chatter.

"If it pleases you, my lady." A man handed Mary a fresh cup of wine. The other man from the study.

Arabella wanted to shout a warning to her warmhearted friend to keep her distance from the handsome foreigner with ice-blue eyes.

"Thank you, sir." Mary smiled at the knight. "Lady Arabella, may I introduce Sir Simon Percival?"

Aside from disliking the golden-haired Percival instantly, Arabella also struggled with her tongue in her first exchange with a man at court.

"How do you do, sir?" She sounded as stiff and formal as in her first days of learning English at Zaharia's knee.

The crafty knight barely heard her, however, in his rapt attention to Mary.

"Arabella," the princess's voice interrupted her thoughts. In her anger over Percival's proximity to Mary, Arabella had almost forgotten her other cause for fear.

She was now face-to-face with the dark-haired knight. Yet as close to him as she had been that day in the forest, his eyes held no light of recognition. Saints be praised.

"This is Sir Tristan Carlisle." Princess Anne spoke in English. "He is the knight King Richard has sent to escort us all to England. He is to be our protector."

"Our protector?" She hoped her disbelief did not find its way into her voice. Blood pounded in her ears as her hands clenched into tiny fists.

"At your service, my lady." Tristan Carlisle bowed before her, then, sweet Jesu, picked up her hand and kissed the back of it.

Gray eyes held her captive. For a moment, she felt a strange awareness of him, just as she had on that day in the ring of trees. His perusal intensified, and his hand lingered over hers.

"It is a long journey to your homeland. Think you we shall be safe, sir?" Snatching her fingers back, Arabella prayed Hilda's magic had rendered her unrecognizable.

"I have pledged myself to the cause, lady."

"Surely you have heard of the recent disappearances of Bohemian noblewomen." She had not heard of them herself until those hidden moments in the study.

Arabella noticed even the princess looked interested in his response.

"I have heard, and will seek answers for myself before we depart. Yet there is no reason to believe the problem will follow us."

She knew very well that was not the true nature of his thoughts, since he'd made a very different answer to his friend. Another lesson to be learned about men. They did not necessarily speak the truth.

"I am sure your king sent you because you are quite capable of ensuring our safety."

"I can only hope that is the reason," he replied, his voice oddly fierce before he turned to Anne. "Your Highness, I must beg your leave. I would see to some preparations before the reception winds down. I have supped earlier with my men."

She made a small inclination of her head to convey her approval and Tristan bowed before her, then turned to Arabella.

"By your leave, my lady."

Arabella felt the heat rise in her cheeks as he stared at her, an emotion she could not guess simmering in his eyes.

"Sir Tristan." Her voice sounded small to her ears. Lingering a moment, he looked as if he would speak further, but just when Arabella's fear peaked, he turned abruptly and strode out of sight.

"Does he frighten you, Lady Arabella?" the princess asked, startling Arabella with her bluntness.

"Nay," Arabella answered, then, seeing the princess's obvious disbelief, she confessed a small portion of the truth. "Mayhap a little. Sir Tristan is certainly one of the most intimidating-looking men in the room tonight."

The princess smiled and winked at Mary. "Granted. But I have noticed many of my young ladies-in-waiting are not in agreement."

"Your Highness?"

"Rosalyn de Clair—"the princess gestured toward a delicate, dark-haired noblewoman a few tables away "—could hardly keep her eyes off him."

All the better for Arabella, although it would not be fair of her to allow an unsuspecting noblewoman to be deceptively courted by an errant knave. Perhaps she should speak to Lady Rosalyn discreetly.

"Mary," the princess continued, "I have heard Arabella has not been to Prague before. I wish you would take an escort tomorrow and show her around. I would not want her to see London before she sees her own Prague."

Surprised and delighted, Arabella promised herself she would not let thoughts of Tristan Carlisle spoil such an opportunity.

"I would be thrilled."

"As would I, Your Highness," Mary added, curtsying in the easy manner of a woman who had grown up around a court full of protocol.

"You must be back early, however, so you will not be tired for our long journey."

Leaving Mary and Arabella to plot their day, Princess Anne moved away to speak with her other guests. And while Arabella was pleased to have escaped Tristan Carlisle's notice this time, she wondered how long it would be before the knight remembered their meeting. Would he compromise her position at court with tales of her uncivilized behavior?

Or did the heated awareness the English warrior incited within her pose an even darker threat?

Across the great hall, Rosalyn de Clair stamped her foot in frustration under the concealing skirts of her richly jeweled surcoat. She watched as Mary Natansia walked off with Arabella Rowan. Rosalyn had been trying to catch Mary's ear so she might gain the simpering twit for an ally at court, but the Rowan witch engaged her in conversation and remained steadfastly at Mary's side.

Rosalyn hoped to appeal to Lady Mary's heralded sympathetic nature with a clever mistruth she had been working on. Everyone knew the emperor doted on his precious ward. Rosalyn just had to make the most of it, and she was sure she could. Hadn't her lover once told her she was the most cunning woman he had ever met? Having clawed her way from her status as a bastard castoff to an enviable position among the nobility, Rosalyn considered those words a compliment.

She turned to find other company for the evening meal. Mary could be cornered another time. There would be plenty of opportunities on the way to England. In fact, maybe she should use the extra time to find an

English nobleman to woo prettily, rather than the Bohemian gentleman she had tentatively marked. Everyone knew no one in Bohemia had money these days. Even King Wenceslas had stooped to sending his sister to England without a dowry. It was a disgrace.

Yes, an English lord would be all the more beneficial. Rosalyn's smiles were restored at this new development of her plan. And, as fate would have it, she had just spied the most delicious Englishman she could have ever dreamed of.

Chapter Three

A bazaar took place once each fortnight on the Vltava River in Prague. Everywhere Arabella looked as their carriage rolled past the marketplace, she saw vibrant colors and lively people. Hundreds thronged the merchants' stands to haggle over vegetables, spices, cloth, animals and tools. Gypsy wagons provided entertainments of all kinds, from dancing to fortune telling.

Astonished by the sights, Arabella thrilled to each new discovery. She was as impressed by the Gypsy street entertainers as she was by the Venetian mosaic of the Last Judgment on St. Vitus's cathedral wall. At the moment, the bazaar caught Arabella's eye and she wanted desperately to take a closer look.

"We have time to stop, don't we? It is all so colorful." Arabella tugged on Mary's sleeve as she asked their driver to stop. She jumped from the small conveyance they had been given for their expedition. Briefly, she wondered whether exploring the market was a suitably ladylike pursuit, but she pushed her reservations about her place at the Bohemian court from her mind. Surely Zaharia would approve. Arabella could almost smell the herbs at a local wise woman's stall.

"I don't know, Arabella. Our driver wishes to take us home before dark."

"We won't stay long. And I would remember this bazaar more than the university or the city palaces, long after we depart." Her gaze already roamed the market-place for anyone selling unfamiliar tinctures or medicinal oils. "Please?"

Mary bit her lip, clearly unsure of herself in the raucous setting.

"If you promise we won't stay very long—"

Arabella gave her friend a quick hug before pulling her to a booth overflowing with fabric samples. Perhaps that would be more to Mary's liking.

"Feel this. Isn't it sumptuous?" she exclaimed over a piece of brightly colored silk with an exotic Eastern design. Mary chose two bolts, giving the merchant her name to have them delivered.

Moving away from the cloth merchant's booth, Mary soon engaged another merchant in haggling over a jeweled comb. Now that Mary was enjoying herself, Arabella hoped she might find the local herbalist. She was searching through the crowd when a large figure garbed in black caught her eye.

Tristan Carlisle.

Arabella was not ready to face the familiar figure striding among the Gypsy booths, speaking briefly with several of the peasant families who ran them. Ducking behind a pie-maker's stand, Arabella watched the English knight as he perused the items of a silversmith.

Observing him while he was not looking at her, she decided his face was handsome enough when he did not have a glower set upon his brow.

His eyes, however, were nothing short of beautiful. A silvery shade of gray rimmed with long, dark lashes. After her few days at court, she already understood the ladies of that realm would have done crime to possess such lashes. The slash of the knight's brows, however, gave him a slightly fearsome aspect even when he did not scowl. The rest of his face could only be described as angular, with a hard, square jaw and prominent cheekbones.

She blushed to realize how carefully she studied Tristan Carlisle when he failed to hold women in high regard. She guessed he was the kind of man her family had warned her about before her trip.

Pausing to finger a delicate bit of silver that he had picked up off the cloth full of wares, Tristan spoke to the boy behind the counter. Arabella could see the knight held a small knife in his hand.

It was ridiculous to stray near him. Yet she found herself walking closer, avoiding his notice but suddenly curious to hear what he asked the Gypsy boy about the blade.

"…from India," Arabella overheard the boy telling Tristan. "I brought it all the way here myself."

While the boy boasted, Tristan took the flat-handled dagger in his palm. Arabella looked longingly at the little weapon, thinking it looked similar to the one she lost before she came to Prague.

"Is that why you can charge an exorbitant amount? Because it weighed you down on the long journey here?" Tristan reached to give the boy's arm a gentle pinch. "You might swing a sword more often. Then mayhap a little knife wouldn't seem like such a burden."

Puffing out his chest, the lad defended himself with the courage of youth.

"It is not exorbitant because it was a burden. It costs much because it is a witch's knife. It is used to draw magical rings for worshipping demons." The boy almost whispered the last words, as if imparting great wisdom to the knight.

Arabella scoffed at the tale. Demons indeed. According to Zaharia, other healers used the weapon in a symbolic way, as if to cut away the world and focus inward to pray.

Tristan laughed at the peddler's ploy. "You may keep your wondrous weapon. I believe I already have a knife that is similar to the one you sell."

The knight produced something from his pocket and held it up for the boy to see.

Arabella's herb-cutting knife.

"Saints!" the boy cried, his dark eyes wide. "I hope you had it blessed. That blade surely came from a powerful sorceress."

Arabella was tempted to run up and snatch it out of the warrior's big hands. How dare he steal it?

"A powerful sorceress, eh? Mayhap she was." Tucking the dagger back in his pocket, he tossed a coin up in the air for the boy to catch. "Thanks, lad. You'll make a fine storyteller one day with tales such as those."

Mayhap she was? What was that supposed to mean?

Arabella wondered if the knight was teasing the boy or if he indeed thought he had come across a spell-casting sorceress in the forest. Thinking back to their strange encounter in the oaks, Arabella imagined she had looked a fright with her hair covered with twigs and leaves, and her eyes wet with tears. Indeed, she had been wailing at the top of her lungs as though the skies were falling, but only because she thought she was alone.

Yes, she'd probably made quite an impression on the English knight.

Thinking she would look at the boy's knives herself, Arabella was about to ask Mary to come with her. But when she turned to look for her friend, the emperor's ward was nowhere to be found.

Arabella tried to remain calm, but she could not see Mary anywhere. All at once, the rumors of stolen women assailed her. She should not have left Mary's side for even a moment. Running down the row of Gypsy wagons, she searched and called for her friend.

Frantically peering into every conceivable corner, Arabella came to a noisy row of Gypsy booths before she turned around.

"May I help you, my lady?"

A man touched her arm.

Stay calm. Arabella bit her lip, hard, to prevent herself from giving in to full-blown fear.

"No thank you, sir." Jerking her arm out of his grasp, she stepped away from him.

"A woman alone must need some assistance." The stranger was a well-dressed Bohemian, but Arabella did not appreciate the steely glint in his eye.

Beyond caring if she attracted attention, Arabella lifted her skirt to run and was yanked back so hard she cried out.

The man's demeanor changed as he shoved her with unexpected force behind a large tapestry for sale at a merchant's booth.

"Help!" Arabella shouted at the top of her lungs, a moment before the brute pushed her to the ground and clamped a ruthless hand over her mouth.

Tristan and Simon were already atop their horses and ready to leave when a cry pierced the din of the marketplace.

Requiring no words, the men sprang forward.

Tristan steered his horse through the crowded bazaar, ignoring protests from people forced to clear a path for him.

With a sweeping scrutiny, he quickly narrowed the possible places the scream could have come from. The two most likely spots were either in the back of a Gypsy wagon in a quiet corner of the bazaar, or behind an arras right next to it. Tristan held his horse motionless as he watched the two places simultaneously and listened with the finely tuned hearing of a man used to stealth in battle.

He heard not a sound aside from the shouts of disgruntled merchants in his wake, but he soon saw the tapestry move a fraction of an inch near the ground. Drawing his sword, Tristan slashed it down and watched it fall on top of two struggling forms.

Dropping to his feet, he turned aside the heavy arras to reveal a middle-aged Bohemian man and a rumpled pile of green velvet and dark hair.

A noblewoman.

"Move away from her now." Though he spoke calmly, he felt the fury of growing bloodlust in his veins. The man wisely scrambled to obey his command.

The villain stuttered his protests as Simon yanked him away from the commotion, but Tristan paid no heed. His eyes were fixed on the woman before him.

Arabella Rowan, the distant beauty he'd met last night at Princess Anne's reception. Only she didn't look so immaculately groomed today. Now that she had been rolling around the ground she looked dusty and disheveled and...

Damnation.

Tristan could not believe his eyes as his vision of aloof Arabella Rowan melded with his memory of the green-eyed enchantress from the forest. They were one and the same.

Her hair, so shiny and luxurious the night before, was a formidable tangle around her head. She was covered with dust and smudged with dirt, recalling her forest appearance.

It was the wild glint in her eyes now, however, that confirmed her identity. Unlike her courtly appearance, she now exuded passion. Heat. Fear and anger radiated from her with palpable force. 'Twas clear at a glance this member of Anne's royal party was not the noblewoman her princess believed her to be.

Arabella knew the instant he recognized her. Really recognized her. The flash of recall revealed itself in the darkening and narrowing of his eyes.

He stepped toward her. Arabella's first response was

to scramble backward but he was too quick. Huge, hard hands wrapped themselves about her waist and lifted her as though she were no more burden than a child. Setting her once again upon her feet, he released her swiftly, giving Arabella the impression the contact had disturbed him as much as it had her.

"You are unharmed, Lady Arabella?" The way he stressed "lady" sounded decidedly unpleasant, conveying his doubt that she deserved the title.

She nodded, her lack of voice betraying her discomfiture.

"The man accosted you?"

Forcing herself to converse with him out of the desire to see her attacker punished, Arabella cleared her throat and met Tristan's hard gaze.

"He offered his assistance to find Mary. She had disappeared from my view for a moment and I became concerned she had met with harm."

"And when you refused his help, he attacked you?"

"Yes."

"When we depart Prague and you are in my charge, you will never wander around without a man to escort you. Do you understand?"

A strange dictate, considering she had been fine today until a man got near her. But perhaps the princess should have asked one of her guards to accompany them, since other noblewomen had disappeared recently.

Then again, perhaps Arabella should not have followed her heart's desires and asked Mary to leave the safety of the carriage for the marketplace. Guilt pinched her hard, perhaps making her words more biting than she'd intended.

"I would hope that once I am in your charge, sir, I will not be attacked by anyone."

"I cannot protect wayward lasses."

Her eyes connected with his and she felt the keen edge of that remark. Tristan Carlisle thought her unworthy of the Bohemian court. He did not think she could be true nobility because he had seen her out in the oak ring, venting her fury to the heavens.

"Wayward?" His remark insulted her grandmother and her heritage as much as it insulted her.

"Arabella!" a small voice cried out moments before Mary appeared from the thick of the surrounding crowd and threw both arms around her friend. "Are you hurt?"

Anger cooling as she reassured Mary of her good health, Arabella decided it would be useless to explain herself to Tristan. He would believe what he wanted.

Heaven knows, most everyone in the Bohemian court already thought she was a wayward lady because of her unusual upbringing. What difference did it make that Tristan Carlisle agreed with their assessment?

What she regretted most about the day was that she had unwittingly broken her grandmother's most important rule. In the course of an afternoon, she had become very much the center of attention.

After spending a fruitless afternoon trying to twist answers out of the Bohemian trader who'd grabbed Arabella, Tristan accompanied Simon back to the keep to continue their preparations for the journey home.

They'd discovered the man's name was Ivan Litsen, but had learned precious little else about his motive. The man had seemed unconcerned about his encounter with Arabella, assuring Tristan that many men of his acquaintance would have done the same had they spied a beautiful young woman unaccompanied in a crowded marketplace.

If such was the case, why had the princess allowed Arabella and Mary to ride about the city? Did Arabella have enemies at court?

"Arabella Rowan is a fair one," Simon observed as he studied the horizon from his horse, trotting beside Tristan's mount.

Simon had been attempting conversation ever since they'd left the alleyway across from the marketplace where they'd questioned Litsen at length and finally given the man into the keeping of the king's guard.

"Passing fair." He had no wish to discuss the woman with his friend, whose appetite for feminine diversion had angered more than one protective father in their rare excursions to the English king's court.

"Are you blind? Such beauty in a lady is as rare as it is striking to the eye."

"She is no lady." Tristan wondered if he could be the only man at court who knew of Arabella's peasant roots.

"I am pleased to hear it. The prospects for our journey home have just begun to improve."

"No." Tristan suspected he was being skillfully manipulated—tested for his own interest in Arabella—but the knowledge did not prevent a surge of possessiveness at the thought of Simon with the green-eyed beauty.

"Pardon? Did the Sultan of Silence speak?"

"She is not your type of woman, Percival, and we both know it. You merely mean to examine my reaction to the wench. Why not just ask?" Irritated to realize he indeed found himself attracted to Arabella—nay, more fascinated than attracted—Tristan had no patience for idle talk of her. Yet he listened because Simon was his brother in spirit, if not by blood.

"I thought I was the picture of subtlety." Simon laughed. "But since you're offering, I am curious what you think of Lady Arabella."

"I met her in the woods on one of the last nights we made camp on the way to Prague, and she bore little resemblance to the lady-in-waiting she plays for her princess." He had not shared the incident with Simon, preferring to remember the encounter in his mind and not pick it apart with questions. "I do not know if the other nobles are aware of a pretender in their midst, or if Princess Anne has purposely gathered as large a retinue as possible, with no regard to the breeding of her travel companions. But either way, Lady Arabella's court facade is a falsehood."

"Perhaps the princess knows nothing of it, and Arabella has merely used that charming body of hers to lure a nobleman to her bed in an attempt to be included in the princess's train."

"Leave it to you to consider the most illicit possibilities." Although heaven knows, Tristan of all people should have been quick to consider such a scheme, after having been betrayed by a woman seeking a higher station in life than a lowly knight could afford.

"Women must use what means they possess. A lesson hard won by us both, Tris, wouldn't you say?"

"There is more." Briefly, Tristan explained about the knife he found after she left. "It may be just an ordinary tool for gathering herbs, but there are some who believe such weapons are ceremonial items for Gypsy wise women or..."

"You don't mean to suggest the girl is—"

"I suggest nothing. I'm merely telling you what I found and sharing the local superstitions."

"You do not believe such rump-fed foolishness."

"I do not fear the girl could turn me into a hopping toad, if that is what you mean. Yet I know she is not who she pretends to be."

They were in a more untamed land, after all. A woman brought up in the Bohemian wilderness among the old ways could be a dangerous influence on the English court, even if her only crime was that of deception.

"'Tis all mumble-minded nonsense," Simon remarked, reining in as they approached the knights' quarters near the main keep. "Arabella Rowan is naught but a wild beauty with unearthly green eyes, and you would call her a Gypsy witch."

"Hardly. Mayhap I will simply call her mine, instead." He had not thought it over before he spoke the words aloud, but the idea had a certain appeal.

"Have you lost your wits? What happened to your aversion to treacherous women?"

"Perhaps my sense of fair play demands I do not allow another ambitious woman to bend the court to her whim." Tristan was no longer the unknown bastard Elizabeth

Fortier had once rejected. After seeing the way his former love had broken the spirits of a much older and far wealthier man following her courtship with Tristan, he had regretted his quiet complicity in her scheme.

He might not have denounced Elizabeth, but he had the power to unmask Arabella Rowan.

Arabella would be the king's problem in England, but until they reached London, Tristan would be wise to keep a close watch on the reckless female with secrets in her past.

"You'd better be careful then, friend." Simon grinned, one brow arched in lopsided mockery as he slid from his mount. "If our young enchantress truly is a powerful wise woman in disguise, you may be in for more than you bartered for."

Tristan did not deny it.

Chapter Four

After days of riding in Princess Anne's specially fash-
ioned carriage, Arabella thought she would expire from
the tedious polite conversation and the confinement of
the padded velvet walls.

There were windows in the carriage at least, to provide
an occasional breeze, but the view was disturbing.

Tristan often rode near the royal carriage, providing
Arabella with too much opportunity to brood over the
man.

He looked more at ease on the destrier than most men
looked on their own two feet. His black hair was caught
in a queue trailing carelessly over his mantle. Dressed
in his customary austere black, he bore no decoration
on his person, no trace of family emblems, heraldry or
garters from the king. As if no ties of loyalty bound him
to anyone or anything.

Why her eyes were drawn to him time and again, she
could not fathom.

He was dangerous. Arabella knew it because her

mother had assured her every man was. And from his crude discussion with his friend, she knew he was accustomed to taking advantage of women. The fact that they were usually widows did nothing to lessen her indignation.

Yet…he'd saved her.

The day at the bazaar had scared her witless. Like a madwoman, she'd fought her attacker with all her strength, the cold certainty that he intended her serious harm driving her to frenzied kicking and pushing.

Out of nowhere, Tristan appeared. In that moment, her heart nearly burst with relief. He seemed larger than life as he loomed over the brute who hurt her. Yes, Tristan Carlisle was dangerous, but all that power and strength had been on her side. She could not forget that feeling of absolute protection.

Unsure how to handle the strange mixture of feelings he inspired, Arabella had done her best to avoid him since they'd left Prague. Her eyes, however, had a will of their own.

Lost in thought as she stared at his broad back, she was caught off guard when he turned and met her gaze, as if he felt her watching.

Flustered, she studied her knotted hands in her lap. Still, he drew closer. Arabella could feel his presence. He reined in near Anne's window, a few hand spans from her own.

"Excuse me, Your Highness. We are in Cologne now," Tristan informed her. "It will take all day to reach the countess's lands. Do you wish to ride straight through?"

"I want to be sleeping under Countess von Richt's

roof this night." Anne smiled warmly. "Think you we will be there for a late supper?"

"We will make all haste so that it may be. I wish you good morning, Your Highness. Ladies." Acknowledging the other women in the carriage by a quick bow of his head, he disappeared to rejoin the head of the party.

As Arabella tried to make sense of the feelings he roused within her simply by his presence, she decided she would make every effort to maintain her distance from him during their stay at the countess's keep. No matter what the leap of her pulse meant when Tristan was near, she was certain it couldn't be good.

"Let the entertainment commence," Countess von Richt announced after an endless supper.

Finally.

The meal had dragged for Arabella, whose seat provided her with an unimpeded view of Tristan Carlisle with Rosalyn de Clair. The sight diminished her appetite even though she had promised herself not to be drawn in by the knight.

"Come, Arabella." Mary pulled her along to the side of the room as the trestle tables were moved aside for dancing.

When the music began, Mary partnered with one of the countess's sons for a dance and Arabella watched, enthralled, as the couples moved by in a graceful swirl of velvets and silks. The lady's dress would swing away from her body with a *swish,* the man's head would incline to hers for a private exchange, and the music would move the pair along the floor. It was so pretty.

"Would you like to join them?" a voice asked from behind, and she knew who would be there if she dared to turn around. Tristan's question caressed her cheek. A shiver chased down her spine.

"No, thank you," she whispered, unable to face him and yet unable to move away.

"Yet you seem to enjoy it." The heat from his chest warmed her back even though they did not touch.

She swallowed hard.

"It is beautiful." Her heart pounded so loudly he must hear it above the minstrels' music. But was it fear exactly? Arabella had known the cold dread of fear after the bazaar attack. This was not it.

"Were you the kind of child to sneak from your bed and watch the entertainment in your family's keep?"

His question confused her. "Oh no. My home is not so splendid as this. I have never seen dancing like this before."

She did not count the times she had danced beneath the stars to the music of the heavens on warm summer nights. Seeing the way others danced brought home how simple her rudimentary steps seemed.

"You do not dance?"

"I do not know how." One of the couples glided by her and she smiled, thinking that her grandmother had been right to send Arabella into the world, even though the experience had frightened her.

It frightened her still. Especially with a powerful warrior at her back and a mixture of confusing thoughts in her head.

"But you would like to learn."

"Yes, but—" she began, until she recalled she could not always speak her mind anymore. "I mean, no. I'd like to someday, maybe…" Her words trailed off because her answer did not sound convincing, even to her own ears.

"I would be glad to teach you." He turned her gently around to face him and her senses spun at his touch.

He looked different this evening. She had realized that earlier when he'd been sitting with Lady Rosalyn. But now that she viewed him close up, she could identify the subtleties of the difference. The dark cape circling his neck was held together with a silver brooch of intertwining serpents. The sapphire eyes of the strange beasts glittered.

The shirt he wore beneath the cape boasted a fine linen, the fabric snowy-white against his darker breeches, the stitches closely sewn. The clean scent of his clothes told her they'd been washed by the maids of Prague keep. She remembered the sweet herbs the washerwomen had used for their soaps.

Merciful heaven, how long had she observed him thus?

"No, thank you, sir." She sounded cold when she had not meant to be. She owed him so much and she had not even thanked him. But sweet Jesu, he unsettled her.

Just then there was a break in the music and a general changing of partners. Rosalyn de Clair extracted herself from the arms of one of Countess von Richt's many sons and attached herself to Tristan's side.

"Tristan, you promised me a dance." The woman touched his arm lightly with a trembling hand.

Arabella vowed she would never let her feelings for

any man appear so obvious. Seizing her chance to escape the confusion Tristan wrought, she hurried from the hall. She did not look back as she found the main doors to the keep and fled down the stairs into the cold evening. It was late autumn, but the brisk night air helped clear her mind after the heady atmosphere in the hall. The nearness of the man and the beauty of the dancers had rendered her spellbound and starry-eyed.

Rosalyn de Clair's arrival had been a welcome slap in the face. The raven-haired noblewoman in the scarlet-red dress reminded Arabella of the nightshade flower that was beautiful but poisonous.

Thinking of the nightshade reminded Arabella that she was alone out of doors, where she could peer around the grounds for some late autumn herbs. How she missed her forest. She had brought along a great variety of herbs from the Rowan lands, but it would be interesting to see what she could find in this part of the world. Mayhap something unusual she would not be able to identify.

The prospect so enticed her that she wandered away from the keep. She found some hawthorn, and some spices, but not many medicinal herbs due to the late season. She used her gown to carry the things she picked.

It was a waxing of the moon, so that meant good, constructive herbs could be collected. Arabella had no cause to gather any other kind. She was interested in herbs for their medicinal value, but knew there were others who used them to wreak harm. Zaharia had met such people before and assured her they could be very dangerous.

The thought of such darkness made Arabella grow

cold, and she waved a small branch of hawthorn in a circle around herself. A tree of good fortune, its twigs could be used to ward off bad spirits.

"Witchcraft is punishable by death in this country, *chovihani.*"

Arabella was so startled she dropped her gown full of herbs to run.

"Not this time, Arabella."

A warm hand yanked her back and she found herself held fast in the strong arms of Tristan Carlisle.

Chapter Five

"*Chovihani?*" she asked, more incensed now than afraid.

It was a Gypsy word for *witch* and Arabella did not appreciate the description, or the implication that she had committed some crime. She struggled to pull away, but his hold did not waver.

"I did not mean to startle you. I wondered where you had disappeared." His voice caressed her ear and she felt her knees weaken just a little as he spoke. And there was that flip in her belly she knew only happened when he was near. She stopped struggling and he released her.

"What do you mean by calling me witch?"

"Imagine yourself as I have seen you." Tristan turned from her to look up into the star-filled sky. "I believe I am in the Bohemian woodlands alone until I hear an awful, gut-wrenching cry, like an animal in pain. Venturing through the forest, I find a beautiful wailing woman in a ring of ancient oaks."

Arabella felt her cheeks heat.

"But she does not look like any woman I have ever laid eyes on." He stepped closer to her. Arabella could not move. "She is barefoot, with a veil of wild hair enveloping half of her body and covered with twigs and leaves. She is like a wood nymph or…an enchantress."

Arabella shook her head in mute denial. "Never, I—"

"Then, when I find her again, she is transformed into a princess of a woman I barely recognize except for the green eyes, but every now and then I get a glimpse of the wild woman out in the moonlight, gathering herbs to make strange potions and waving sticks around her head in some sort of ancient ritual."

"I am no *chovihani*. If some people choose to believe medicine is an art of witchcraft, that only shows their lack of knowledge. But I think you know better." Or, she hoped he did. She spied intelligence in those gray eyes of his, even when he called forth unexpected feelings from deep inside her. "Call me *drabarni*, herb woman, mayhap. That name would be more fitting."

"You are a healer?" he asked, eyes narrowing.

"I try to be. There will forever be some things that are impossible to heal. But I try to find cures and relieve ailments, and in some instances I have been granted the grace to really heal. But even when I can't heal, I can usually help."

She took pride in her skill and had worked all her life to be as knowledgeable as her grandmother in the healing arts. She saw no reason to hide her talents.

"You possess a great talent," Tristan said, his voice hinting at genuine admiration. "From years of battlefield experience, I can appreciate a good healer. It is painful to watch a man die whose time has not yet come. England has great need of you."

"Perhaps she needs me, but will she want me?" Arabella peered up at the partial moon as a chill crept over her skin.

"What do you mean?"

"Will England welcome me, or will her people make the same mistake that you did and shun me because of my calling?"

"Others have made such an error?"

"Indeed sir, you are one of the few who have even bothered to admit their mistake. Most people feel more comfortable with their superstitions, even when the truth of my gift stares them in the face. Were I somewhat less skilled, people would not accuse me of witchcraft. It is because I am exceptionally good at my art that I make people uncomfortable."

Tristan frowned. "After witnessing your abilities, I would think most people would be grateful."

She shrugged, powerless to understand human nature.

"I really must return to the keep."

"Wait." His fingertips reached out to curl lightly over hers. "Let me show you how to dance."

Tristan had not planned to ask her as much. He scarcely knew what had made him chase her through the keep. In part, he had wanted to elude Rosalyn de Clair's company, since his head warned him away from her obvious advances. But he supposed Arabella intrigued him more than she should. He'd wanted to maintain a boundary between his knights and the Bohemian noblewomen, but she called to him on a gut level, no matter what his reason had to say.

Now he found himself playing courtier to her when what he really wanted was far less chaste.

"I should not stay." Her eyes told him a far different story, however. And her feet—remaining firmly planted on the dark earth of a rocky hillside—were even more telling.

He would not take advantage of her. But he could linger with her.

"We will stay but a moment. Would it not be useful for you to learn the steps of our dances out here, where there are no witnesses but the trees? The great halls of the English king's keeps might be less forgiving."

She bit her lip and his mouth watered. He knew he played unfairly with her. And yet it was *she* who had left the safety of the countess's hall. She who had put herself in this most vulnerable position.

"Do I have to wear my slippers?"

Tristan laughed, drawn to her untamed spirit. They would be well matched in so many ways that he ached at the thought.

"Nay. You do not need your slippers." He drew her a step closer, trailing his thumb over the back of her hand to savor the delicate skin. "Allow me."

Sweeping Arabella off her feet and into his arms, he strode to edge of the clearing. She started to protest until she seemed to realize his intent. Gently, he sat her down on a large, flat rock and knelt to remove her shoes.

"I do not blame you for wanting to be rid of these shoes your princess has all of you wearing." Forcing himself to keep his touch gentle, he skimmed his hands over one ankle in the space between her hem and her shoe. It was only a thumbnail's width of her that he stroked, but the knowledge of how easily he could take more was enough to make the touch sweetly passionate.

"I—" Arabella's breath caught in her throat as he trailed a finger down the arch of her foot. "The curled toes are a bit awkward for me."

Tristan removed her other shoe quickly before he scared her out of the clearing. He would carry this only so far—at least for tonight.

"The ground is smooth here." He offered his arm and guided her a few steps away toward a patch of open ground. "Do not stray from me, lest you step on a root or fallen branch."

Not that he would release her long enough for her to go that far.

He explained the pattern of the dance—the step together, step kick alternating—and then moved her briefly around the clearing to demonstrate. When they were ready to begin, Arabella faltered for a moment.

"What?"

"What if I miss a step?" She peered down at their feet, his heavy and booted, hers small and bare. "You will surely break my foot."

"You will be safe as my partner." Tristan squeezed her hand, reminded anew of her innocence despite her earthy appeal.

"Shall I sing the minstrels' tune to guide us?" Her green eyes were dimmed under the dark sky, the stars reflected in her gaze.

"You have such a gift for song?" He could not even recall the music, let alone repeat it, yet a tune hummed from between her lips, light and sweet.

Gently, he steered her forward to begin their steps, the song wrapping them in the moment. She followed him easily, although her focus remained directed at her feet for the first few passes as they wove their way around the clearing. When at last she looked up at him, a smile lit her face.

The knowledge of her joy damn near robbed him of his breath. Her happiness made him regret his duty to inform his sovereign of the rumors about her. Indeed, in that moment, he found them difficult to believe himself.

Moments passed before he realized her song had faded along with their steps. They stood frozen in the moonlight, their breathing evenly matched.

"Thank you." Her simple gratitude humbled him at a time when his thoughts already strayed to a future date when she would resent him for revealing her past. Her family.

By all that was holy, he already resented his position himself.

"It was my pleasure." He bowed over her hand, recovering his wits. "Shall I deliver you back to the keep?"

"Only if you promise to safeguard our encounter as a secret. I would not have my princess think that I am as wayward a lady as you once believed." Arabella's scent drifted on the cool breeze, her gown and her hair bearing a hint of spring flowers despite the lateness of the year.

"If I protect your secret, you must agree to keep

mine." He would be damned for taking advantage of her. He knew it, and yet he could not stop himself.

"I know nothing of you to remain quiet about." She shivered from the chill in the air, or perhaps from her body's awareness of his.

He hadn't missed her response to his nearness as they danced, as her gown was a tighter fitting affair than the costumes customary for English noble-women. Heat suffused his limbs, calling him to advance upon her and show her exactly why her cheeks burned and her soft breasts tightened whenever he touched her.

"You must never tell anyone about this...."

Lowering his mouth to hers, he brushed a kiss across her lips. She made a small sound in the back of her throat—whether it was a squeak of surprise or protest, he did not know. But he did not lock her against his body and she could easily back away.

She did not. Her cry faded into a sigh of pleasure before she relaxed against him. She parted her lips and only then did he pull her into him, wrapping one arm around her waist and lifting her off the ground to stand atop his boots. He gathered the dark masses of hair flowing down in his other hand and gently tilted her head back. Arabella followed the subtle demand, arching her back to offer him a better taste. The effect of her breasts flattened against his chest stole his last intelligent thought and steeled every inch of his flesh.

He ran his tongue along her lower lip before allowing himself the sweet reward of her mouth. He let go of her hair and stroked the length of the silken tresses, feeling the curve of her spine right through the soft locks. When his hands reached her rounded hip, Tristan summoned every scrap of restraint to resist a more carnal touch. Instead, he reached up to touch her face, his fingers none too steady from the force of blood pounding his veins.

He half waited for her to push him away, to find some sense of maidenly outrage. But instead she wound her arms about his neck and held tight, forsaking all control of the situation. Raw lust swamped him, testing his honor and his will, until a noise sounded in the forest very close to them.

A light, animal snuffle.

Tristan stilled, gripping Arabella's arms tightly as he shot her a warning look. Only when he was certain she understood did he turn to peer into the surrounding woods.

Responding to the slightest movement to their left, Tristan charged into the forest only a few feet behind a dark figure. He knew he would quickly overtake the person who lumbered awkwardly through the night, but just before Tristan laid his hands on the spy, the fleeing man reached a scrawny horse. The lout leaped onto the mount and urged the nag as fast as it would take him.

Devil take the rutting hound.

"Tristan?" Arabella called from much too near and he realized she had quietly followed him through the trees. He had to admire her speed and soundlessness, though her feet would no doubt protest the trek.

Tristan swore a mild oath as he trudged back to where she stood.

"You're going to need to be very careful, Arabella. I don't know who would be watching us secretly, but I have to believe whoever it was could be following the princess's retinue."

"Of course." She swept her hair behind her ear, her silver circlet askew. "I will return to the keep with all haste."

"Not without an escort." Tristan halted her quick retreat with a restraining hand. "There will be no more late-night escapes from the rest of your party or secluded searches for herbs unless you are with me. Do you understand?"

Her curt nod told him that he had wounded her feelings, yet he could not temper his warning when her safety depended on it. He had been idle-witted to allow himself to touch her, to allow himself to forget for a moment his purpose in escorting the princess's women. The mission that had started out as a courtier's errand had turned into a critical duty with high stakes.

No wild and reckless beauty would tempt him away from it, no matter how sweetly she danced for him in the moonlight.

Rosalyn hid herself behind the small wardrobe when she heard the door to Tristan's chamber open. She tensed with anticipation as she heard him step into the room and close the door behind him. Too bad she had to resort to such drastic measures, but Tristan had disappeared after their dance. Afraid he had gone to find the Gypsy Rowan woman, Rosalyn decided she would waste no more time. She needed to lie with him tonight.

It was fortunate that the captain of the English guard had been given his own chamber in the castle, rather than sharing quarters with the other knights. Tristan's quarters gave Rosalyn the opportunity to see him in private and to consummate their relationship before her condition developed more noticeably. With the help of a few restraining garments, her waist remained tiny. The only hint of her upcoming babe was the new weight in her breasts that enhanced her figure. She smiled in the darkened room, knowing that she had already won this battle.

Surprised Tristan had not already lit a candle and discovered her, Rosalyn wasn't sure how to proceed. Should she wait for him to spy her in the moonlit room, or should she announce her presence? He might not notice her at all and she could slide into bed beside him after he lay down. She decided to do just that if he did not notice her on his own, and watched in breathless anticipation as he removed his houppelande and the tunic underneath.

Rosalyn ran her tongue around her lips as her mouth went dry. The man was magnificent. His broad chest boasted great strength. The muscles that his tunic had hinted at were now clearly revealed to her hungry eyes. Sitting on the bed, Tristan removed his boots and let them fall to the floor. He was about to remove his breeches when she stepped out from the shadows in her scarlet gown, one sleeve already slipping purposefully down her shoulder.

"What are you doing here?" His stillness was not the response she had expected.

Taking a deep breath, she called upon devices her mother had taught her long before Rosalyn turned away from her father's fallen whore to claim the nobleman's protection. Rosalyn arched her shoulders enough to press her breasts more fully against the seams of her surcoat.

"Are we back to being strangers, Tristan?" She draped herself across him. "I thought we were better friends than that," she purred into his ear.

"Mayhap we could have been. But I fear you are sweetly attired trouble."

He had spoken softly, but his words cut her almost as much as his obvious imperviousness to her offer.

She slid from the bed and stared him down.

"What are you insinuating?" Rosalyn's mind raced, wondering how he could have guessed her plan.

"I mean no insult. But I fear 'tis not me you really want. Are you using me to hurt someone else? Another lover, mayhap?"

She spun away from him as though in the throes of emotion, although she needed solely to conceal her surprise. He missed the mark on her intentions, but— truth be told—not by all that much.

"No. I have no other lover, although mayhap at first I spoke to you to take my mind off of a cruel man who misled me." Sniffling, she turned back to face him and thought his stance appeared slightly softened.

"He was a fool," the English knight assured her, his taut muscles bronzed by the golden glow from the hearth.

"A man of noble standing in Bohemia led me to think he wanted to marry me and I foolishly let him pay court to me at our home." Heaven knows, her father hadn't helped her obtain the match. De Clair thought he'd given her all she deserved when he'd opened his home to her six years ago and had graced her with his name.

"The matter of marriage is often fixed long in advance. Perhaps your father had hopes that you would ally yourself with another."

Someone well beneath her, no doubt. But Rosalyn would not be sold off so cheaply.

"I cannot say, because I forgot all about the Bohemian nobleman and my father's wishes when I saw you." She reached out to touch him and smoothed her fingers across his chest—a most pleasurable diversion. Something stirred inside her and it was not her fledgling bairn.

Trusting her womanly senses, she trailed her hand down his bare stomach to the waist of his breeches and beyond. Only then did he reach out to restrain her, holding her hand in midair.

"You are a beautiful woman, Rosalyn." The hoarseness in the knight's voice made her hopeful. "But I am without lands and a title. Your parents would not approve of me."

"But you are well respected by your king. Your undertaking here proves that. King Richard will reward you when you bring him his bride." And by the saints, she had affected him. She could see it in the impressive rise of his garments.

"The English king rewards knights who win battles, not knights who guard royalty. I am afraid I will receive no such reward, no matter how valuable the princess is to my sovereign."

Something in his answer did not settle well upon her ears. She had told enough lies in her time to recognize one when she heard it. Tristan was obviously a strong warrior. Anger swelled in her belly where desire had been. With an effort, she forced a few tears from her eyes, desperate to make her ploy work.

"I am rejected again, no matter how prettily you spoke to me at dinner." With a broken cry, she lunged for the chamber door, hoping he would stop her. She even paused on the threshold.

"Good night, my lady." His feet remained firmly planted until Rosalyn had no choice but to leave. She would try another approach tomorrow, or perhaps she would shift her attentions to Tristan's second in command.

Departing the chamber and closing the door softly behind her, Rosalyn heard a startled gasp in the hall. She turned around to see a wide-eyed Mary drop her eyes quickly to the floor. Of all the blessed, wonderful good fortune.

Hiding a smile, Rosalyn feigned embarrassment as she straightened her drooping gown and wiped false tears from her eyes.

"Oh please, Lady Mary," she begged. "Do not tell anyone."

Chapter Six

Arabella stretched contentedly in her bed beneath the sun's warm rays. She must have slept late for the sun to be so high. She was loath to wake because her dreams were so inviting. So hopelessly inappropriate for a woman who did not wish to draw attention to herself.

Throwing off the covers, she walked to her chamber door and peered out into the corridor, just in time to see Tryant Hilda bustling toward her.

"Well, look who we have here. If it isn't the sleeping beauty. I was beginning to think we'd have to call in a prince to wake you, Arabella." Hilda pushed her way into Arabella's chamber after calling for a maid to help her dress. "I hope you don't mind I didn't wake you for the hunt—"

"Hunt?"

"I could not imagine you wanting to shoot down a wild boar, so I let you sleep on."

Arabella could not envision herself shooting a wild boar either, but she knew the party would be hunting on horseback, and she would very much have liked the chance to sit her own horse.

"Did Mary go?" Arabella asked, thinking her gentle friend would not want to participate in the bloody sport.

"Yes, my lady. But I think it was more for the arm of the knight who asked than for the sport itself." Hilda winked.

"A knight?" Memories of her moonlight dance rushed over her, filling her with a warmth she knew she should not feel. Her mother had warned her all her life, yet Arabella had foolishly made herself vulnerable to Tristan's touch.

His kiss…saints preserve her, she did not know how she would ever put those heated moments out of her mind.

"The English guard's second in command. Sir Simon Percival, I believe."

Arabella nodded, although she only had one knight on her mind this morning.

"Did anyone else stay behind?"

"Hmm…I think several women did not go. And the English captain stayed behind. Of course, very few of the servants were needed."

Tristan had not gone. Arabella wondered if he would have ridden if she had.

"May I go down now, Hilda?" Arabella asked. "I am frightfully hungry now that it is so late."

Obtaining the lady's approval, Arabella excused herself to steal a muffin from the sideboard in the great hall, but she did not bother to sit down to break her fast. She wished to wander about the grounds, although she would stay close to the keep since Tristan had warned her away from solitary walks.

Besides, who would wish to steal her from the countess's home? Arabella might possess a noble connection, but she did not have any great wealth. Mary might have to be more careful as the emperor's ward, but Arabella Rowan did not fear for her own safety, especially not in the comfort of woodland terrain where she knew how to keep herself safe.

Outside the keep, she could almost forget she was halfway across Europe from her Bohemian home. The forest surrounding Countess von Richt's home was beautiful. More lush than the woodlands Arabella had known, the forest seemed alive even in the middle of December. The sun's warm rays felt more like those of early autumn, and the dense trees beckoned. The smell of the woods and dry leaves soothed her. Arabella realized how much she missed the quiet solitude of a forest after the endless days in a carriage full of other women.

She had wandered into the trees when she remembered her muffin. Taking a bite of the still-warm pastry, she hastened ahead, enjoying the crunching of the leaves under her feet. But as she listened, that sound mingled with another, more threatening noise.

Hoofbeats.

Someone approached at a breakneck pace. Turning to see the rider, she discovered Tristan Carlisle astride his fearsome beast of a horse. Her muffin dried in her mouth at the sight. He did not look pleased.

"What in the name of all that is holy are you doing out here?" He halted a mere foot in front of her.

"Gathering the herbs I dropped yesterday, when you scared me out of my wits." She dusted the crumbs off her hands and peered about the clearing.

"Do you not remember my command that you leave the keep only with an escort?"

"I can see the towers from here." She pointed to the roofline, where the countess's men-at-arms guarded the walls and could surely see her. "I purposely remain close to the keep."

"And you expect those men to protect you?" He slid from the back of his horse and stood a hand's span from her. "What makes you think one of them would not spy you alone out here and decide your foolishness makes you fair game for their sport?"

She blinked. "We are guests of the countess—"

"The von Richts are under no obligation to protect Anne's contingent, Arabella. I am. That means you will cease your dizzy-eyed games and do what I command of you, lest you find yourself dismissed from the court." Anger steamed off him and for the first time she feared the repercussions of her actions.

Zaharia expected her to prove herself as a noble-woman, not to be sent home in disgrace. Bad enough she had allowed kisses in the moonlight. She could not afford to bring royal displeasure on her family's name.

"I did not mean to—"

"You would have been attacked last night if it wasn't for me, and you promised you would not go out without an escort."

She recalled him asking for such a promise, but she did not remember making it. How could the man have plied her so sweetly with kisses the night before and yet condemn her so quickly this morning?

"And I thought I honored your request by remaining within sight of the keep. I do not understand what makes you think the man last night meant to harm me, when he could have just as easily wished to do injury to you. Or perhaps he wished to steal from the countess's home. But his presence had nothing to do with me."

"And if he proves to be the same man who grabbed you in Prague?"

She hated to be thought foolish, yet she had not seriously considered that the same man might have followed the company all this way. Their journey was long and arduous. What would tempt a mere thief to go to such lengths?

"You think this man in the woods could come so far? I have no dowry to offer any man. I am not worth the fortune that other women in the court are."

"Perhaps not, but since we do not know his reasons, we must be careful. Some men attack women out of lust and simply leave them ruined."

"As if a man could ruin the soul of a woman with mere lust." Still, the image made Arabella scan the grounds with a more wary eye. "I did not comprehend the full extent of the dangers you suggest, but I understand well enough that I will have to be far more careful to protect myself from those wishing to do me harm."

She could not help but think Tristan posed a more real threat than any phantom in the woods. Not that he would hurt her physically, but she could already see how easy it would be to be swept away by his kisses, only to be faced with a cold stranger the next morn.

"Aye. And now you will come with me." Mounting, he reached out to lift her up beside him.

He settled her none too gently in front of him atop the big black beast, his thighs bracketing her bottom while her legs trailed off to one side of the saddle.

"The Fates will frown upon you for not letting me collect my herbs." She gazed longingly at the fields all around them and the forest behind them.

"Herbs or no herbs, you would be wise in the future not to contradict me," he murmured in her ear as he set the destrier in motion. "You will find I make a dangerous adversary."

Arabella, recovered somewhat from his threats to send her away, twisted around and glared into his fierce countenance.

"Ah, but you forget that while you may be dangerous to others, I am a powerful *chovihani* according to you. You pose no danger to me." She tossed his accusation back at him, frustrated by her lack of freedom.

"You'd do well to hide your questionable lineage once we reach England, Arabella. I do not think my king will find your upbringing very amusing," Tristan warned, his gray eyes cold as flint.

She turned from him quickly and said no more as Tristan guided his mount through the trees. She would simply stay close to Anne's guards for her herb gathering ventures and medicine making. Because while she could not afford to be sent home in disgrace, neither could she ignore her calling as a healer. She had trained her whole life to be a wise woman and she could not lose that along with her home. Her family.

Besides, she would need to demonstrate her skills early on in Tristan's homeland if his countrymen were as distrustful of her art as she feared. She would cure every ailment in England to prove herself.

Caught up in her thoughts, she did not realize they were not heading back to Countess von Richt's until they were deep within the forest and the sun was almost obscured by the dense trees.

"Where are we going?" Her anger fled as she looked around the expanse of rich green pines. She felt a rush of pleasure at this unexpected opportunity to explore.

"I was beginning to wonder if you had even noticed." Tristan smoothed her hair off her shoulder while the horse slowed its progress over a treacherous patch of tree roots. "I did not seek you out today simply to have quarrelsome words. I discovered an unusual place in the forest early this morning that reminded me of you. I could not help but think that you would like to see it."

Curious, Arabella looked up at him as he steered the horse under a low branch. It was becoming difficult to make any progress now, the trees were so thick.

A place that reminded Tristan of her? Perhaps a patch of herbs. But Arabella recognized the spot Tristan wanted to show her the moment they reached it, and it was no remote herb garden.

A clearing in the woods greeted her eyes, with huge oak trees planted in a careful circle in the middle. The place appeared so eerily similar to the ring of oaks where she'd first spotted Tristan, it gave her chills. But then she felt so overcome with longing for her home that tears threatened at the corners of her eyes. She hadn't even been gone a full fortnight.

"Well?" Tristan stepped closer to her side, peering into her face to gauge her reaction. "Don't you like it?"

"Of course. I'm just missing my home. Could we go see it?" She had to ask since she would not be able to leap from the horse without his help.

Once they'd dismounted, she hurried ahead to the ring. She was still breathless from her haste when he joined her in the shady circle.

"I guess I thought I had the only perfect ring of trees in the world. I always fancied my ring of trees must be magic."

She had played games within her trees as a child. She had not been lonely, since her grandmother and mother both spent more time with her than—she now understood—many noble parents spared their offspring. And yet she had often longed for a sister or friend her own age, and it had been because of her longing that she'd formed a close relationship with the woods and nature. Her grandmother had understood this, but Arabella did not share the sentiment with the knight beside her for fear he would think her foolish. When he did not speak, she ran her hand over the bark of one bare tree and turned to him again.

"Don't you think it is strange that I would have a perfect ring of oak trees in Bohemia and that there is one here, too?" She slid to sit on the forest floor at the tree's roots.

"Nay. I think that they were both planted purposefully and for the same reasons." He sat beside her, keeping a steady watch outside the ring while he spoke. Arabella realized he still believed they might be followed. "My guess is that our ancestors sometimes liked to gather out here as opposed to in a hall or a chapel, so they planted perfect rings of trees with the same careful attention we would use to build a keep or a sanctuary today."

"I suppose that explains why there is more than one perfect oak ring in the world." She noted the girth of the trees and guessed the massive oaks to be hundreds of years old. "But do you think that the ring in my forest could still be magic?"

"I will admit I thought it was magic when I first spied you there."

Her heart skipped a beat and then sped its pace. The sudden heat between them made her wonder at the wisdom of being alone with him, after all he had warned her about and after all she had already experienced at his hands.

Unbidden, her gaze darted to his broad palms where they rested, one on his sword and one propped on the tree beside hers.

"You need not fear me, Bella." Somehow he had read her thoughts. His use of her family's name for her unleashed an unexpected ribbon of pleasure through her heart.

"I do not understand your purpose in seeking me out."

A smile spread from one corner of his mouth to the other. It was a sight she had not truly seen before.

"Do you not? Then I should be commended for my restraint where you are concerned. Any other man would have…" He stopped himself and leaned back on the ground beside her to stare up at the sky.

"Tristan?"

When he did not answer her, Arabella leaned forward slightly to glance down at him. He slung an arm over his eyes.

"Are you all right?" she pressed, venturing one hand to the dark houppelande that covered his chest.

He did not answer right away. Arabella wondered if he played a jest upon her. But then the large forearm slid from his face and he opened his eyes.

A strange expression greeted her. Perhaps she had been right in her first reaction to run from him, but it was too late to go anywhere now. Trapped in the intensity of his gaze, Arabella could not tear herself away even if she wanted to. The pull of Tristan Carlisle was much too strong. His eyes lured her forward to press her lips to his. His mouth was hard against hers as his tongue coaxed her lips apart. It was the sweetest sort of invasion and she felt a warm languor take hold of her body. He tasted of wind and sun and pine.

Liquid heat shot through her and when she whimpered, she could feel him turn raw and possessive, his tongue exploring her mouth. Her insides melted as her body conspired to quiet any doubts she had. His kiss made clear thought impossible and her mind was a jumble of incoherent reactions to his roving fingers. Dear heaven but she wanted him to touch her more.

Ached for him to touch her more.

Arabella assured herself she would give in just for a

moment, just to feel what it would be like. His arms pressed her hard against the length of his body, and she marveled at the feel of his masculine frame. He was so hard everywhere, his body rigid and rough where hers was soft and smooth. She could have been swept away by the mere feel of his body rubbed against hers, but there was so much more to his embrace than that.

His hands traced the outline of her form through her velvet gown, exciting every nerve and awakening her to a heightened level of sensation. Any place he stroked came alive and her skin tingled with anticipation. If only she could feel his hands upon her bare skin...

As if reading her mind, Tristan untied the laces of her gown down her back and softly eased the velvet down the curve of her shoulder. The combined voices of her own reason and what she'd been taught shouted at her to put an end to the liberties he took with her person, but her curious nature and her desire to control her own fate conspired against her. He ran his finger down the valley between her breasts, and she shivered in his arms. Arabella saw the intent way he watched as the gown brushed over her breast to reveal a taut pink nipple. Slowly, skillfully, he unveiled the other breast to his eyes. Arabella knew she must cease this madness now. Before she could not.

"Tristan?" She feared the powerful ache inside her that went against everything she knew to be right. "I am afraid—"

He broke away from her slowly, regret evident.

"Do not be. I am sorry for allowing myself such intimacies, but I am certain we were not followed, the way we were last night. There is no one nearby and it is easy to perceive visitors in the daylight."

"Nay. I am afraid of my own longings," she whispered, studying his face as she willed her breathing to return to normal. Her whole body hummed with want and the frustration. Where would those heated sensations lead if she allowed things to take their course?

She had thought that lust was a demon known only to men, yet she was certain she must wrestle the beast as fiercely as any man. It was a surprise to discover she might have more in common with this fierce knight than she did with the reserved women she'd studied in the princess's court.

"By all that is holy, Arabella, you should not say such things. And yet— Hell." He growled at the back of his throat before he seemed to shake off his thoughts. "I do not mean to frighten you."

He smiled at her, although the hungry look in his eyes lingered. He pulled her dress back over her shoulders and she relaxed a little as the folds of fabric slid along her body, putting at least that fragile barrier between her and temptation.

"Here." Tristan sat her up and went about lacing her gown into place. "I promise you I will behave myself. I brought you here so that you would enjoy yourself, not to scare you." His task done, Tristan sprawled on the forest floor beside her and rested his head in his hands.

"Now tell me—if it pleases you, my lady Bella—all about you and where you come from. I am most eager to know what had upset you the day I found you in a ring of trees very much like this one."

* * *

He took deep breaths and hoped like hell she would take him up on the offer, since he didn't think he could form any rational conversation on his end. And by the saints, he knew he wouldn't be able to face the ride back to the keep with her between his thighs just yet. Thankfully, she took the opportunity to explain her path to Prague, including some details about her mother and her grandmother Zaharia, who seemed to be of tremendous importance to her.

She did not claim Gypsy heritage outright, but he thought he discerned the Romany look in her features. Apparently her father had been a Bohemian nobleman, making her claim to a place in Anne's retinue legitimate. But Tristan gathered her female forebears possessed a different perspective altogether from the women of the court.

Every so often she would try to ask him about his life, but he steered their talk back to her. When she asked anything about England or the wars he'd fought in France, he would give the briefest answer possible and encourage her to tell him more about life in the Rowan household. Partly, he was curious about her upbringing, which she talked about with such warmth. Having no family of his own and a childhood he'd rather forget, he found her experience intriguing and he hated to dole out pieces of his past for comparison.

Arabella soon lost herself in her subject and while Tristan listened carefully, he could not help an occasional slip into more carnal thoughts. He had come so close to taking more than he should from her today. And while the idea of stealing her innocence had not bothered him when he first identified her as the woman he'd met in the forest, he had to admit his conscience pricked him now.

Did she not deserve the chance to embrace her noble heritage and see what England held in store for her? And yet, there was a quality about her that stirred a man's blood, an earthiness he could not deny. What if Tristan did not pursue her, only to leave her to another man's attentions? The thought rankled. At least—if Tristan succeeded in wooing her—he would ensure their encounter did not impede her ability to study her healing arts. He could make sure she found a place to practice her work safely.

He would not allow her passionate nature to leave her with nothing, the way another man might.

"It is almost moonrise, Tristan." Arabella's voice interrupted his thoughts as she pushed to her feet and Tristan realized the lateness of the hour. "Perhaps we should go."

"Aye. 'Tis a dangerous time of day for us." He rose and called for his horse, still uncertain whether or not to pursue her. "Perhaps you will pay me the honor of your company another day?"

He still intended to keep a watch over her since he feared for her safety, given her penchant for roaming free. That in itself put him in an untenable situation, since it left her alone with him in private places. His pulse quickened, along with his hunger for her.

"I would consider it if you will share with me something of yourself, after all I have revealed to you."

She waited for him to mount and then allowed him to help her up. The nearness of her hip to his thigh forced him to draw one ragged breath after another. Perhaps understanding the dangerous position she put herself in, Arabella held herself rigidly forward to prevent her body from brushing against his. Wise woman.

The falling twilight brought with it a suggestive spell and Tristan struggled to think of a way to distract himself until they were back at the keep. He honestly did not know if he could restrain himself for their trip back to the countess's, let alone during the rest of the journey to London.

"So you think you have done more than your share of talking today?" He slid his arm around her waist to hold her securely in the saddle.

"I have offered up a great deal of my life to your curiosity, including some of my grandmother's most secret herbal remedies, and yet you have remained quiet."

"I vow your tincture mixtures are safe with me, since the instructions are already muddied in my head." Truth be told, he'd missed much of what she'd shared with him today in his haze of lust for her. "But I will entertain you on the way home, my lady. I only wish I knew something more amusing than tales of battle and the life of an English knight."

"But I know nothing of a knight's life."

In between the killing, there was a lot of craving for women, Tristan thought grimly. So he wouldn't be sharing tales of his own life with Arabella. Bella.

She had a beautiful name to match her unique appeal.

"I heard a story while I was on a diplomatic mission to the French court some months ago. I recall it well because the tale is about my namesake, Tristan, and his lady Isolde." He stroked Arabella's hair as he spoke, unable to keep his hands from her. After Elizabeth Fortier had deceived him, Tristan had kept away from noblewomen, since he had no interest in marriage and no lands to offer. He had not missed the complications a noblewoman brought to his bed, but he had missed the softness of such a woman—the perfume and song, the delicate body and smooth skin.

"That would be fine. It has been many moons since I have heard a new story." She did not remove his hand from her person but slanted a charming glance up at him with her green eyes before turning forward once more.

"Well, this Tristan was a great warrior in England." He skimmed a knuckle down her cheek. "He had many adventures, but his greatest concerned Isolde, who was daughter to the Queen of Ireland. Tristan fell in love with the beautiful Isolde while on a royal mission to ask for Isolde's hand for Tristan's king. So Tristan had to ask the woman he loved to wed another man."

Arabella nodded, the shift of her hair sending a sweet smell to his nose.

"A loyal and faithful knight, Tristan won the hand of Isolde for his king, as much as it hurt him. Isolde did not know King Mark, but she was a dutiful lady and went with all good intent to meet her husband. Unbeknownst to Isolde, her mother packed a love potion for Isolde to drink with her new husband, so that the two would fall in love and live happily ever after."

"I do not think there are herbs that would incite love, but I have heard that some sages believe thus."

He smiled and let his head drop closer to her ear for the tale—and so that he could catch her scent again.

"But alas, Isolde did not realize what the strange potion was for and drank the libation with Tristan."

"What happened?" Arabella turned to look at him, eyes wide and suddenly closer than he expected.

"They were bound together forever in endless passion. But of course, Isolde was obligated to King Mark. Tristan and Isolde were forced to pursue their love in secret, slipping away from Mark's court and meeting in dark places."

"I thought you said they were both dutiful people."

"They were, Arabella. But it is an impossible situation to be married to one person when you feel such ardor for another." Tristan trailed his hand over her belly, then adjusted the horse's reins.

Arabella drew in a sharp breath at the touch and turned her face from his.

"But one must suppress it," she insisted, though her reply lacked conviction.

"How could you possibly suppress it?" Tristan spoke into her ear, allowing his lips to skim the soft flesh as he spoke.

"One would have to. Everyone has obligations and responsibilities they are not necessarily happy with, but good people fulfill their duty anyway."

The horse stumbled just then, jerking Arabella backward against Tristan. She scrambled to regain her seat, her wriggling against him a sweet torment that called to mind the heat that had nearly flamed out of control in the forest earlier.

"Even if that duty means you must deny yourself the love of a lifetime?"

"Yes. I did not want to go to England, but I had no choice. I had to fulfill my family's obligation to the crown."

"But you did not leave behind the overwhelming passion of your life, did you?"

"Well…my study of healing, in a way."

"That is not what I mean. My point is that you did not leave behind a man who could render you senseless with desire and satisfy your deepest longings."

Arabella's heart pounded beneath his arm and the knowledge that he affected her thus tempted him as much as any more overt touch.

"You did not leave behind such a man, did you?"

"Of course not."

"Until you have experienced such intense devotion, I do not think it is possible to judge."

Arabella's cheeks flushed with hot color and he would have given his sword arm to know the precise direction of her thoughts at that moment.

"What happened to Tristan and Isolde?" She turned her attention out to the fields as they cleared the edge of the trees.

"They lived many years as lovers, though eventually Tristan took another woman to wife. But as he lay dying, he sent for Isolde so that he might see her one last time. If Isolde was on the ship that sailed to him, a white flag was to be raised. If she were not on the ship, a black flag was to be flown. The ship arrived, and it did fly a white flag, but Tristan's wife reported to him that it was black, and thereupon the brave knight died from his sorrow. When Isolde arrived at her lover's side, she died from her grief as well."

"How sad." She ducked her face with a sniffle and he remembered how many emotions he'd seen in her since meeting her.

That wealth of feeling was something he'd never seen in a noblewoman, but perhaps he could help her to channel it so that she would not reveal too much of herself to others.

"Aye. But the tale reminds us not to put off our happiness." He steered the horse down the slope to the keep as the gates came into view.

"How so? They were lovers as it was. I would think the story shows that unlawful passion should not be heeded."

"Mayhap. But I know that if I were fortunate enough to be granted such a love in my lifetime, no power on heaven or earth would part me from her."

"You could not defy your king," she replied.

"Perhaps I would spirit my beloved away to where no king would have power over us."

As they neared the courtyard, one of Tristan's men— young Henry Mauberly—came running toward them, shouting Tristan's name.

"You'll wake the dead," Tristan admonished him as he drew up, already surveying the courtyard for signs of trouble. The hunting party must have returned by now, but he was certain none of the women would have been stolen, with Simon in charge of the group's safety.

"I wanted to warn you." Mauberly jerked a thumb toward the keep. "Princess Anne is searching for you. Apparently she wishes an audience with you at once, although I have not been able to discover why." Henry's forehead creased in worry, but Tristan remained unconcerned.

"I will see her immediately and find out what is afoot." Tristan urged his horse forward as he shouted his thanks to Henry for the warning.

"What do you think she wants with you?" Arabella waited for him to dismount before she held her hands out to him.

He could not help but savor the way she came to him unquestioningly. Sweet heaven, but he might have to indulge this one selfish need. His hands tightened briefly on her waist before he let her go.

"Concerned for me, little one?"

"Nay. But it is not like the princess to call on you for no reason. I am sure if she is taking pains to find you right away, there is something important brewing."

"I will soon find out." He handed the reins to a stable boy. "In the meantime, you must remain safely inside. If you wish to go out, you must wait until I can escort you."

She nodded, though she could not hide her reluctance.

"Is it really so difficult for you to spend the day in the company of Anne's other women?"

A smile tweaked her soft cheek. "Aye."

"Still, you must wait for me." He let his gaze remain locked with hers for a long moment to ensure she understood his meaning.

And in that moment, he decided he had put off his own wants long enough. Arabella had all but admitted she did not belong with the other women. She did not enjoy the life of a noblewoman. She savored her independence. Tristan could give that to her if she became his.

"Ah. Just the man I have been looking for."

Tristan and Arabella looked up to see Rosalyn de

Clair in the door to the keep. Although the woman was smiling, Tristan perceived a coldness in her eyes as she nodded at Arabella.

"I am on my way to see the princess," he assured her, wishing he had been harsher with her the night before. While he had not wished to hurt her overmuch, he also did not want her to view Arabella as a rival.

"I have been seeking you as well, sir." Rosalyn smiled at Tristan and took his arm.

Before he could extricate himself from her hold, Arabella made her excuses and hurried inside the keep. Tristan watched her disappear, hoping he could make her forget this unpleasantness tomorrow before they continued their journey. Now that he had made up his mind where Arabella was concerned, he saw no reason to wait.

Rosalyn leaned closer as they passed the great hall and moved into the family's living quarters.

"Tristan, please don't be angry with me. It's not my fault, I swear."

His senses hummed with warning at the fear in her tone. He halted his progress and spun her to face him under a low stone arch leading into the countess's apartments.

"What do you mean?"

Before she could answer, a door near them opened into the corridor.

"Oh. There you are." Mary Natansia, the emperor's ward who had captured Simon's eye, rushed forward from a chamber that looked like a lady's solar. Her manner now lacked the warmth of their first meeting in

Prague, as she held herself stiff. "We have been looking for you, Sir Tristan. Would you join us?"

Beyond Mary's shoulder, he could see the princess, along with Countess von Richt and two of her sons, milling around a stone hutch. Tristan could scarcely refuse them an audience, but by now, his skin itched unpleasantly with the sense of imminent doom.

"Of course." He followed Mary into the brightly lit solar, where silk-covered benches sat in a formal row before long, arched windows. Despite the lateness of the hour, some sunlight still filtered through the panes of leaded glass, while torches already burned from their seats in iron rings that rimmed the chamber.

The princess motioned for Tristan to take a seat on the embroidered cushions, a pained expression etched on her young face. He hardly felt at his leisure in the feminine space, with peacocks and garlanded unicorns staring out at him from the rich tapestries.

"Please, sir. I need to speak with you about a matter of the utmost importance." She waited for him to sit while the countess sat near a small sideboard with her hulking sons.

"I trust no one was harmed in the hunting party?" Tristan knew Mauberly would have informed him if such had been the case, but he couldn't come up with any other reason for this strange council to gather.

"Nay. Seeing Rosalyn here, you must know to what I am referring." Anne stared at Tristan.

He grew more uncomfortable by the minute. Anne and Mary looked at him expectantly, as if he could guess their thoughts. Damn it to hell, why had

Richard sent a warrior as his envoy, instead of a pasty-faced courtier who might actually know what these women wanted?

"No, Your Highness. I have no idea to what you are referring." His answer seemed to fluster the princess and Mary, but he noticed that Rosalyn stared demurely into her lap, her hands folded on the beaded skirt of her voluminous surcoat.

She knew what the princess wanted and she had been scared of his reaction, judging by the way she'd spoken to him in the corridor. Did it have to do with Arabella? Remembering the cold look Rosalyn had cast her way, he wondered if the women had begun to question Arabella's place at court.

Anne stood abruptly and positioned herself behind Rosalyn's chair, her own surcoat simple compared to the intricately woven birds and beasts that adorned Rosalyn. Anne placed her hands on the other woman's shoulders and spoke very quietly.

"I am referring to your paramour, Lady Rosalyn. She carries your child, sir, and if you will not offer marriage, I am in a position to demand it."

Tristan's jaw fell open at her words as a ringing started in his ears. His gaze flew to Rosalyn, looking to her to refute the dizzy-eyed claim, but her eyes were still cast down at her folded hands, as if the matter did not surprise her in the least.

The devil take him for a clay-brained idiot. The woman must have instigated this whole bit of stupidity. Bolting from his bench so fast that he knocked the cushions askew, he fixed Anne with an unwavering eye.

"I swear on my honor, I have never lain with this woman in my life."

The countess's sons swarmed to the princess's side, their swords present at their hips even if they did not lay hands upon the hilts. No doubt Tristan looked ready to do murder, but he knew better than to wreak revenge on a group of noblewomen.

"We have the lady's word as well." Anne's expression remained resolute.

The anger churning through him demanded an outlet, but he feared an ill-advised outburst now would only worsen the situation. He was in the Bohemian court now. No one here knew the depth of his character, the way they did in his homeland.

"And you will take her word over mine because she is one of your own?" He had not meant to sound quite so disagreeable, but it took every scrap of his reserve not to howl his fury in Rosalyn de Clair's faithless face.

Anne's pursed lips admonished him even as she kept her tone even. "There is also a witness to Rosalyn's early-morning departure from your chamber, Sir Tristan."

When the princess's gaze slid to Mary Natansia, Tristan understood the matter more clearly. He had no doubt that Mary had seen as much. Mary's scruples would have demanded that she see Rosalyn married to the man whose bedchamber Rosalyn had visited in the night, assuming the man to be the father of her child. If, indeed, she was even with child.

Tristan had little cause to believe anything the de Clair woman claimed.

"Your Highness, I have only been among your retinue for the last fortnight. And the only time Lady Rosalyn visited my bedchamber was last night. I assure you, I did not invite her, nor did I touch her."

"Her realization of her condition is early, I'll grant you. Sometimes a woman just knows. Her honor is ruined anyhow, sir, as you can surely understand."

"But not by my doing. I told you, I have never even lain with this woman and I will swear that before a priest."

Mary rose from her chair to face him.

"Sir Tristan, I saw Rosalyn slip out of your chamber early this morning. I saw her disheveled clothes and her fallen hair. I am not so innocent as to think she arrived in such a state of disarray."

Tristan knew a lost cause as he met Mary's clear-eyed stare. He could see the disillusionment and anger there, along with a certain amount of righteous certainty that she had done the right thing. He understood her position, recognizing that some people were too good to believe the worst of others. Knowing this, he did not bother to explain that Rosalyn's clothes were disheveled from hiding behind a wardrobe or rubbing herself against him in a manner meant to tempt him.

"I will find a way to prove my innocence. I am an honorable knight and I would never defile an innocent noblewoman." As it happened, his morals had stood strong against the temptation of Arabella Rowan, and she could not even claim full nobility.

"We trust in your good name, sir, and will wait for you to make the honorable decision." Anne nodded, subtly dismissing him.

As eager as he was to leave the chamber, Tristan could not resist one last comment.

"Until then, I hope you will consider assigning each of your maidens one of your older women as escorts, lest we find another man falsely accused during our journey."

He took his leave to think through his options, before Rosalyn's lies created more trouble. He had not climbed from ignoble beginnings to his current station only to be brought low by the very kind of scheming woman he had sought to avoid.

Unsettled by her talk with Tristan as much as by her fear that something was amiss, Arabella wandered through Countess von Richt's sprawling keep instead of returning to her chamber. They would depart Cologne two days hence and she found herself eager to be underway, despite her distaste for the long hours of travel in a confined space. At least the party would be moving. The days in Cologne stifled her as they passed, for the most part, inside thick stone walls. Arabella had never felt so far removed from the earth and the herbs that provided her with the tools she needed for her work.

As the corridors narrowed and she reached a dark portion of the keep, she heard a shriek of pain nearby. The torturous sound broke off and then surged again, louder than before. She moved in the direction of the noise, remembering her own screams when a strange man had grabbed her in Prague.

A servant hurried by her and Arabella stopped the woman in her path.

"What is it?" she asked the maid, who nearly spilled the pitcher of water she carried.

"It is Marta. A kitchen maid, my lady. She is having her baby this night and the pains are coming fast. The countess cannot be disturbed and we do not know who to—"

"I am a healer and I can help. My chamber is two doors down from the princess's solar. Do you think you can find it and retrieve the leather pouch near my palette for me?" Arabella took the pitcher of water from the maid and gave the younger woman a gentle nudge in the right direction. "Make haste. I will attend Marta."

Arabella wasn't surprised to find out a baby was trying to make its way into the world on the eve of the full moon, and she hastened to the chamber the maid had pointed out. The work was intense and complicated by the baby's awkward position within the womb, but as the night wore on, she delivered her first baby without her grandmother's aid.

Arabella felt more fulfillment than she had ever known in her life, and she understood at that moment that she had left her Bohemian home at precisely the right time. She was ready to be a healer on her own and she was needed elsewhere. To stay in the little village in Bohemia, which was already graced with one healer, would have been selfish. She needed to use the skills Zaharia had taught her to save many other people. She had never felt so blessed as when she held Marta's crying son in her hands and passed him to the equally teary-eyed kitchen maid.

Happy but weary, Arabella stumbled out of the room a few hours later. She had given Marta an herb to help her sleep and had passed the babe into the care of

Marta's younger sister, who would sit by her sister the rest of the night. The countess had also visited the birthing room briefly and said she would check on the girl again before morning.

As Arabella made her way back to her own chamber, Rosalyn de Clair stepped into her path, looking as fresh as a newly picked flower. A nightshade, Arabella reminded herself.

"Congratulations, Arabella." Rosalyn smiled as she paused beside her. "I hear you delivered a squalling babe for one of the kitchen maids this eve."

"Aye." Arabella tightened her grip on her pouch of herbs, wary of the rumors she'd overheard regarding her work as a healer.

"Perhaps you can deliver Tristan's babe when I give him a fine son before the next harvest." She smoothed a hand over her flat belly. "Then again, mayhap it would make you uncomfortable to deliver Tristan's baby, when you fancied him yourself."

Rosalyn patted Arabella's arm before she swished past her down the hall, leaving Arabella to contend with a knot in her stomach and her heart in her throat.

Tristan's babe? She must have misheard the woman's comment. And yet— Hadn't Rosalyn made a point of showing her favor for him?

Arabella couldn't remember finding her chamber or readying herself for bed. She was only vaguely aware that she was at last lying down, safe from the malicious little nightshade with the taunting dark eyes.

Perhaps you can deliver Tristan's babe when I give him a fine son before the next harvest.

The words seemed caught in a permanent echo, ringing back to her time and again, growing louder all the while. Tristan's baby. The cruel and smug Rosalyn was to bear Tristan Carlisle's heir. It could not be.

But as much as Arabella's heart would have her deny it, her mind screamed the undeniable possibility. It was early for Rosalyn to know she carried Tristan's babe. Especially as a first-time mother. Could Rosalyn have lied about it?

And yet how could she doubt the matter, when she herself had so recently fallen prey to the knight's persuasive courtship? Hadn't she lain beside him just that afternoon, thrilling to his every caress as if she were a woman with nothing to lose? What had made her think that her charms were any more special than any other woman's?

Her anger with herself grew right alongside her fury with Tristan. She had been a hasty-witted fool to be taken in by his attentions and his story of undying passion. Not for all the world would she trust him again. Nay, she would not even allow him near her, no matter that for one frozen moment tonight she had almost wished she had been the one to know Tristan's traitorous touch.

Chapter Seven

A persistent knocking woke Arabella the next morning. Try as she might to ignore it, it wouldn't go away.

"Arabella. Please let me in."

Arabella recognized the voice as Mary's even through the heavy velvet hangings around her bed, but she still didn't move to open the door, since that would bring her all the closer to facing the day. Facing Rosalyn de Clair and, worse, facing *him*.

"Arabella, there is someone here who wants to see you," Mary called.

"Nay." Could Tristan Carlisle be at Mary's side? Arabella picked at a golden tassel looped around one of the bedposts. She had not grown accustomed to the wealth of the countess's keep.

"Arabella, don't you want to see the precious little boy who owes his life to you?" Mary asked.

Heart softening at the memory of the beautiful baby she'd helped guide into the world, Arabella yanked the tassel to draw aside the bed curtains. She wrapped herself in a small length of fur draped over the edge of the bed and flung the door wide. Mary held a tiny creature whose eyes blinked in wonder.

"Oh." Arabella reached to take the little bundle. "He's so beautiful. Did Marta name him yet?"

"No." Mary settled herself on a bench at the foot of Arabella's bed. "She wants you to name the baby."

"No." Arabella's heart squeezed tight at the suggestion of the honor.

"'Tis true. The countess and I spent time at her side this morning after prayer. Apparently, Marta did not marry the babe's father and she has no family of her own, so she hopes that you will name him, since she credits you with her life and her babe's."

The darkness in Arabella's heart over Tristan and Rosalyn eased at this sweet reminder that she could make a difference in people's lives with her healing. She would not let the news of Tristan's faithlessness rob her of her strength.

"Well?" Mary prodded, stroking the soft down on the baby's head with the back of her finger. "What will you call him?"

"Stefan." Arabella wanted the first baby she had ever delivered on her own to bear a very special name. "It was my grandfather's name. I never knew him, but my mother has told me there was never a man stronger nor truer. Do you think she will like it?"

"Aye." Mary smiled as they gazed at the little boy, who was just beginning to fall asleep. "We must bring the babe to his mother as soon as you are dressed. Let me hold Stefan while I speak to you of some unpleasantness with the princess's retinue."

Dread pinched her as she awaited the news. She could scarcely bear to hear it all over again. Handing Stefan back, Arabella reached into her traveling chest for a fresh kirtle.

"I have heard the rumors of Rosalyn de Clair's babe and— The man who fathered the bairn, as well." As she slid into the gown, she wondered if the lout had lingered in the beds of any other Bohemian nobles.

"I am glad you've heard. I wanted to be sure you knew, since the princess held the English knights in high regard until she learned the truth."

"She is certain it is true?" Arabella had not realized she held out some small hope that Rosalyn had told a mistruth until the question fell from her lips. Bending to her trunk again, she unearthed a blue surcoat embroidered with butterflies and small birds. As she tugged it free from the trunk, the sweet herbs she'd packed around her clothing released the scent of her beloved homeland in the full bloom of summer.

The ache that went through her was so strong her eyes burned with it.

"*I* am certain it could be." Mary's words were tinged with a bitterness Arabella would not have expected. "I saw the lady emerge from Sir Tristan's chamber myself, or I would not have believed it. I had taken a liking to Sir Simon and viewed them both as men of honor."

Sensing that Mary battled a hurt not unlike her own, Arabella stopped fussing with the ties on her surcoat to comfort her friend.

"We cannot blame ourselves for trusting men who were sent to protect us." She squeezed Mary's shoulders while a party of revelers from the day's hunt walked past the chamber door, singing a lively tune. "We saw how nobly the English knights guarded us that day in the marketplace when I was taken by a strange man."

"Aye," Mary agreed, her voice soft with emotion. "I did not expect coarse behavior of such men."

Arabella regretted not speaking out about the conversation she had overheard that day she'd hidden in a chamber at Prague Castle. Yet Rosalyn de Clair was no widow. How could Arabella have guessed that Tristan would overstep the limits he'd set regarding the princess's women?

"Now that we are aware of their capabilities, we will remain distant and safe from them. I am sure the English king will punish them suitably."

"The princess hopes to resolve the matter herself before we leave the countess's keep. We might linger here longer than expected."

More laughing revelers filled the corridor outside Arabella's chamber and she made haste to finish dressing so that she could help bolster Mary's spirits.

"Then we will help the countess get ready for the night's feast, which she has promised will be the most lively yet. What say you? Shall we deliver Stefan to his mother and then show the countess how good Bohemian honey gingerbread is made?"

Mary smiled and Arabella promised herself she would not allow her friend's thoughts to stray toward an English knight any more often than she allowed her own to do so. No licentious foreigner would steal away Arabella's chance to prove her family's honor to the world.

Later that night, Tristan moved silently through the keep's gardens to contemplate the second-floor balcony that opened off Arabella's chamber. A warm glow emanated from her windows, but he could not tell if the light came from the hearth or if her taper still burned.

She had heard the rumors of his dalliance with the de Clair woman. He could tell by the way she'd avoided his eyes in the great hall while the company dined. Of course, many of the princess's other women had avoided his eyes, as well, proving to him that the matter of Rosalyn's false accusation had spread like the plague among the nobles. Tristan cared little for anyone's opinion here, save Arabella's and Princess Anne's. Of course, his king would have the final say on his future, so the monarch's opinion would be more important than anyone's. But until they returned home, Tristan would have to contend with the Bohemian noblewomen and the way they viewed him. He hadn't been able to think of anything else all day—even when he'd received word from Prague that Ivan Litsen had escaped.

Now, more than ever, he needed to be vigilant to ensure the safety of Anne's retinue, yet his thoughts were elsewhere.

Determined to make Arabella see the truth, Tristan tested the branch of a nearby fruit tree to see if it might hold his weight. Though the trunk seemed slim and the wood was brittle with cold, the tree held him until he could grab the ornamental stone rails surrounding the balcony.

Hauling himself over the barrier, he peered through the narrow pane of blue glass beside the door to her chamber. Within the apartment, he spied Arabella brushing her hair, her fingers smoothing the unbound locks behind the wide bristles. A taper burned on the chest near where she sat. The folds of a blue velvet chamber robe spilled onto the floor at her feet, and heavy white lace at her throat provided an enticing hint of the night rail beneath.

Tristan had not meant to interrupt her at such a private moment, but neither could he regret the sight before him. Still, his presence here—now—would surely make her nervous, and that he did regret.

He swore under his breath, but the sound must have been enough to alert Arabella, for she turned toward the balcony door. After placing the brush beside the taper, she moved toward the glass pane.

Retreating into the shadows, he avoided her glance until she opened the door into the night. Then, reaching out to her before she could react, he folded his hand over her mouth and held her to him. She stiffened. Softly, he spoke into her ear.

"I will not hurt you, Arabella. 'Tis Tristan and I need to speak with you."

He'd been hoping she would find comfort in the knowledge, but he was disappointed. She trembled beneath his hands and he released his hold on her mouth but not her slender waist.

"Is this how you approached the last maid you led astray, sir?" She stared daggers at him in the moonlight as she peered over her shoulder at him.

"Nay." He let go of her waist, his hands missing the feel of her even before his fingers were fully free of the velvet. "But then I know well that Lady Rosalyn was no maid that night she hid herself in my chamber."

Bitterness clogged his throat and he swallowed it with effort.

"Do you have any idea how you are compromising me by being here right now?" Arabella peered down into the empty garden before pulling him into her chamber and out of the moonlight.

"Aye. I understand completely, since the de Clair woman used the same scheme upon me for her own ends."

Arabella was quiet a moment and he wondered if she had taken the time to consider a scenario no one else had bothered to ponder. His hope faded when she shook her head.

"It is not up to me to determine your guilt or innocence, sir. Better women than I have that responsibility, and it seems your appeal did not sway them." She glanced over her shoulder toward the door leading out to the corridor before bending to move a heavy bench toward it.

"Let me." Easing her aside, he repositioned the bench to guarantee their privacy, only partially surprised that she would lock herself within her chamber while he remained with her. Clearly, her good name meant more to her than any fear of what he might do while they were alone.

"What are you doing here, Tristan?" She tugged a linen from her bed and draped it around herself, tipping the candle enough to rock the heavy silver base but not enough to knock it over.

"I have come because I need your help." He cursed

himself for noticing her pink toes peering out from under the layers of blanket, robe and night rail. Her bare feet reminded him of her vulnerability and the intimate state in which he'd found her.

Dangerous thoughts for a man already accused of untoward behavior where women were concerned.

"What do you mean?" Her grip on the blanket rendered her knuckles white.

"I need the aid of your healing skills, Arabella, but not until you've heard all I have to say."

"You are hurt?" Her expression shifted from wariness to concern. Her eyes narrowed as she seemed to search his body for injury.

And what did it say about him that his body reacted to her interest on the basest level, despite the royal wrath hovering over his head?

"Nay. But your healing knowledge might help me understand Rosalyn's claim. I needed time and privacy to relate my tale, since you avoided me today."

"I think I have good reasons, when you would woo one woman while bedding another." She scrubbed a hand over her forearm as if to warm herself, despite the blaze in the small stone hearth.

"You are wrong. Your princess is wrong. And although I understand why Lady Mary believes I have done such a thing, I swear to you that she has drawn the wrong conclusion as well. I am *not* the father of Rosalyn de Clair's child, nor have I ever touched her beyond a courtier's politeness witnessed by the entire Bohemian court."

"Do not forget that I know better than some how persuasive your touches can be." Arabella's cheeks flushed, but whether her high color was due to discomfort at the topic or outright anger, he couldn't be sure.

"That does not mean I would apply them to every passing maid." Frustration crawled over his skin. If Rosalyn was a man, he would defend his honor with a sword. But in this battle with a woman, what weapon could he choose? "My king would not trust such a man to safeguard a hundred women halfway across the continent."

"Tell me then, Tristan, why do you think Rosalyn would do such a thing? If you are not the father of her babe, why would she not simply point out the proper man to the princess?" She stood so close to her curtained bed that Tristan could not help but think how easy it would be to pull her into the privacy of those heavy velvet hangings.

"Mayhap her lover is someone whom her family disapproves of. Or it may be that he has grown tired of her. I don't know, but the first time I even noticed her was the day we set out from Prague. She made it her mission to ride next to me whenever possible and presented herself to me in a way that conveyed she was no innocent."

At that moment, Tristan heard voices in the corridor. He placed his fingers lightly over Arabella's lips in warning. When the feminine laughter faded away, he removed his hand from her mouth and drew her farther from the door.

"Yet you did not simply take what she offered?" Arabella peered at him, a dark emotion in her eyes.

Surprised by the forthrightness of the question from a maid, Tristan reminded himself Arabella did not possess the same social sensibilities as her peers because of her unusual upbringing.

"Even if I had wanted to lie with her, I would not have risked it while she remained under my protection. There is the matter of my honor. And I have reason to believe my king will recognize my service after this mission, so I would be cautious for that reason if no other." Before his death, the Black Prince had promised Tristan lands and a title. Now, five long years later, Tristan knew young King Richard would have to either produce those lands upon Tristan's completion of this duty or else free him from service to the Crown to seek his fortune elsewhere.

Arabella seemed to weigh those words for a long moment before, finally, she gave a small nod as if to acknowledge the truth she found in the idea. Or was that wishful thinking?

She paced a few steps from him and toyed with a small pouch. He recognized it as a token she carried with her constantly.

Curious, he stepped closer to watch her crush the pouch between her fingers. The velvet sack released a fragrance he'd come to associate with her. Flowers? More of her precious herbs?

"What would you have me do, Tristan? You said you came here to ask for my help." Placing the small bag on a chest, she stared up at him. Her green eyes glowed brightly in the dim room, the golden light from the hearth picking out the flecks of amber.

"You are a healer. I heard that you acted as midwife to one of the keep's servants last night. You must know enough to be able to tell whether a woman is months or mere weeks with child, right?"

"It is not always easy. Some women do not betray signs for months, others much sooner."

"I am willing to bet that Rosalyn is much further along than she pretends." Tristan had watched over the women in Anne's retinue well enough for the past fortnight to know none of them would have had the opportunity for any encounters save with his men. He trusted this had not happened, so that meant Rosalyn had been with child before they departed Prague. "I want you to find out just how much further."

"You cannot be serious."

"My honor and my future are both at stake, Arabella. I am deadly serious."

Arabella paced the floor of her chamber as footsteps echoed in the corridor once again. Tristan tensed at the activity in the keep. He should be overseeing the guard on the princess instead of tending to personal matters, but hellfire, Rosalyn's scheme would destroy all he'd worked for if he didn't stop her. And if there was any small chance that one of Tristan's knights had committed this deed, either before they left Prague or after, that man might prove an insidious threat to Anne's companions.

"Do you think, like the rest of Anne's followers, that I am some kind of sorceress who can peer into a cup of tea leaves and discern such things? Tristan, to find out something like that, I'd have to have Rosalyn's permission to examine her. I'd need to touch her belly or—" She made a helpless gesture. "You don't just walk up to a body and grab them."

"I know what you would need to do, Arabella. If I could arrange the opportunity, would you do it?" He tried not to notice the way the blanket she had thrown about her had slipped off one shoulder.

"She hates the sight of me. She'd never agree to such a thing. Especially if she really is further along than she says, she will not give us a chance to find out the truth."

He made no comment, unsure whether Arabella would agree with his plan.

"Unless you're not planning to obtain her permission?" she asked.

"I am unconcerned with her permission."

"Sweet, merciful saints. Tristan, I could not. She would have to be willing or I—"

"What about me? I am not willing to marry a woman I have never even touched, and yet your princess gives me no choice. But I will not marry a scheming woman just because she has envisioned me as a useful husband." He did not wish to frighten Arabella with the depth of his feeling, but the anger simmering in his blood would not be cooled until he'd revealed the false-speaking wench for the liar he knew her to be.

Finally, Arabella nodded.

"You might wish to give her an herb that will relax her if you hope to convince her to see a healer." She reached into the wooden chest beside her bed and pulled from its depths a small leather sack tied with a strip of dried weed. "A pinch of this is no more than a midwife would give to an expectant mother to ensure peaceful rest, so it will pose no harm to an innocent babe. It might help relax Rosalyn enough to listen if you ask her to seek care for her child."

"Thank you." He took the pouch and stuffed it in his tunic. "I am more deeply in your debt than I can say."

He watched her tuck a tray of herbs back inside the chest before she closed the box again, locking it with a key she kept at her bedside.

"Then, I pray you, please make sure I do not find myself on the wrong end of Anne's wrath should she discover your plan."

"I vow my thanks will be more substantial than that, should I find an opportunity." The desire to kiss her loomed large, but given his current situation and the fact that he'd sneaked into her chamber, he guessed that wasn't a desire he should act on. Still, he brushed his lips across her forehead before backing toward the window to leave.

"You will fetch me when you need me?" She followed him to the balcony and opened the door for him.

Moonlight spilled into the room, casting shadows of the tree branches along the cold stone floor.

"Count on it." Bowing low to Arabella, Tristan couldn't help but think how he'd assumed her strange upbringing meant she would welcome the kind of dalliance Rosalyn de Clair had obviously indulged in with another man. Tristan hadn't seen past Arabella's wild eyes and untamed ways to the noble heart beneath her earthy nature.

And while he regretted his false impression of her, he would make sure that no one else at King Richard's court made the same mistake. Arabella's kindness toward him when he probably didn't deserve it had earned her the most vigilant protection in London, where the cruelty of a royal court could be far more dangerous than any bandits they might encounter on a trek across the continent.

Chapter Eight

Arabella did not have long to wait for Tristan's call. She raced to Lady Rosalyn de Clair's chamber the next morning after being roused from a fitful sleep by Tryant Hilda, who had been sent by the princess. Apparently Lady Rosalyn had taken a fall that morning while out riding and Princess Anne wanted assurance both Rosalyn and her babe were uninjured.

Had Tristan concocted the story to hide the sedative he'd given to Rosalyn? Or had she truly fallen? Uneasy with her part in Tristan's scheme, Arabella quickened her pace. When she arrived at Rosalyn's chamber, the princess, Mary and two serving maids were already at the woman's bedside.

"Thank you for coming so quickly," Princess Anne greeted her as Arabella went straight to the bed where Rosalyn lay.

"What happened?" Arabella asked as she lifted the woman's eyelids and peered at her. The laces on her saffron-colored gown had already been loosened.

"We're not certain. Sir Tristan brought her to us. Apparently they went out for an early ride and Rosalyn fell." Mary wiped a damp cloth across the other woman's forehead.

"Did her horse rear?"

"No." The princess seated herself on the room's only other furnishing, a small bench beside a door that led out onto a balcony similar to Arabella's. "They were not mounted when the accident occurred. I believe they were walking to their horses after stopping by the river when Rosalyn stumbled over something."

Arabella paused in her inspection of Rosalyn's head to glance at the princess.

"I do not see a head injury besides a small bump." She would not lie for Tristan's sake.

"Neither did we, Arabella," Mary murmured. "But we thought you might want to check the babe after the fall. Sir Tristan seemed concerned for the child's safety."

Nodding, Arabella loosened the rest of Rosalyn's gown and shook off her mixed emotions about this exam. Tristan could not have asked for more ideal circumstances. Lady Rosalyn was ready to be examined and both Princess Anne and Lady Mary were present to learn the truth about Rosalyn's child.

Gingerly, she touched Rosalyn's abdomen. She was surprised when her fingers met the stiff material of binding beneath her kirtle. Gesturing to one of the serving maids for assistance, Arabella loosened the garment.

Once the bindings were cast aside, the shape of Rosalyn's distended belly was clear. Rosalyn de Clair had clearly known about her impending child for longer than she had claimed. She had hidden her poor babe beneath an armorlike undergarment.

For a moment, Arabella remained too stunned to continue, but Mary came to stand by her side and urged her on.

"For the babe's sake, Arabella," Mary reminded her friend as she fought back her own tears. "And for Sir Tristan's. I have accused him wrongly."

Arabella checked Rosalyn over and determined the child to be at least three full moons, perhaps more. Since Rosalyn had attempted to hide her form beneath her gowns, chances were she was not eating nearly enough.

"She needs rest and food." Arabella packed away her herbs, since Rosalyn did not require any. "I will check on her later if you would like me to, but she may not want to see me."

"Thank you, Arabella. We are grateful to you for coming so quickly." The princess clasped Arabella's hand but exchanged looks with Mary. "It seems we will have to apologize to Sir Tristan."

After gathering up her things, Arabella left the room to the serving maids and headed back to her own chamber. She was not surprised when a large hand reached out from the shadows to touch her shoulder before she reached her room.

"Arabella." Tristan stepped into the corridor from the shelter of a hidden stairway she had not noticed before. The scent of cedar and balsam drifted up through the stairwell and she wondered if the passageway led outside.

She did not have time to ask, however, as the

English knight opened her door and stepped inside her chamber with her.

"What is her condition?" He turned her to face him, his fingers clenching her shoulders.

Arabella was ready to protest his grip, but changed her mind when she saw the stern set of his features and the cold purpose in his gray eyes.

"At least three moons, perhaps more. She has been hiding her child to her own detriment and likely the detriment of that innocent babe."

Tristan released her arm. "While I am sorry for her poor health and the fate of a child who deserves better than this, I can not help but thank God for allowing the truth to be known."

"The whole keep will know it soon enough. The princess and Mary both saw her condition for themselves."

Tristan's eyes narrowed. "And yet it will be you she blames when she awakens."

"There can be no help for it. She did not like me before I revealed her secret, either." Arabella hid her herbs behind her bed while Tristan watched, and her sudden awareness of him warmed her skin.

"I would not have her blame you for what is my fault. I know firsthand that she is a dangerous enemy." He stepped closer to her and Arabella's breath caught in her throat. "I will protect you from her. From anyone who tries to hurt you."

Arabella watched as he reached to stroke her hair. He plucked at a lock, twining it idly around his fingertip.

Before she could stop herself, she inclined her head ever so slightly toward his touch.

"I will not need protection from Rosalyn de Clair." Arabella did not wish to feel indebted to a man who unsettled her greatly already. "Although I did not wish to make this journey, I have since realized that it will be good for me to find my own strength. I can't do that if I allow you to protect me."

His caress paused and he tipped her chin up. The heat she saw in his eyes sent a bolt of want straight through her core.

"Will you allow me to kiss you, Arabella?" His invitation was soft and warm on her lips, his mouth already close to hers.

"I dare not." She swayed on her feet in spite of herself.

"You have dared a great deal more, to our mutual enjoyment." His hand trailed down her neck to trace the shape of her shoulder. His thumb dipped beneath the neckline of her kirtle.

Arabella gasped softly, knowing she needed to banish him from her chamber but unwilling to halt the pleasure he could bring her.

"Or are you afraid to admit how much you liked what we have shared?" At his words, a quiver raced down her spine and caused a stirring all over her body. She felt a warmth in her womb and a weakness in her knees, and did not even try to stifle the little sigh that escaped her lips.

"I am not afraid to admit it, only afraid of where it will lead when you are so deeply opposed to taking a wife." After seeing the lengths Rosalyn de Clair had been driven to in the hopes of procuring the protection of a husband, Arabella realized she could not afford to allow her passions to rule her. In her newly claimed position as a noblewoman, she did not have the love of her family nearby to bolster her. Unwed women with children were outcasts. Even the maid Marta had been stripped of her post with the countess before her babe had been born.

All around her, Arabella saw warnings not to give her emotions free rein.

Tristan stiffened. But then, as a man, he would not share her concerns.

"Fair enough." He released her, the warmth of him disappearing from her skin. "I would not have you fear the consequences, when I owe you my freedom."

"And I would never want you to think I tried to steal it away after you found it again. It is better if we do not tempt ourselves."

She didn't like the idea that there would be no more moonlight kisses and no more stolen touches. But she possessed naught to recommend her to any man—no riches and only a shaky claim to noble lineage. And for a man like Tristan, who did not wish to burden himself with a wife in the first place, Arabella knew her appeal did not extend beyond fickle passion.

Chapter Nine

"We need to break up the group for the crossing." Tristan pulled Simon aside at the marketplace in Calais. They should have sailed for home three days ago. They'd left Countess von Richt's after the princess decided Tristan needn't wed Rosalyn de Clair immediately, though she had assured him she would address the matter with the king when they arrived in London since there was still the matter of Rosalyn having been seen leaving Tristan's chamber.

With the threat of marriage no longer looming, he'd been able to devote his full attention to protecting the Bohemian retinue, a job that grew more complicated with each passing day.

"Have you gone mad?" Simon pulled Tristan closer to the shoreline where boatmen waited with seafaring vessels for the crossing. "We cannot afford to divide our limited numbers. What if we are set upon while separated? We would be easier to defeat that way."

"But we are easier to follow this way. Herding a

hundred women across the continent attracted constant attention." Although at least the sheer number of people had helped keep him away from Arabella this past fortnight. He was determined to honor her wishes, but her eyes still followed him every day, her regard a steady, if invisible, caress.

"Think you we will be attacked during the crossing?" Simon gawked at him as if he'd turned into a lunatic. "My God, man. We are a stone's throw from our home shores. Let us cross as soon as possible and be done with it. The winds are with us today and the chill of the journey is beginning to take its toll on some of the women."

Tristan understood the need to finish their journey, but he could not rid himself of the sensation they were being pursued. Some of the French king's guard had joined their number three days ago in a sign of diplomacy, after the king had made a final effort to waylay Princess Anne into an alliance with him instead of with his English enemy. Tristan had resented the king's tactics, but the princess had dissuaded him simply and tactfully. Now the French men-at-arms swore they'd spotted men riding behind the Bohemian party at a distance when they'd first seen Anne's retinue.

"We cannot discount the possibility of attack at sea if men follow us with intent to intercept Princess Anne. I will not allow impatience to thwart a mission that has been a success thus far."

Successful, at least, as far as his duty was concerned. On a personal level, the past moon had been a dismal failure, since he had frightened away the most intriguing woman he'd ever met. Simon had suggested that Tristan should welcome this new estrangement from Arabella, given the whispers of her Gypsy heritage and mysterious past, but Tristan missed her. He missed talking to her and—even more—he sorely missed the feel of her lips beneath his.

He peered back toward Arabella and found the place she'd been standing vacant. Mary Natansia stood beside the princess, just as she had moments ago, but Arabella Rowan was nowhere in sight. He scanned the market-place for signs of her or the blue traveling gown she'd been wearing. He found nothing.

Cold dread gripped his gut even as he prayed she had merely wandered off to some abandoned hillside to feel the earth beneath her heathen feet.

"Hellfire." Tristan called to his horse as he turned on his boot heel. "Prepare the party for an overnight. Arabella's gone."

"Rosalyn, I do not think we should move any farther from the group." Arabella reined in her horse, refusing to follow the other woman any deeper into the surrounding woods. "You really shouldn't be riding anyhow, and the princess has offered you her carriage."

Rosalyn de Clair turned to face her with open hostility in her dark eyes. Her purple surcoat swept down one side of her mount's flank as she rested sideways in one of the new sidesaddles that Princess Anne had made popular among her women.

"It is she who asked me to speak with you, Arabella Rowan. Would you deny your princess her wishes? Or are you so poorly raised that you do not know better than to displease the royal family?" Rosalyn had not forgiven Arabella for revealing the truth of her bairn's age to the Bohemian court.

Arabella knew as much from the glaring looks Rosalyn had cast her way during the past fortnight. She had not bothered to tell the woman that she had not needed to explain Rosalyn's condition to the princess. Princess Anne had seen the proof with her own eyes in Rosalyn's unbound belly.

"I have followed you because I wish to honor Anne." Arabella tamped down her anger at the woman as she glanced back toward the marketplace. They hadn't strayed far from the group, but Arabella knew Tristan had stressed the importance of remaining together.

She had tried to obey that rule, truly she had. But the close quarters of that kind of travel had made her all the more disposed to grant Rosalyn's wish to speak with her privately, especially since Princess Anne wanted the two of them to make peace.

When Arabella turned back to speak to Rosalyn, however, the other woman was moving her horse out of the small clearing while another rider entered the same patch of rocky ground. A man.

Nervous, Arabella was turning her horse around to return to the group when another mounted figure galloped toward her, cutting off her escape.

"Rosalyn!" She called out to the other woman, but she seemed to have disappeared.

Had she gone for help? Or was there some chance the woman had led Arabella astray on purpose?

Arabella met the eyes of the first rider and realized her folly as she recognized the face of the criminal who had tried to attack her at the bazaar in Prague.

Ivan Litsen.

Too late, she urged her horse away from him, but she was hemmed in by her pursuers. Heart battering against her chest, she screamed, thinking her voice might carry as far as the marketplace.

Her horse danced beneath her and she wished again for the little knife she had lost to Tristan Carlisle that day in the ancient oak ring. If only she had a weapon of some kind.

Digging her heels in the horse's flanks, she steered the animal hard to the right. Before the mare could gather speed, the unknown rider caught up to her and yanked her out of the saddle and onto his mount. She kicked and flailed, but Litsen's friend was a younger man, strong as an ox with muscles as thick as tree trunks. The brute had her immobile, her mouth muffled with a restraining hand, in mere moments.

Her back bent awkwardly over the man's knee as he pinned her.

"Well, my lady." Ivan Litsen's voice reached her ears before she saw his boots and his horse's legs from her awkward vantage point. "How nice to see you under more favorable circumstances."

Breath burning her lungs while blood rushed to her head, Arabella couldn't imagine what this man could want with her. No man would travel hundreds of miles for the sake of ruining one woman. This man was up to something far more cunning. And why hadn't they chased Rosalyn? Unless there were even more attackers she had not yet seen?

The thought made her blood chill.

"I cannot say the same, sir," she choked out between clenched teeth before the beast who set her upright on the horse.

She could see now that her other captor was tall and fair-haired. He possessed chiseled features and no emotions to animate them, while his eyes were a muted, muddy color she could not identify.

"I will hold her." The man spoke to Ivan while scarcely moving his colorless lips. His words were in English, yet his accent was not that of a native speaker. "You must obtain the other one while the party disperses to look for this one."

"Aye. I might have to wait until after nightfall, but I will be back with her." Ivan sweated profusely and smelled of his own nervousness.

"If you don't secure her tonight, we'll salvage our losses with this one." The tall man touched Arabella's cheek to turn her face upward. His gentleness with one hand while he imprisoned her with the other made her ill.

"She will be worth our trouble, Thadus." Ivan seemed to be waiting for a sign from the tall man before he left.

"She meets my approval. Now make haste, lest I take her for myself and leave you behind."

Ivan kneed his horse and Arabella was left alone with the man called Thadus. She was almost sorry to see Ivan leave. For all of his slimy ways, he seemed less of a threat than the cold man staring at her now.

"Get down."

Arabella hesitated for just a moment.

"Get down." Thadus yanked her arms downward and she sprawled on the ground. Arabella tried to collect her wits as fast as she could, knowing her only hope was to outsmart this man.

"Stand up, wench. And if you make another sound, I will slit your friend's throat when Ivan returns with her. Your value alone is enough to make my trip worthwhile, and I will do whatever I need to in order to keep you compliant."

Arabella's knees wobbled at the cool warning and she knew by the lack of humanity in his eyes that he would carry out his threat. Of course, she did not know whose throat was at risk. Rosalyn's? Or another woman from the Bohemian retinue? Not that it mattered, since Arabella would not risk any of them.

Thadus retrieved a length of chain from a pouch tied to his saddle and used the heavy metal links to bind her hands. While he was busy, Arabella had a moment to look at her captor unnoticed. He was almost as tall as Tristan and every bit as broad shouldered. Everything about him was pale—his hair, his eyes, his skin—and exceedingly well-groomed. A nobleman? Even his hose were neat. Thadus's clothes smelled vaguely of spice… mugwort, mayhap.

When he finished with the chain, Arabella's hands were tied together from wrist to elbow in front of her. Thadus held his own length of the links so that he might drag her along.

Standing inches from her, he admired his handiwork before lifting his gaze to her face. He ran his finger along the tops of her breasts, which were forced together by her bound arms.

"Don't worry, love. You will find our company is not entirely unpleasant."

She hid a shudder, hoping to dissuade him with lack of response. If she were of some sort of value to them, as they had said, she hoped they would consider her worth all the more if they did her no harm.

He dropped his hand from her person before tying her chains to his horse's reins and then lifting her up on his mount again. Arabella tried not to panic as he urged the animal deeper into the woods.

The Bohemian party would probably be discovering her absence now, if they hadn't already. Rosalyn must have returned to the group safely, since the men hadn't discussed her. Tristan would be very angry with her for allowing herself to be separated from the group and she did not blame him. She'd been foolish to listen to Rosalyn, but the woman's story had seemed likely enough, since Princess Anne wanted peace in their group. Would Tristan come to look for her himself, or would he send one of his men? No, he would definitely come for her himself, if only to berate her for disobeying his orders.

But even if he guessed which direction Arabella had set off in, he'd never be able to find her in the dense forest Thadus was leading her into now.

If only she could leave him a clue…

Arabella remembered her pouch full of crushed flowers. She always had some with her to scent her clothes a little bit, but she had even more than usual today, as she had found several late-blooming flowers dried on a well-concealed vine in a thicket close to town. She just needed to open the sack before they were too far into the woods.

Gingerly, she tested her bonds and found that she could not move her fingers very much, but she could move her tied hands together fairly well. Of course, moving her tied hands and arms to one side might catch Thadus's eye, but she deemed it a risk worth taking.

She twisted her body slightly on the saddle to make access to the dangling pouch easier. Then slowly, so as not to draw her captor's attention, she laid the burden of her bound hands over the sack and slipped two of her fingers inside. She began to flick one flower after another out onto the ground, hoping by the time Tristan looked for her it would not be too dark to see them. The chances he would find a little trail of flowers out in the middle of nowhere were small, but then Tristan Carlisle was a clever man.

Her heart ached at the thought of him. She had struggled to keep her distance from him since they'd left Cologne, but heaven help her, no amount of distance could convince her eyes not to linger on the man. She watched him in spite of herself, until the small changes in his expression each day had somehow become of interest to her. Along the road, she had made it a game to anticipate his moods and interpret the swift clenching of his jaw versus the downward swoop of both eyebrows.

Her grandmother would call her a foolish girl. Arabella consoled herself by recalling there'd been precious else to occupy her mind over the long journey.

Now, she tucked her bag of crushed flowers back into the folds of her skirts as Thadus reined in his mount in front of a pile of branches and leaves. Dismounting, he tied the horse and smiled before he pulled Arabella's chain so hard she fell to the ground. Without her hands to break the fall, all of her weight landed painfully on one shoulder.

Scrambling to her feet, she ignored the burn in her arm. Perhaps if she never lay on the ground, her captor would have less opportunity to attack her. For now, Thadus led her to the pile of branches, which she realized was a crude shelter with barely enough room to squeeze inside. Large limbs had been tied between three trees about six hands from the ground. Those branches had been covered with smaller ones, along with leaves and moss for a roof.

"You have to enter on your knees anyway." Thadus used the toe of his boot to give Arabella a shove forward. For what seemed like the tenth time in the past hour, she fell again. Once she was inside the shelter, Thadus crawled in after her to tie her to one of the supporting trees. She debated a swift kick to his temple when his back was turned, but knew she wouldn't be able to accomplish anything after that. Thus, she remained still as he tied her and prayed Tristan would find her soon, so she could warn him that her captors planned to steal a second woman.

"I will return after I've found sustenance." Thadus removed a knife from a sleeve at his waist and held the blade up for her to see. "Once my hunt is fruitful, I will return. Do not move and do not call out, or I may be tempted to hunt closer to home."

He bared his teeth before he backed out of the shelter, leaving her alone in the hour before twilight. She didn't realize until he'd been gone for several moments that she'd been shaking.

Who was Thadus, anyhow? And why would he bother following the Bohemian retinue all the way across the continent? Did he mean to steal the princess? Arabella could see the sense of that, perhaps, since Princess Anne held a great deal of political importance. But then why abduct Arabella? She did not even bear her father's name and the noble who had fathered her was a man of only marginal standing, from what Zaharia had told her.

Darkness had fallen by the time Thadus returned. After throwing a freshly killed rabbit on a stone just outside the entrance, Thadus crawled into the shelter and unfastened her chains before backing out again.

"I am hungry, wench. Prepare the rabbit while I make the fire.".

Arabella hastened past him, her fingers tingling with pain now that she could move her hands after all this time. No sooner had she emerged from the shelter than a noise sounded nearby. Pausing, she peered into the woods.

An animal roar erupted from the undergrowth.

It took her mind a moment to catch up with the rapid movement of a dark figure barreling out from the cover of the trees.

Tristan.

Relief flooded her veins at the sight of him charging through the forest, a look of ferocity on his face she'd never seen before. And sweet merciful heaven, how she welcomed that fierceness even as she feared for him.

Sword drawn, Tristan rammed into Thadus. Brandishing a small dagger, Thadus deflected the sword but lost his blade in the leaves. The sickening thud of bodies colliding surprised her.

Thadus shouted curses in a foreign tongue, his hand reaching out to wrench Arabella backward. Screaming, she scrambled out of his grip while Tristan's blade slid across the other man's back, doing little damage because Thadus was so low to the ground.

Thadus reached for his own weapon, the large knife he'd waved under Arabella's nose earlier. Scuttling through the leaves and sticks on the barren ground, she kicked the blade to one side while Tristan dropped his sword and used his fists to pummel her captor.

Curses and blood flew while they grappled. Spittle spewed from Thadus's mouth as Tristan's fist connected with his jaw. Fear clogged her throat as she struggled to draw breath through her fear. Thadus fell against the shelter, bringing the pile of sticks to the ground.

She leaped to her feet, hoping to ensure her captor did not harm Tristan, even though Tristan appeared well in command. Still, the evil she'd seen in the other man's eyes had her frightened. She danced from one foot to another, scared and anxious, while the men grappled in the pile of sticks and debris.

Tristan's fist cocked and fired repeatedly until his opponent moved no longer. The sight chilled her even though she was grateful for Tristan's victory. Still, as the sound of dull thuds mingled with the crack of an occasional bone breaking, Arabella found she could bear no more.

"Tristan, he begs for mercy." At least, she thought he did, but she couldn't trust her hearing, given the pounding of her pulse in her ears.

Tristan paused at her words and for a moment, she thought he did not recognize her. His eyes were dark and intent, a cruel expression in their depths.

But then his face cleared and Thadus begged for mercy in English.

Tristan sighed deeply and released his quarry long enough to reach out to Arabella. Grateful for Tristan's safety as for her own—she ran to him, falling into his arms.

"Thank you. I'm so glad you found me." She hid her face in his houppelande, breathing in the scent of him, familiar and foreign and so welcome. "Did Rosalyn retrieve you? They mean to take another woman from Princess Anne's company."

"Rosalyn de Clair? She remained safely with the other women when I departed to find you. We must make haste to return." He brushed a kiss across the top of her head and she felt tears of relief burn her eyes. "What do you mean *they?*"

He looked down at her while Arabella struggled to understand why Rosalyn had said nothing of her capture. Her lungs burned with the effort to catch her breath.

"Thadus was not alone. Ivan was with him. He went to the shoreline to—"

A whistling noise made her halt her words. All at once, Tristan's expression changed. His eyes widened and he stumbled forward.

"Tristan?" Terror seized her.

Behind him, Arabella caught sight of the small silver blade protruding from Tristan's back. Beyond that, she saw Thadus wavering from the effort to sit upright. He must have thrown the blade end over end across half the clearing.

As Tristan fell against her, his great weight toppled them both to the ground. Thadus's face peered like an evil demon before he, too, collapsed on the forest floor.

Arabella screamed.

"Tristan!" She had never been made ill by the sight of blood in all of her years at her grandmother's side, yet her stomach churned now as she edged out from beneath Tristan's prone form.

"Please God, let him be all right," Arabella prayed as she took hold of the knife and withdrew it carefully from Tristan's back, making sure that she did not move it a hair's width to either side of the original wound so as not to do any more damage. It was a long knife but had not gone clear through his body. And, thankfully, it had not gone to his heart, being positioned just above and a little to the right of that precious organ.

After stuffing the wound until she could make some better bandages, Arabella tore up parts her skirts, loosened Tristan's tunic and searched his bag for water. Occasionally she struck Thadus over the head with his own knife handle to be sure he remained unconscious. If the hellbound bastard dared awaken, Arabella swore she would kill him with her bare hands.

Forcing herself not to think about the fact that Tristan's injury was all her fault, Arabella struggled to assume her role as a healer. Remote, detached, quick thinking. She tore off Tristan's houppelande and tunic to assess the damage done. Already, the rags she had stuffed into the gash were soaked with blood. Blood loss would be the biggest threat at this point. He could recover from this injury, Arabella felt sure of it, if only he didn't lose too much blood now and if infection didn't set in later.

As quickly as possible, she removed the blood-soaked rag from his back and rinsed out the wound. She then laid several layers of iris petals from her herb pouch over the deep gash, and covered those with the bandages she had torn from her linen kirtle. The iris petals would help to stanch the bleeding.

But how to get him to safety?

He would need constant attendance for the next week and a comfortable place to recover. How could she move this giant of a man?

Arabella was trying to figure out whether she could somehow haul Tristan onto one of the horses without doing him greater harm when she heard a single set of hoofbeats.

Ivan.

Was he returning to camp with whatever other unfortunate victim he'd set out to catch? She picked up Thadus's knife and prepared to take on Ivan. She would kill him if she had to.

But when she leaped out in front of the rider with her knife drawn, she came face-to-face with Simon Percival.

"Thank God." Relief flowed through her veins like wine and Thadus's knife clattered to the ground. "You must help me quickly. Tristan's been injured and—"

"What has happened here?" Simon turned to Arabella as if he already knew where to lay blame. His eyes narrowed.

The guilt she felt doubled under Simon's condemning stare. "I know I should not have left the rest of the party at the shoreline, but—"

Simon cursed as his glance landed on Tristan. He slid off his horse and strode to Tristan's side.

"If he dies, my lady, you will be one very sorry woman." Simon lifted his friend over his shoulder, even though Tristan was a larger man.

Arabella went to Tristan's horse to mount as well. "I will ride behind him. He needs—"

"He doesn't need you or your foreign medicines to dull his wits." Simon whirled on her and shoved her away from Tristan's mount. "If I see you near him, I cannot be responsible for what I might do." His warning hung in the air between them, and then Simon turned from her to tie a rope around his injured friend, securing him to his horse.

Arabella didn't know what to say. If she hadn't strayed from the rest of the group and had heeded Tristan's warnings, none of this would have happened. But Simon didn't realize that she could help Tristan, *had* to help him, for him to recover.

"But—"

"You will ride with me." Simon pulled her up to the saddle behind him and grabbed the reins of Tristan's horse so he could lead the animal. "We will cross as soon as possible and I will let Tristan's king decide whether to call a surgeon or a Gypsy witch to heal him."

With Simon's cruel words chasing round her memory, Arabella sat very still as they picked their way through the trees to return to the shore. All the while, Arabella kept her ears alert for any sound from Tristan, whose life she might have cost with her plea for mercy.

Chapter Ten

Cursing the cold dampness of her new lands along with the cold hearts of everyone around her, Arabella vowed to find Tristan two days later, after they reached Canterbury, where Princess Anne's party was greeted by the Earl of Buckingham. No one had listened to Arabella about the threat to the Bohemian party she had learned of out in the woods. They felt comforted by the fact that their journey was almost over and that they were on British soil, where the number of knights protecting the women had doubled.

Rosalyn de Clair swore she had gotten lost while escaping Ivan and Thadus, and she thought Arabella must have beaten her back to the group waiting for them on the shoreline in Calais. She was as surprised as anyone else to discover Arabella was missing, but she had not seen the men clearly enough to say who might have followed them.

Simon had taken pains to keep Arabella away from Tristan, even putting her on a separate boat for the crossing from Calais. This morn he had called for a local doctor to tend Tristan, but after seeing his friend settled, Simon had to leave for Princess Anne's introduction to the earl, who was the king's uncle, and some other nobles.

Not daring to question anyone regarding the whereabouts of Tristan's room, Arabella stole through the small Canterbury castle, looking for his chamber. After several mistaken guesses, she spied a maid leaving a tower chamber with a large kettle in her hand.

"Pray, tell me," Arabella inquired, glancing behind her to make sure they weren't overheard, "is this the chamber of the wounded knight in need of a doctor?"

"Yes, my lady," the maid answered as she moved the pot to her ample hip. "Is he on his way?"

Arabella bristled at the assumption that *she* was not the doctor, but knew from her conversations with Princess Anne that life here was very different from life in Bohemia. Women were not expected to assume the same duties that they had in her homeland.

"I am the doctor's wife. The doctor won't be able to make it for days, as he is tending an outbreak of an infection several days' journey away. But I have come in his stead to help where I might." Arabella doubted the maid would believe her, due to her foreign looks and the fact that she surely lacked the proper accent.

So, not waiting for an answer, Arabella went up the few remaining steps into the small chamber to find the bed curtains drawn and a deathly stillness settled over the narrow room. As her eyes adjusted to the darkness, she was able to distinguish Tristan's large frame laid out

on a large bed. It took a moment longer for her to realize
that he was not lying prone, as he should be due to his
injury, but flat on his back.

"Who is in charge here?" Arabella turned to another
maid, who was wiping Tristan's brow with a damp cloth
as she leaned through the velvet hangings.

"We are caring for him until the doctor arrives." The
maid straightened, blowing a hank of dark hair out of
one eye.

"Who laid him down on his back?" Arabella
demanded. How on earth could anyone be so dull witted
as to set a body down on its most injured part?

"Sir Simon's men brought him in here." The red-
faced maid appeared as irritated as Arabella felt, perhaps
because of the extra duty of caring for a sick man.

Arabella changed her tack, hoping for a few moments more of the woman's goodwill.

"He is lying directly on his wound. Would you help
me to move him?"

If either of the maids thought it peculiar that the
doctor's wife knew without looking where the knight
was injured, they did not speak of it.

The two younger women hurried to her and, between
them, they managed to turn him onto his side so that the
deep gash on his back was accessible.

"I'll need more warm water and clean linens." She
also longed for a guard posted at the door to let her know
when Simon returned, but this she did not ask for. She
would tend Tristan as long as she could.

Flinging open the bed curtains as soon as the maids
departed, she moved to an ancient arrow slit covered

with a tapestry and shoved that aside to let at least a sliver of daylight into the chamber. She needed to check the wound carefully, and she did not subscribe to the idea that a body needed darkness in order to heal. Turning back to Tristan, she recognized the signs of a serious fever, although the wound did not look infected. She would sew the gash up neatly after she'd made him more comfortable.

Tristan's pale skin nearly burned her hand. She reached for her bag of herbs and picked out the pink flowered centaury plant to lower the sickly heat. Choosing seven of the largest flowers, she crushed them into a small bowl at Tristan's bedside and sang soothingly to him in her native language.

When the remedy was complete, Arabella fed him the substance in a base of water and then sought out some yarrow for its power to heal wounds. She used three stems for a paste to be applied directly onto the wound and kept three aside to mix with some angelica for a tonic to drink. Angelica was good for almost any ailment, and these particular stalks had been picked at the height of their full glory last June.

Behind her, the maids had returned with the water and linens and stood hesitantly at the chamber door. She waved them inside, but not before she noted the wariness in their eyes. No doubt the women had overheard her singing in a strange tongue and suspected she was not who she claimed to be, but she managed to procure the supplies they brought before hustling them back out the door.

She watched over Tristan for hours in the tower room

until she heard heavy footsteps barreling down the hallway, accompanied by a woman's murmur.

"She would not dare."

Simon Percival's voice drowned out that of the woman and Arabella guessed her presence in the sickroom had been discovered. Knowing Tristan's suspicious friend would try to throw her from the chamber, she rose from the bedside and softly bolted the door.

The footsteps echoing on the tower steps reached the chamber seconds later. Simon let loose a stream of oaths she'd never heard before and then proceeded to threaten her with exposure to the king. But then the woman began talking softly to Simon again. Arabella crept back toward the door to hear what she was saying.

"She'll not harm him, I swear it—" a familiar voice intoned.

Mary's voice.

"Mary?" Arabella called through the door. "He may perish without me. He is very taken with fever right now."

Simon interrupted her with another series of curses and demands to see Tristan for himself. Arabella didn't bother to speak but let Mary calm him down once again.

"Simon says he wants other doctors to look at him," Mary finally said.

"Simon let his men lay Tristan on his back to the detriment of his wound. I am loath to trust doctors he recommends after such callous care."

Arabella turned her attention from the door to Tristan. Mary could take care of Simon Percival. Right now, Tristan needed her. She did not leave his room the rest of the day.

Lingering in fever, Tristan teetered deliriously between life and death. He called out for a woman named Elizabeth more than once, but never for Rosalyn, which Arabella was glad of. She tried not to let herself wonder who the mysterious Elizabeth might be and continued to speak reassuringly to him as he battled for his life.

Long after twilight, he opened his eyes and reached out for her, his grip strong.

"Arabella."

She started, almost dropping the wine jug she carried.

"Tristan?" Settling the jug by his bed, she knelt beside him. His color was still off, his features flushed and his eyes bright. "How do you feel?"

"Furious. I keep seeing a pale man's face and I'm so angry I want to—" He broke off, frowning. "Who is the man?"

"His name is Thadus and I do not know where he is from, but he has followed the retinue since we left Prague. Ivan Litsen attends him."

"He abducted you." Tristan's eyebrows knit together as he seemed to struggle to remember what happened.

"Aye. You saved me and I begged you not to kill Thadus, but I was a fool because the knave rose up and slipped a blade in your back afterward. I would never have guessed he could move after the way you beat him and I'm so sorry—"

Tristan's fingers clamped over her lips, halting her words.

"It is no matter. Does Simon know these men follow us still?"

Guilt nipped at her heels. "He is so angry with me

for running off that he has not listened to me. I had to lock him out of the chamber to even attend you."

"Make him listen." He cupped her cheek in a surprisingly fierce grip. "Bring him to me."

He moved to right himself before his body contorted with pain.

"Pray do not move." She placed a quieting hand on his shoulder. "I will talk to him, Tristan, I swear, but do not injure yourself further."

"You are a healer." He seemed to relax at the thought, his eyes sliding closed once again. "I am certain you will repair the damage. You must find Simon before harm comes to the princess."

She recoiled at the idea, knowing Simon had come to see her as the enemy in the moments after he'd found her with Tristan's injured body. She should have talked to him that night, mayhap, and made him see the truth. But her lack of experience with men—nay, the fear her mother had instilled in her from a young age—had kept her silent in the face of Simon's anger.

Where had her silence gotten her?

"Rest, Tristan." She retrieved the wine pitcher and poured him a cup. "Drink this and then sleep. I will see Simon and set everything to rights."

She hoped. Calling for a maid, she sent a note summoning Mary to the chamber. She hoped her friend could make Simon Percival see reason where she could not.

Late that night, there was a soft knock on the chamber door. As Arabella advanced warily toward it, slippers shuffling along the clean reeds, she heard Mary's voice.

"I'm alone. May I please come in?"

Arabella did not hesitate, knowing Mary to be a true friend. Quickly she unlatched the door and confided her worries about the men following the princess's retinue, along with Tristan's insistence that Simon be made aware of the threat.

Arabella did not add her own fears that Rosalyn de Clair knew more than she admitted. She refused to test Simon's threshold of belief.

"I will tell him. Do not concern yourself with the princess's safety. She is guarded by many more knights now that we are in the king's domain." Mary squeezed her. "I've been so worried about you."

"I'm fine. It's Tristan we need to worry about. The fever must break soon or I fear he will be lost."

Mary's face paled as she twisted the long lace sleeve of her kirtle. "He mustn't be."

"I know, but it is up to him now. I have done all that I am able to."

"It is not only his life I fear for, Arabella, but yours."

"I do not understand." Arabella poured wine for Mary and a cup for herself. Her arm shook under the weight of the pitcher and she realized she hadn't eaten all day.

"There have been rumors since we arrived here. Apparently some of the maids heard you in here singing to Tristan. I'm sure you were singing a Bohemian song, but the girls had heard some of the gossip about your past and have told everyone you sang a witch's chant while you mixed up strange potions for Tristan."

"Sweet, merciful heaven. Can I never escape such foolishness?" She imagined Rosalyn de Clair had been only too happy to spread hateful talk. "People have long spouted thus about my family, Mary, and I have yet to suffer more than frustration for it."

"No, Arabella." Mary drank deeply from her wine cup. "It is different here. If the English nobles heed the rumors, there is a chance…they could imprison you."

The words hung in the air like a bad jest.

"But if Tristan lives…"

"His life will testify to your skill as a healer. You might be accused, but his good health would refute any accusation of evildoing."

"And if he dies…"

"He mustn't."

Arabella did not contemplate the matter then, as Tristan seemed to be calling out for something.

"I'll leave you alone," Mary said as she edged her way toward the chamber door. "And I will speak to Simon."

When Mary left, Arabella latched the door behind her.

"Chovihani."

Tristan's gray eyes gleamed with an unnatural light as they came to rest on Arabella.

She sank down on the bed next to him and let him run his fevered hand over her eyes and cheeks and lips.

"Didn't you know I would come after you?" he asked, his eyes closing with the exhaustion of speaking and moving.

"Yes." She knew he referred to their time in Calais, since he seemed to be reliving that day in his fevered dreams. "But I didn't mean to leave the group. Rosalyn wanted to speak with me and I thought she wished to make peace."

"Trust no one."

She wiped his forehead and his chest for the thousandth time. His lips moved as if he would say more, but the silence between them stretched until at last she discerned one word.

"Sing."

And so she did. She sang the lovely Bohemian lullabies her mother had sung to her as a babe, no matter what any lurking maid in the corridor might think of them. She did not cease until his fever broke shortly before dawn and she fell into an exhausted slumber at his side.

Tristan's dreams were so wickedly pleasant he did not open his eyes even when bright sunlight warmed his face. The feminine form beside him stretched languorously, as if calling him to linger in his bed. And although his limbs ached with exhaustion, he could not help the stirring in his blood at the feel of lush curves beneath his hands.

The floral scent of the woman's hair floated across his cheek and he swiped the locks from his face, kissing the top of her head.

Arabella.

He knew her by her scent, although how she'd found her way into his bed, he could not be sure. He dreamed, of course. And knowing that, what would it hurt to slide his hand beneath her kirtle to feel one slender thigh?

She moaned softly at his touch, a sound that affected him as deeply as any physical caress. She stirred in his arms, her hips shifting against his thighs.

A surge of possessiveness took hold of him as he steered her hips where he wanted them. He reached higher to skim his hand along her full breasts—until a white-hot pain knifed through his shoulder.

In a flash, the dream dissipated. Fire simmered behind his eyes as the sweet female form vanished.

"Tristan?"

Her voice calling to him seemed real enough and he forced his eyes open to see her peering down at him, her hair bed tousled and her kirtle askew. His realization that she'd been sleeping next to him almost drowned out the remnants of pain rippling through his body like waves.

"You were in my bed and I was too damn weak to enjoy it." His voice sounded hoarse in his ears and the effort to speak raked his dry throat.

"To the contrary, I think you probably enjoyed it a little too well." She smoothed a hand over her kirtle to straighten the neck. "I fear we both did."

"I dreamed of you. You sang to me." The pain receded and he wished he could have remained a prisoner of those dreams a bit longer.

"That was no dream, any more than me being in your bed." Her cheeks burned with such a deep hue he almost regretted waking with his hand up her skirt.

Almost.

"Arabella." He sensed time lapsing between his words, but he could only gather his thoughts slowly, as if he was still in a dream. "I do not know how you will fare in my homeland, but I am glad you made the journey safely."

"What do you mean? You think I will not thrive in your cold country?" Her voice had taken on a strangely fearful note and he wondered what he'd said to upset her.

"You are so different. I sometimes fear you will attract

too much notice." He took a cup of wine from her and drank deeply, willing away the hunger for her that persisted even now that she'd removed herself from his side.

"I hope that is not the case." She bit her lip and straightened up from his bedside.

His gut told him something was wrong and he cursed the injuries that had kept him away from his duties. His head spun.

"How long since I found you in Calais?" He ran his hand across the scruff of whiskers on his jaw to guess at the number of days.

"Three days. We have been waiting in Canterbury while you recover and will move on to London as soon as you are well."

"Three days?" His world felt tipped askew and he resented the weakness in his limbs. "I am ready this morn."

"You must not rush your recovery." Her green eyes darkened with worry.

"I will not delay. The sooner the princess weds, the sooner my obligation is fulfilled."

He had not considered how Arabella might interpret those words until he'd spoken them.

"I fear we have been a burden to you. Me more than most," she replied. She opened the door to the chamber and called for a maid to bring food to supplement the weak broth she'd fed him the night before.

"You have come to my aid more than once and I will not forget it." Thoughts of Rosalyn de Clair made his head throb more than the pain in his back. "Richard may yet force me to wed Rosalyn merely to keep peace between our people, and I do not look forward to that. But we cannot afford to linger in Canterbury with Ivan and the other man— What was his name?"

His memories of what had happened were disjointed and the effort of talking made him as breathless as a dizzy-eyed old man.

"Thadus."

"Aye. Send for Simon so I might make our plans." Injured or not, Tristan had to secure the traveling party on this last leg of the journey and make sure Simon understood the threat still present. "I might call you to explain what you heard while you were held captive."

He would thank her properly later, when he knew the company had arrived safely and he'd completed his mission. Until then, he would do everything in his power to regain his strength and ensure Richard could not withhold the property that should be Tristan's reward. He'd drink all the cursed tasteless broth Arabella gave him and sleep like the dead if it would make him heal faster.

"I will. But first, I would like my knife back." She tucked a stray lock back into the keeping of a silver circlet decorated with birds of prey.

"What knife?" His head buzzed with a wealth of concerns all needing his immediate attention.

"My blade, which you found in the clearing that first day we spied one another. I have wished for it many times since then, especially while I was a captive to a cruel man."

He stiffened. "Did he hurt you?"

"Nay. But next time I would prefer to have a knife in my possession."

"There won't be a next time. I will retrieve your

blade once I find the clothes I wore the day I came after you. I have carried it with me since we first met."

Perhaps he should not have revealed how close he'd kept her token since first discovering the knife. Arabella had affected him in ways he would not have anticipated before he made the Bohemian journey and he did not relish the thought of any woman possessing that much sway over him.

But she simply nodded and backed away.

"I have left a potion beside your bed for when you are ready to—sleep again." Her gaze dropped to the floor and he had the feeling she was remembering the way they'd woken up intertwined.

The memory would haunt him today as well, along with that overwhelming anger he'd felt at the thought of another man touching Arabella. He needed to break free of her spell soon, as they would part company in London.

"Soon enough." He sat up and reached for his tunic, then scowled at the sight of her hurrying toward the door. She had cared for him in close quarters while he recovered but ran from the sight of his naked chest? "What kind of healer does not assist an injured man in dressing?"

He had expected a sharp retort or an impassioned denial, so he was surprised when she met his gaze directly.

"In caring for you, I may have injured my honor as thoroughly as your enemy wounded your back, sir. I did not realize to do so would earn me the enmity of the people in your cold little country." She closed the door behind her, leaving Tristan to wonder what in Hades had happened these last few days to put a fearful light in the eyes of a wild woman who once carried her own blade and made the woodlands her home.

And he could not help but think it was not a mistake for Anne's royal retinue to try and tame his *chovihani* into a noblewoman.

Chapter Eleven

In London several days later, Arabella stared with longing at the open chest beside her bed that contained most of her possessions.

She knew the yearning to run away was a childish wish she would ignore. But heaven help her, she could not help but indulge that small flight of fancy for just a few moments before attending the princess at the evening meal. Arabella's dream of freedom was probably the only thing that kept her tongue civil and her pride stuffed down her throat when she wanted only to run through the countryside with the wind at her heels and the earth beneath her feet. If she didn't please the princess, she would be sent home in shame, and disappointing her grandmother was a fate worse than endless suppers with too much food, too many drunken men and shoes that pinched her feet.

Slamming the lid shut on her chest and her dreams for at least a few more hours, Arabella hurried out of her chamber and into the passageway she hoped would lead to the great hall. Her brief trip to Prague had prepared her somewhat for the grandeur of castles and cathedrals, but she had still been amazed by the beauty of Westminster and charmed by London. King Richard and Princess Anne were to be married in the great cathedral three days hence, and tonight they dined together in the spectacular hall of Windsor Castle.

As she navigated her way through the keep, she passed several of the women from the court, all of whom seemed to have forsaken her in the days since Tristan had been hurt. She'd never been well accepted by them, but now—except for the princess and Mary—all of the women avoided her. She did not need their approval, and yet the slight hurt. At least Simon Percival had extended a grudging apology to her the day before, after Tristan had explained what had happened to her in the forest outside Calais.

Now, as she slid unseen into a seat at a table in the back of the hall, she took in the company, searching for Tristan. Princess Anne and King Richard were seated on the dais, their happy countenances genuine reflections of their new affection for one another. Mary sat beside Simon Percival and Arabella knew the two had become closer in the sennight since Tristan had been harmed. But even as the food began to make its way around the tables, she did not see Tristan. Had he obtained his property from the king? Had he left the retinue, now that he'd delivered the women safely to London? She worried at the thought, even as she reminded herself the foreign warrior represented a danger to her position.

Her feast was interrupted by a messenger from the

king with notice that she was to attend a private audience this evening with him and Princess Anne. She gulped back a rising fear that King Richard had already learned of her reputation as she tried to imagine what the meeting could be about. She noted that the same messenger made his way over to Rosalyn de Clair and, finally, to a weary-looking Tristan as he at last arrived for the meal. A curious threesome, but mayhap the messenger had stopped to request the presence of several others before Arabella had noticed him. Unless…

In all the chaos of her abduction and Tristan's fever, she had forgotten about Rosalyn de Clair's baby. Princess Anne had said that she would let her new husband decide the matter of a husband for Rosalyn when they reached England. Would the king assign a husband to the noblewoman in his private meeting tonight? To send her home in disgrace could cause ill will amongst her many friends within the Bohemian court.

Arabella barely noticed the rest of the meal, although it was filled with extravagant entertainments. She tried not to stare in Tristan's direction, but found her eyes drawn back to his large frame, grown leaner in the days of his recovery. He should be resting to regain his strength. But whether she thought that as a healer or as a woman who felt something more tender for him, she couldn't be sure.

One thing was certain, however. Any desire for the English knight needed to be stamped down as ruthlessly as her urge to flee home. Because although Tristan might woo her sweetly and kiss her until her knees grew weak, he had made it very clear that no woman would ever stake a claim to his heart.

* * *

The English king was no warrior.

Hours after supper ended, Arabella studied the young king surreptitiously as she waited in the large private chamber for the evening meeting to begin. At fifteen summers, he was not quite as old as the princess. He wore his fair hair trimmed to his chin. He had changed his garb since the evening meal, abandoning purple velvet robes for a fur-lined scarlet houppelande with white undersleeves.

King Richard's private chamber was a large hall within his guarded apartments. He and Princess Anne were seated at the head of the room, engaged in animated conversation. Arabella was overwhelmed by the sheer luxury of the space. Everywhere she turned, Richard's colors of red and white appeared in one fashion or another—the tapestries that hung from the ceiling, the coverings of the sumptuous chairs, the royal robes. The room's most striking feature was the brilliant tapestry depicting a crowned white hart covered in laurels. When Arabella exclaimed over the piece, Mary—who had also been summoned to the meeting—explained the white hart was a symbol of Richard's mother, Joan of Kent, which the king had taken to using himself.

After studying her surroundings, Arabella noted the other guests. Several of Tristan's knights were present, along with Rosalyn, Arabella and Mary. Tristan joined the group bearing a thoroughly fierce expression. She glanced to see Rosalyn's reaction to the grim knight, but she remained solemn, her gaze downcast. She was finally wearing garments that were a bit loose through the middle, no doubt at the insistence of Princess Anne, but she looked as beautiful—no, even prettier—than before. She was lovely enough to have nearly any man she wished. If she had any sense, she would not attempt to maneuver a man so opposed to marriage.

King Richard greeted Tristan personally, bestowing his attention on him alone. Seeing the two men together, Arabella couldn't help but compare them. What a fine ruler Tristan would have made. He was a natural-born leader of men, while the king appeared a mere boy.

Soon, King Richard waved for silence and the already somber group grew completely still.

"You are well come, my friends," he began pleasantly enough. "I have called you here this night so that we might settle some overdue matters before my nuptials. Princess Anne has brought to my attention her lady, Rosalyn de Clair, who is with child. We would see this woman well settled before her expected date, as she is now one of our own."

Richard bestowed one of his smiles on Rosalyn, who returned the gesture prettily.

"Sir Tristan Carlisle," the king continued, now turning to direct his comments to the knight in question, "Rosalyn claims you as the father to her child. What reason have you for not taking her to wife?"

"Several. The first of which is that the child is not mine." Tristan rose as he addressed the king, and Arabella winced with the pain the stubborn man did not show.

Or, possibly, she winced at the idea that Tristan might still end up sharing his bed with Rosalyn de Clair for the remainder of his days. Arabella was surprised the king had raised the question when she'd thought the matter settled back in Cologne by the sight of Rosalyn's unbound form.

The king looked about the room thoughtfully for a moment until he spied Mary.

"But, my goodly knight, another noblewoman witnessed the same woman departing your chambers early one morning." Richard seemed to lift his brow in question at Mary and she hesitated only a moment before nodding. "How would you respond to this, sir?"

"She did indeed, sire."

"So you do not deny her presence in your bedchamber in the middle of the night some weeks ago?" Richard seemed to be giving Tristan a second chance to explain himself.

"No."

Why wouldn't Tristan explain what had happened? And why didn't the king call on her to find out what she knew about the age of the babe? But, Arabella reasoned, the king might not do so unless Tristan himself called on her to be a witness to that fact.

"But it is against your wishes to marry the same woman who was in your bedchamber in the middle of the night?"

"Yes."

All at once, Arabella understood Tristan's pride was keeping him from defending himself. The same stubborn pride that had forced him to stand in the king's presence when he should have been abed. She had not recognized the depth of his pride while they journeyed across the continent, but she saw it here, in a court full of powerful men. Tristan would not beg for his freedom from a king who could not yet grow a beard.

King Richard seemed at a loss for words for a moment, but recovered himself after an exchange of glances with Princess Anne.

"I vow that whosoever takes this woman's hand will win my appreciation along with lands belonging to the Crown."

Arabella's breath caught at the king's promise of such a prize. Was that not what Tristan had hoped for himself?

All of the knights turned to Tristan as if waiting to see what he would do. When a long moment passed in silence, one of his men stepped forward, helmet in hand.

"I'd like to ask for the lady's hand, Your Majesty."

Rosalyn scoffed openly as her face grew red. Arabella did not know the man who came forward—a young man with freckles and hair as red as Rosalyn's cheeks.

"Are you claiming to be the sire to Lady Rosalyn's child?" asked the king.

"Nay, but it is well known that Tristan Carlisle is not the babe's sire, either," the tall knight asserted, still kneeling before his king.

Rosalyn started to speak, but perhaps thought the better of it after seeing Princess Anne's warning expression.

"The Crown owes you a debt, sir." The king gestured to the other man to rise. "I will provide you with a deed to a small property on my northern border after your wedding."

Surprised at the strange proceedings, Arabella was nevertheless relieved for Tristan's sake. She wondered how soon she could depart the gathering now that the matter had been settled, but the king waved his hand for quiet once again.

"One other matter has been called to my attention." King Richard frowned, as if this next issue was even more troubling than the first. "I have been deeply concerned by recent rumors among my court regarding the influence of the Unholy."

A hush fell hard on the small room. Arabella could not breathe for a moment.

"I will not have this talk of heathen influence among my nobles as the Crown has served its people peacefully alongside the church for hundreds of years."

All eyes turned to her.

Of all the wag-tailed lies Tristan had heard spewed at a royal court, this had to be the worst. And curse it all if this one wasn't partly his own fault.

"By your leave, Your Majesty, the rumors infecting the court have been my doing." Tristan stood again to address the king even though he felt weak as a foal on knock-kneed legs. His argument would be less impressive if he fell on his arse as he spoke, but Arabella deserved someone to speak on her behalf after all she had done to save him.

"What do you mean?" The king reached for Princess Anne's hand and Tristan wondered at the strange connection between the two of them, as they had only known each other for such a short time. Their affection did not seem like pretense. Indeed, they had no reason to feign a fondness they did not feel.

"The talk of Gypsy magic has been my fault, Your

Highness." He'd been appalled at Simon's misinterpretation of what had happened the day he'd been wounded, but apparently Simon was not the only one among them who thought Arabella an unusual woman. "There has been speculation among the court about my seemingly miraculous recovery from a recent injury. I was grievously wounded outside of Calais, Your Highness, but I was tended by an incredibly skilled healer."

He turned to acknowledge Arabella and was pleased to see her head held high despite the obvious tension in the chamber.

"Lady Arabella Rowan, I have learned, has been training all her life with a noted healer in Bohemia. And although my cure at her hands might seem nothing short of magic, I can assure you her feat was brought about by great knowledge and not dark arts. I see now I have not praised Lady Arabella's skill sufficiently, while others have falsely whispered about her. My only excuse is that I am long a stranger to the ways of court life, and I had forgotten how tales can be exaggerated with every telling. I owe Lady Arabella and Your Highness an apology for bringing about these rumors."

Hellfire. That had sounded painfully close to a speech. He was turning into a flattery-spewing courtier in spite of his intentions. He consoled himself with the thought that a man couldn't always draw his sword to fight a battle, a fact he'd learned well after Rosalyn de Clair's false accusations.

And perhaps this way he would earn some token of thanks from Arabella. The notion cheered him.

The king, however, frowned. "The Crown might

accept your apologies, but I believe you owe Lady Arabella much more than that."

Tristan straightened, immediately alert. His back throbbed all the way through his shoulder and down to his fingertips, but not so much as the ache in his head that crawled over his skull with this new worry. What more would the king have of him?

The king called Arabella before him and Tristan watched her move toward the dais before bending her knee to the royal couple. Never had she appeared more different from the first time he'd seen her. Somewhere on the journey to London, Arabella had developed a quiet grace that effectively hid her wildness. This eve, she merely looked like an exotic beauty plucked from foreign lands.

"Is she not lovely, Tristan?" King Richard smiled over Arabella's bent head and Tristan experienced a surge of possessiveness that ignited unreasonable anger toward the boy king.

"Aye." The word stuck unpleasantly in his throat and Tristan wondered if he'd ever be able to spirit her away for another moment in private, now that they'd returned home.

"I am glad you find her pleasing, sir, for there is an obvious solution to the rumors of witchcraft you have brought upon my court. Since you have claimed responsibility in front of witnesses for Lady Arabella's dishonor, you will now take responsibility for correcting the harm done by taking her to wife—"

Arabella drew a sharp gasp and reached to steady herself, her hand connecting with Tristan's forearm.

"But I will not stay in England forever, Your Highness." Arabella's words were softly accented by her native tongue, but the tone rang with disillusion that would have translated in any language. "I have obligations to my family in Bohemia."

Tristan placed his hand on her shoulder in the hope his touch would quiet her. While the king might appear amenable, he had inherited enough of the Lancaster temper that it would not be wise to disobey him.

The king overlooked Arabella's words to focus on Tristan.

"As this is a match we favor, the Crown grants you the property of Ravenmoor in Northumbria, which we decree an earldom in your honor. We are well pleased with your service these past fifteen years."

And with those words, the king offered everything Tristan had struggled for all his life. He merely had to marry Arabella in order to obtain it. The move was judicious and served multiple royal purposes. The fact that it would break Arabella's wild heart and would chain Tristan to a lifetime of obligation to a woman who yearned for freedom would never cross the king's mind.

"I am humbled by your gift." Tristan forced himself to speak the words, even though his head already rebelled at the uneasy partnership the king had created.

"I'm sure you'll understand why this needs to take place as quickly as possible, since these rumors must cease. You can wed tomorrow, directly after Lady Rosalyn exchanges her vows. Then you and your lady may make haste to Ravenmoor, safely away from the gossip of the court."

It wasn't until Tristan had agreed to the terms and the king had dismissed the party that Tristan realized Arabella had maintained her grip on his forearm during the proceedings. She remained kneeling, her hand locked around his wrist, until he tugged her to her feet and pulled her into a private antechamber.

Her skin was pale, her pupils so wide that the green rims were scarcely visible as she stared up at him.

"You are so horrified at the thought of marriage, *chovihani?*"

She shook her head in mute response for a long moment before she called up hoarse words.

"You would call me this even now? Even after my name has been publicly denounced for…" She shook her head again and her eyes glistened with unshed tears.

Regret kicked him soundly in the chest. No armed opponent had ever struck so keen a blow.

"You are right." He did not bother to remind her that he had not used his name for her in front of anyone else. "But you may be consoled to know that I am being sent to Ravenmoor to protect the king's northern borders after rumors of a Scots alliance with the French. I will have little time to disturb your studies if you wish to pursue them."

"You will make war on your neighbors while I heal them."

"You may not have the opportunity to heal the enemy, but there will be villagers who will welcome a healer." The thought made him thirst for the journey to begin, no matter that Arabella wept for their unwanted union.

She would grow to appreciate the untamed land, far

from court, that matched her own in rugged beauty. As for himself, he had not planned ever to wed, after the rebuff from Elizabeth and the wound to his pride that had ensued. But he was a different man now and his position would require a wife. Arabella might not be his choice, given her headstrong ways, but he could not deny he'd long been attracted to her. He would welcome the chance to touch her while knowing she held no illusions of love.

"You will not allow me to heal your enemies?" She looked up at him, genuinely dismayed, and he wondered how such innocence could coincide with such a passionate nature.

"Welcome to the world's most civilized kingdom, Arabella."

The emotions in her expression seemed to disappear as if she'd shuttered her expression, and Tristan mourned the loss of the woman he'd met in a leaf-strewn clearing last autumn. His wife would not be the same wild-eyed Gypsy, and he knew he was as much to blame for that as the rest of the court.

Still, as he offered her his arm to leave the antechamber, he could not help but savor the fact that tomorrow night she would at last belong to him, not for a few stolen moments, but all night long.

Chapter Twelve

Rosalyn found it exceedingly difficult to break free from her groom on their wedding day.

She did not miss the irony of the situation. All of her maneuvering for a favorable husband had ended with her being keenly maneuvered herself. By Tristan, by Arabella and, ultimately, by the English king. She knew the arrangement should have angered her, but in the increasing exhaustion of carrying a babe, she found herself simply grateful to have found the security of marriage to a man who—on the surface at least—did not seem to mind that she'd taken a lover in Bohemia.

"Where have you been?" Ivan Litsen waited for her outside the chapel where she had just exchanged vows with a towering Scot who'd found favor with the English king.

"It is not a simple matter to vanish from one's own wedding." She owed Ivan a great deal, since he had helped her convince an aging Bohemian nobleman that she was his child. But Ivan had pushed the limits of her gratitude with his request for a private audience today.

He stood behind a peddler's cart, a hood over his face. He blended in with the rest of the people in the courtyard, who remained busy with trading and the polishing of armor, even in winter.

"Does the Rowan girl know of your connection to me?" Ivan had alliances with political factions Rosalyn did not begin to understand, and he had been forever asking her questions about whom she'd met ever since she'd successfully joined the Bohemian court some three years ago. Her "accidental" pregnancy had been—in part—a bid for freedom from the awkward secret meetings he was always demanding, but that plan had failed in a spectacular way when the babe's father rebuffed her.

"I do not think so." She'd been quick to escape the skirmish in the woods the day she'd led Arabella away from the shore in Calais. "If she does, she has not voiced her fears to the court."

"Keep it that way, lest you find your new husband apprised of your roots." Ivan lowered his voice as a boy chased an escaped hen through the courtyard.

"I have served you well for three years across the continent and under the watchful eye of two kings and an emperor. Do you not think I have already earned my place?" The distress from marriage to an unknown man and her advancing condition had made her tongue sharper than usual.

Ivan's eyes narrowed and she remembered why she should be more careful around him. He might be aging, but he'd been in the old emperor's private guard and he had the might to enforce the whim of his quick temper.

"You are beholden to me for the rest of your days and you would be wise not to forget it. Do not forget you risk more than your own neck. Your babe will make an easy target if you cannot fulfill your end of our bargain."

His eyes sent a chill through her that she feared even the marriage bed would not warm. She had risked the growth of her babe for three moons in the hope of securing a protector. Or at least that was what the Rowan woman would have her believe about binding her thickening middle. Rosalyn had not intended to inflict harm on an innocent, and she surely would not risk her child to the wrath of Ivan.

Nodding, she wrapped her arms about herself to ward off the cold. Her jewel-encrusted sleeves bit into her palms.

"I will make sure no one learns of our association."

"Excellent. We cannot strike in London. The risk is too great. But we have heard rumors the Rowan girl rides north."

"I have heard the same." Despite her envy of Arabella, Rosalyn did not relish the idea of harm coming to her. Arabella had provided her with herbs that eased Rosalyn's roiling belly without asking for so much as a favor in return and the gesture had seemed uncommonly kind. Rosalyn would not have thought such softheartedness lurked within her, but something about new life growing inside her had changed her perspective.

"We wait to strike there." Ivan drew his hood around his head as another peddler drew near. He reached into his cart to hand Rosalyn a scrap of lace from his wares and raised his voice enough to be heard by anyone passing. "Until then, God bless you on your wedding day, yer ladyship."

Rosalyn snatched the lace from him, grateful to be freed from the unsavory meeting. Her new husband would wonder at her whereabouts and—despite his lack of refinement and his harsh accent—she feared she already nursed a small tenderness for the man who had accepted her when few others would have. She would reserve final judgment until she discovered if he would beat her or otherwise make her life more difficult. But for the first time in too many years, she could not squelch a small sense of hope for her future as she entered the keep.

As long as she continued to feed Ivan Litsen the answers he craved, she might yet know happiness. She just prayed Tristan never found out the depths of her deceit where Arabella was concerned.

In the village near which Arabella had grown up, weddings were celebrated with both families present. Gifts were exchanged. A goat from the bride's father or a treasured urn from the groom's uncle. After seeing those simple but heartfelt celebrations among loved ones, Arabella found it difficult to rejoice over a marriage her family did not even know about.

The small private chapel at Windsor glowed with the warm, flickering light from hundreds of candles and the simple altar had been adorned with brilliant green ivy. If Arabella had been amenable to marriage, she would have thought it a beautiful place to wed, certainly preferable to the soaring heights of Westminster Abbey where the king would marry Princess Anne.

But this marriage was not welcome. Oh, she appreciated Tristan's chivalry in assuring his king that she did not bring the dark arts to plague the people of Britain. His words about her healing skills had been noble. Thoughtful. But there had been no talk of love between them, no explanation of who Elizabeth was to him, no word on whether he still plotted with Simon in dark corners about what women they would woo to their beds.

Arabella had always thought she would wed a man devoted to her alone, a man who believed that love could coincide with marriage. Her upbringing might have been unconventional, but the Rowan women married for love alone. They chose the men. Their mates had never been chosen for them.

"Do not be nervous, Arabella." Mary hovered at her side, picking at the cream-colored cotehardie the princess had donated to Arabella for the exchange of vows.

Gold beading outlined the neck and elaborate golden stitching ran down the back of the gown to cover the many tiny fastenings. It fitted close to the body until just beneath her hipbone. She also wore a jeweled belt encrusted with emeralds and rubies, another donation from Princess Anne for the occasion.

"I wed a man who will not love me and in exchange I am taken away from my homeland forever." The king's solution to the rumors about Arabella sat uneasily upon her shoulders along with the weight of the heavy garment. "I think it is a good time to be nervous."

"I hope to speak to the princess about traveling to Northumbria with you, so perhaps you will not be as alone as you fear." Mary's nimble fingers adjusted Arabella's hair, which Hilda had adorned with a wreath of dried flowers.

"Really?" Arabella's heart caught at the words and the show of friendship. "You would travel to the end of this cold island to be at my side?"

Mary tugged her deeper into the nave while a handful of the princess's women gathered to witness the ceremony.

"It would be my pleasure if the princess will part with me."

"How could she?" Arabella's hopes sank a bit. "You are the highest ranking noblewoman in her retinue. She will need you in London while she tries to win the hearts of the people."

Mary's cheeks flushed with color. "I will remind her that I hope to win the heart of one of Tristan's men, who will travel to Northumbria, as well."

Arabella's fears about her wedding fled at the thought of this new puzzle.

"Not…"

"I know you are not fond of Simon Percival, Arabella, but—"

"We must speak." Arabella recalled the conversation she had overheard between Tristan and Simon that night in Prague Castle and knew she must warn Mary the knight could be toying with her tender heart.

Ah, but was Simon's view of women so different from Tristan's? She would have been wisest to listen to her own counsel instead of scaring Mary away from a man who—perhaps—could at least learn to love in a way Arabella feared Tristan might not. If only she could have found out before agreeing to such a match.

"They are coming," Mary whispered, turning her to see the knights entering the nave.

The arrival of Tristan and his men made Arabella's breath catch. They wore their standards over their houppelandes, their colors bright beacons atop the staid black and gray of their outfits beneath. Tristan stood proud and straight, his shoulders a formidable barrier despite the grievous injury he'd sustained.

But she set aside her instincts as a healer for a moment and looked at him strictly as a woman would.

Beneath the red standard that must signify the Ravenmoor seat, he wore black, his attire ever efficient and functional. Arabella had never seen him wear anything that would have prevented him from wielding a sword or riding his horse at a moment's notice.

The houppelande he wore tonight was thigh length, with heavy dark hose beneath. He did not wear a sword into the nave, but she guessed he carried a knife concealed at his waist. His dark hair had not been tied back and it touched his shoulders. Arabella had never seen it thus.

Joining him before the holy man who would unite them in the Church's eyes, Arabella tried to listen to the priest's words. In truth, she heard little the elderly man said. Her mind whirled with imagining what would happen after the ceremony. Would the group break bread and celebrate or would she simply return to Tristan's chamber, now that she was his wife?

Unable to rein in her thoughts, she used her time in the holy place to say her own small prayer that she would know how to set things right between her and Tristan. No matter that he might love another woman or that he had not chosen Arabella; she wished to be a good wife. Perhaps then he would one day allow her to return to Bohemia, if only for a short time.

Soon, the priest's withered hand fell upon her shoulder, coaxing her to face Tristan. His gray eyes were unfathomable in the glimmer of candlelight.

Tristan reached for Arabella's hands and held them in his own, although she did not recall the priest having told them to do so. His hands were warm and a little rough as he gently massaged her palms with his thumbs. The gesture sent a shiver through her as she remembered vividly how vulnerable she was to his touch. Heaven help her, she would have to guard her heart carefully with this man, when he could strike a chord deep inside her so easily. With her passions so close to the surface, it would be too easy to lose herself in the touches he doled out so readily, too easy to let herself think he could one day care about her.

And now the priest was looking at her, as was Tristan, expecting an answer…

"I will," she managed to whisper, and she thought she felt Tristan squeeze her hands.

Now oblivious to the ceremony, Arabella could only think about Tristan's hands holding hers and the battle she would have to wage in his bed to keep herself in check.

After the short mass was complete, the priest turned the couple to greet their guests.

"The Earl and Countess of Ravenmoor." His pronouncement rolled over her with new meaning.

Her life had been irrevocably tied to Tristan's.

While the small gathering cheered, Arabella attempted to withdraw her hand from his grip, but instead of releasing her, he drew her to him. The sudden heat of his body against hers chased away any awareness of their audience. He lowered his mouth to hers, taking full advantage of her parted lips, the kiss darkly intimate. She swayed on weak knees, clutching his houppelande to keep her balance, but the kiss ended as suddenly as it had begun.

Blinking, she attempted to gather her wits while Tristan moved away to greet the king.

Mary and Princess Anne reached her at the same time to draw her, laughingly, away from the private family chapel and deeper into the keep.

The princess sniffled and hugged Arabella. "You make such a beautiful couple."

"And Tristan is such a gallant, Arabella. He took your hand so gently—"

"To feast!" the king exclaimed, waving the gathering toward a smaller hall where cold meats and cheeses, dried fruits and ale weighed down the trestle tables.

Arabella tried several times to speak privately with Mary about her fears regarding Simon Percival, but her efforts were cut off by one well-wisher after another. The party had grown between the chapel and the reception hall as Rosalyn de Clair and Sir Henry joined them with the guests from their own nuptials earlier, and Arabella greeted what seemed like hundreds of people.

Occasionally she stole a glance in Tristan's direction. He seemed in good spirits for a man just forced to wed, but Arabella supposed he celebrated his new-found wealth more than his added burden of a wife. Then again, mayhap the nuptials did not weigh on his mind, since he would have as much freedom as he ever had. On the other hand, the laws of his land—and, really, hers, too—were so deeply in men's favor that she would be beholden to him no matter how he treated her.

Her thoughts taking an unhappy turn, Arabella withdrew from the party to find some fresh air. Slipping past a throng of revelers who seemed surprisingly drunk, considering the feast had just begun, she eased unnoticed into the low arched corridor with halls and chambers branching off on each side. When she reached the door that she hoped would lead outside, she was surprised to see it crack open and an elegant purple slipper slide through.

Rosalyn de Clair stepped into the keep, her cheeks bright red from the cold. The gray light of a winter day shone around her, highlighting features that were still delicate despite her thickening middle.

"Congratulations on your wedding day, Lady Rosalyn." Arabella nodded in greeting, wary of the woman after their strange talk in the forest that had led to Arabella's abduction while Rosalyn escaped unscathed.

"And to you." Rosalyn remained in her path. "You wish to go out unattended?"

"Exchanging vows with a man by the king's decree has made for a tense day, as you probably know. I hoped fresh air would renew my spirits." She removed the dried floral garland from her hair, tired of striving for approval she might never achieve.

Rosalyn did not move out of her way. Instead, she put her hand on the door as if to delay Arabella's departure.

"You do not wish an escort after what happened in Calais?" Rosalyn's fear sounded almost genuine. "I have heard the men who took you are still at large after wounding Tristan. I think your husband would have even more reason to hate me, should I allow you to roam the courtyard free."

"And I have heard the king's residences are always guarded by many knights." Arabella did not know what to make of the woman's sudden interest in her well-being. "I think it would be difficult for two foreign men to elude so many protectors."

Straightening, Rosalyn nodded, her purple surcoat glittering with jewels that winked even in the scant light of the corridor.

"Do not be so sure. Two men might probably hide themselves where an army of two hundred could not. But I will not stop you if you insist. I only hope you remember my effort the next time one of our company whispers that I led you astray that day in Calais on purpose."

Arabella felt the keen edge of that remark. No doubt Rosalyn had heard that Arabella thought her actions had been strange that day.

"I will. Although it occurs to me now we never were able to speak that day." Nodding, Rosalyn moved out of her path.

"Aye. But I only hoped to make peace as the princess

wished, Arabella." She darted close and kissed Arabella's cheek. "Godspeed in your marriage and may you be safe."

Amid a rustle of skirts and shuffling slippers, she was gone. Arabella laid a hand on her cheek where Rosalyn had kissed her and she wondered anew at the other woman's motives. Could she truly have wished to make amends that day?

Zaharia had always said a woman with child often became more subject to the whims of her humors. Some women turned more ill-tempered, while others found depths of warmth and contentment they had never before known. Could Rosalyn have experienced that kind of happiness now that she had reconciled herself to her babe?

She opened the door to the courtyard long enough to assure herself that all looked harmless enough. A few children ran about chasing an escaped hen and a mangy dog. Some squires wrestled on the cold ground, cursing and laughing as each tried to best the other. An old peddler pushed a cart, his hood drawn so far over his head his face was not even visible.

All seemed quite safe. She moved to step into the fresh air when hands clamped about her waist from behind her, halting her. She was about to scream the keep down when a voice behind her rumbled in her ear.

"Do not even dream of escaping your wedding day, Arabella."

Turning, she met the angry eyes of the man she'd vowed to obey for the rest of her days.

Tristan had not needed to look far for his Gypsy wife

when the princess had remarked on her absence. As he suspected, she'd run for open skies and the earth beneath her wild feet. Yet it frustrated him that he would have to look for her at all on the day of their nuptials.

"You seek to be free of me so soon?" Pulling her back inside, he closed the door to the courtyard, sealing them in privacy at the end of the corridor. The air remained cool between them and he wondered how long she'd been standing in the breach, one foot in both worlds.

What made him think he would be able to tie her to him when she was forever slipping away?

"I sought only a bit of fresh air after the…" She seemed to forgo that line of defense and took up another. "I am not well suited to conversing sweetly around tables full of people with dreams that bear no resemblance to my own."

The honesty of the answer appeased him somewhat, although he still planned to keep a closer eye on his fleet-footed wife in the weeks ahead. He would not be able to leave Ravenmoor until he was certain she understood what he expected of her. Until he was certain she would not risk her neck again for the sake of herb gathering or fresh air, or whatever other excuse she fed him.

"I do not relish dancing attendance upon the king myself." He shifted his hands to her shoulders, marveling at the sight of her. Her dress might be borrowed, but the rich fabric could not have been better suited to her. From her proud bearing to her keen, intelligent eyes, Arabella had been born with an inherent strength and nobility. "You are not any more pleased to play courtier than I am."

He grinned to realize they had this in common. A sudden longing to spirit her away seized him and he wondered what their life on the edge of civilization might be like.

"We care about many of the same things," Arabella observed, her thoughts mirroring his own. "If only we possessed the potion of Tristan and Isolde that we could drink together to find—"

He pressed her lips together with his thumb, striving to be gentle but unwilling to hear her fanciful notions now that they pertained to him. It was one thing to spin romantic notions when he only sought to woo her for a night or two. But now that they were joined forever, it would serve no good purpose for her to have illusions about their future.

"We should not wish that pain on ourselves." Memories of his own foolishness for the sake of love still burned hot if he allowed himself to remember them. "To know love is to open yourself to the greatest suffering imaginable and it is not a fate I would wish upon someone I'm sworn to protect."

Arabella blinked, her expression troubled. Confused.

"I do not understand. I thought you believed such love was worth safeguarding at all costs. Even to the displeasure of your king."

Cursed by his own idiocy. He remembered spouting something about never letting go of love if he happened to find it and wondered how he could reconcile words as idle as kisses with the more reasoned principles that guided his life.

"Aye. But I think that such love is as likely as the existence of magic potions that inspire it. They make for good tales and that is all."

Arabella lowered her eyes. When she lifted them again, her expression was cool. Shuttered. The same remote distance that lurked in every other noble-woman's eyes.

"Of course. How foolish of me to think otherwise. I hope you'll understand why I will not remain long at our wedding feast, since it is one thing to celebrate undying devotion and quite another to celebrate the legal loss of my independence."

She brushed past him like a cold breeze, her beaded skirts scraping the wool of his hose. He thought about stopping her, but what could he say to ease the biting regret he'd heard in her words? He would not give her false expectations when he had no intention of giving up his heart to her.

Tonight, he would introduce her to the rewards of marriage. The passion they'd glimpsed between them could now be fully explored and he suspected the night would bring heady pleasures for them both. Perhaps Arabella would not mourn the loss of love once she discovered the full scope of delights that awaited her in the marriage bed.

Chapter Thirteen

In spite of her threat, Arabella remained at the wedding feast for some hours. As much as she wished to distance herself from Tristan's disheartening view of their union, she realized that to leave the feast early would only lead her to her husband's bed all the sooner.

A daunting proposition.

The night that awaited her might be less worrisome if she could find pleasure with Tristan without fearing for her heart. After the hours they'd spent together in Cologne and the hints of passion she'd glimpsed there, she knew the marriage bed would hardly leave her cold. Indeed, the thought of baring herself so completely to Tristan filled her with heart-racing warmth. But how could she experience such intimacy without giving up a piece of herself to him?

And to do so would be dangerous, since Tristan had made it clear that theirs would be a loveless union. Did he harbor feelings for the woman he'd called for during his recovery from the knife wound? She had not forgotten the name—Elizabeth. Perhaps this other woman held his heart.

After consuming a bit too much wine, Arabella departed the revelry quietly. Seeking her own chamber, she pushed open the door and found her quarters alive with activity. Mary and Hilda were already there, and Mary rushed to hug her as she entered. Hilda urged her to a bench and began brushing her hair.

"It was a beautiful wedding, Arabella." Mary stored the garland of flowers Arabella had dispensed with earlier, perhaps thinking she would wish to save a token. "You are fortunate to be wedded to a man who was so intent on defending you to his king. I think he cares for you."

Arabella did not contradict her, although she knew Tristan's view of her—of marriage—all too well.

"Are you nervous?" Hilda unwound two thin plaits she had woven into Arabella's hair earlier that day.

"No. Because of my training as a healer, I know what to expect." Still, seeing her bed looming nearby made her think of where she would be spending the night in Tristan's chamber.

"Ach." Hilda waved away her words as she combed through the wavy sections of Arabella's hair. "Delivering babes only shows you the painful results of the marriage bed. I vow the wedding night is far more enjoyable."

Arabella smiled, touched that Tryant Hilda would offer her the consoling words a mother might speak to a daughter on her wedding night. The thought instilled a lump in her throat as she thought of her family.

A knock sounded at the door while Hilda chuckled and Mary opened it to admit one of the maids.

"The princess sends a gift with her regards, my lady." She thrust a wad of creamy fabric into Mary's hands and bent her knee quickly before hurrying away.

"Oh, Arabella. Look."

Mary unfurled the fabric to show them a night rail of the finest linen Arabella had ever seen. The garment practically floated as Mary shook out the wrinkles. White and delicately sewn, the garment's voluminous sleeves were interwoven with pale blue ribbons. More silky ribbon wound about the elbows to secure lightly brocaded lace to the wearer's arms. The bodice was simply yoked, with a skirt that fell to the floor and ended in a thick swath of more lace. Two pale blue birds had been embroidered along the hem, their elaborate tails intertwining with a flourish.

"It's perfect," Mary whispered, touching the linen reverently. "This must be one of the gowns sewn for the princess."

"I cannot accept such a treasure." Rising, Arabella plucked at the embroidered hem to admire the stitching.

"You must." Mary and Hilda spoke at the same time and then Mary let Hilda continue. "The princess would not send it if she didn't want you to accept it, Arabella. It will please her most to know that you are pleased."

Arabella stared down at her jewel-encrusted gown and then back to the night rail.

"She is too generous by half. But I will admit that I am sorely tempted."

Amid admonishments from Hilda and encouraging

words from Mary, Arabella dressed in the night rail and allowed herself to be escorted with all swiftness to Tristan's chamber.

The light mood in Arabella's room had nearly succeeded in driving away her worries about the night ahead. But they came flooding back when Tristan flung open his door to Hilda's light raps.

Her breath caught in her throat at the sight of him. He appeared even more fearsome half-clothed than when he was astride his enormous horse with sword in hand. Although she had cared for him during the night his fever broke, she had not appreciated the full extent of taut muscle that covered his body, perhaps because he had been in repose. Now, Arabella's companions urged her forward into the chamber past her husband. Hilda tucked her into Tristan's bed where the dark blue curtains had been fully opened. A fire crackled in a small granite hearth, the flames glinting off the polished chain mail that he had not worn on this, his wedding day. While Arabella slid between the cool linens, Tristan stalked from one end of the spacious room to the other, never looking in their direction.

With a final reassuring pat on the hand from Mary, the women hurried out and closed the door behind them. They were barely outside the portal when Tristan lowered the bar to bolt the door, locking them together in this masculine domain.

Arabella sat up and leaned against the silk-tasseled pillows piled high against the headboard of the high, carved bed. Waiting. Even with her eyes averted, she could sense his movements across the stone floor covered in clean rush mats, see his shadow moving ominously along the polished wooden beams of the high ceiling. It occurred to her that the chamber had likely been decorated for their nuptials. Extra tapers burned. There was an abundance of pillows that appeared freshly beaten, and dried flower petals had been strewn across the end of the bed.

Unfortunately, none of those thoughtful touches eased her worries.

Venturing a glance toward him, she saw him settle into a chair across from the bed. Though his body seemed at ease, his gaze was intense. Her heartbeat quickened.

For a moment, she recalled the first day she had seen him, in the oak ring. Like then, she could now only stare at him, unsure of herself in the presence of a powerful man…or was it that she was unsure of herself in the face of this powerful attraction between them? Heaven help her, she could not look away.

"Was it very hard for you to enter this chamber tonight?" A strange light danced in his eyes as he watched her, as if waiting for her to make a wrong move. He retrieved a dully shining object from the table next to him, where three tapers burned, and held it out for her to see. "I began to wonder if you might make a run for the mountains."

The object he held was her knife, lost the day they had first seen each other. He turned it over as if to better observe it. Arabella did not know how to interpret his mood. She watched his hands trace the edges of her blade.

"I do not plan to flee into a countryside rife with danger and men who wish to harm me. Thank you for retrieving my blade. It was a gift from my grandmother and a token that I treasure."

"You come to my chamber only to arm yourself?" He lifted a brow as he replaced the knife on the table near a wash basin. Although he jested, his eyes looked as weary as she felt.

"I came because—whether you will it or not—I am your wife." She wished they could dispense with the enmity between them for tonight at least. But then a moment of insecurity made her blurt, "Are you so sorry that it is I in your room this night and not Elizabeth?"

She had not intended to ask him about the woman, but perhaps a deeper jealousy gnawed at her than she had been willing to acknowledge.

Across from her, Tristan stilled.

"What would you know about Elizabeth?" The quiet request came with a seriousness she had not expected and now she wished she had remained silent.

"Nothing. You merely called out for her in your bout of fever. But most people battling life-threatening illnesses do not call out for persons of no consequence to them. I guessed Elizabeth is your…lover." She had not expected the confession to tweak her insides with a sharp pain. She had thought of Tristan's plea for the faceless woman numerous times since his fever, but she hadn't realized how much she'd resented his desire for another woman until she spoke the obvious conclusion aloud.

Elizabeth was his lover.

Some of the tension seemed to leave his broad shoulders. Was he unconcerned that she had guessed the truth?

"At least you did not find me attempting to flee

during the wedding feast." He rose from the chair to approach the bed and her mouth went dry.

As he stalked closer, she forced herself to find her wits.

"That is ridiculous. I have already told you—"

"If I were to draw the kinds of haphazard suspicions that you have, I might be tempted to believe you departed for a tryst in the woods today before I discovered you." He lowered himself to sit on the bed beside her and her skin warmed at his nearness.

Only now that he sat a few hands' spans away did she notice the clean and slightly foreign scent of his soap. The muscles in his arms bunched and flexed in odd places as he spoke, as if alive with charged feeling even before he touched her.

"You know well that was not my intent." She did not know what he sought from her, but she refused to be baited by his game.

"I know little where you are concerned, other than your propensity to roam and your passionate nature." He reached to touch the sleeve of her gown, his fingers tracing the pattern of brocade lace along her forearm.

"I have given you no reason to doubt my honor." She cursed herself for trembling at his touch, but she could no sooner stop her shiver than she could halt her racing heart.

"Nay. Nor have I given you reason to doubt mine." He leaned closer to skim his hand up her shoulder, his fingers landing lightly on her cheek. "Do you think we might both endeavor to remember as much?"

A humming vibrated along her skin and her flesh seemed to come alive under his touch.

Nodding, she arched closer to him, seeking the source of heat.

"Good." He bent to brush a kiss over her lips and she realized that she wanted to know the feeling of his mouth on hers again.

"But Tristan?" She spoke softly in the scant space between them, his lips already touching hers. "I cannot give over myself to you fully when you would—when you have made it clear that there is no hope of mutual regard between us."

She did not think he would care, and she did not know why she felt the need to make him aware of her reservations.

"You are assuming that you will be *able* to hold back." A soft flick of his tongue along her lower lip sent a dizzying rush through her limbs. "You do not think I can persuade you otherwise?"

The fire in her blood seemed to leap at his words. She had been too long without Tristan's touch and now, suddenly, she recalled the pleasure it inspired. Heaven help her, she submitted to this brief contact, this taste of passion.

That gentle kiss twisted into something new over the space of one heartbeat, turning from gentle reunion to something much more. He bound her to him with one arm, pressing her body to his so that she was at once blazingly aware of him from hip to shoulder. Her breasts tightened as he sealed her against his bare chest.

Caught by surprise, she cried out, only to have him deepen the kiss. His tongue penetrated her mouth, stirring an ache so wicked she could not describe it. Heat pierced her womb as his hand moved lower down her spine to the curve of her rump. Here he paused, exploring the contours of her hip with that strong, heated touch.

Her head spinning, she put her hands to his shoulders to ease herself back, away from him, to gain a moment to catch her breath. But the brush of his skin, hot and smooth beneath her fingertips, enticed her. Supple flesh encasing solid sinew. And soon she lost herself in the task of exploring it. She could not understand how quickly he had turned the tide of her needs from a desire to hold back into a simmering craving for more of him.

When his fingers plucked up the hem of her night rail and his palm ventured up her bare calf, she realized that she needed to act. Fast. She would be swept away if she allowed this to continue, unable to find herself again after this sweet incineration.

She tore her lips from his, breathing hard. "Wait. I—" She could not make sense of what she wanted, her thoughts scattering as fast as her sense.

Tristan did not release her fully. He merely trailed kisses down her throat, burning a path to the juncture of her neck and shoulder, a place that proved incredibly sensitive to his wicked skills.

The persuasive pressure of his mouth left her reeling, her whole body tingling in response to a kiss placed in such an unexpected place. She felt the effects of that kiss in the tightness of her breasts, the flutter of her belly and the restless itch of her thighs. That magic wrought through her whole body made her think there was much she did not understand about the healing arts and the way a body responded.

"Tristan." His name escaped in a plea as she became captive to his will.

Her fingers lifted to stroke his face, straying into his thick, dark hair.

He answered her by drawing her out of the covers and draping her over his lap, his powerful legs bracketing her bottom.

"Don't hold back from me, Bella." He cupped her face in his hands, forcing her gaze to his. "Not tonight."

She searched his eyes, hoping she would find some hint of tender concern, but she found only desire. His breath rushed noisily from his lungs the same way hers did. She took some comfort from the knowledge that she affected him.

"What you ask is impossible." Already, she had given up her freedom. Her hope of returning home one day. Her wish to one day know love.

"You desire this as much as I do." His thumb stroked her cheek as she became slowly aware of the hard length of him pressing against her hip.

"I—" She wanted more. But she could not express herself with so many emotions tumbling together and her body so hungry for his hands. "No."

"You watch me." His fingers skimmed down her neck to the bodice of her night rail, where he unwound the first ribbon that held the garment in place.

"Do not ask me for something I cannot give."

"Your eyes follow me. I feel them on me when I walk into a room. I sensed them on me all the way across the continent." He unveiled the valley between her breasts and gently explored the terrain.

Her eyes fell shut as she remembered those days of watching him, trying to make sense of what she felt for him. Her pulse drummed in her ears, the noise drowning out her thoughts as he spoke to her.

"And you tremble at my touch." He unfastened another ribbon on her gown and the linen slid from her shoulders.

Her eyes flew open at the realization he had bared her breasts. The night rail pooled around her waist, still shielding her legs and her hips, but she was naked from the waist up.

Tristan held himself perfectly still, perhaps wanting her to feel the tremors in her body that he'd spoken of. As if she did not already know.

"Even the king's most celebrated knight cannot win every battle." The words seemed like an empty taunt when she was already half naked and sighing in his arms, but her pride demanded this last stand against his will, no matter how inadequate.

He laughed softly as his thumb circled the taut peak of one breast.

"We shall see, Bella." He crossed the tip of that distended crest then, his caress slow and deliberate until her eyelids fluttered from the rush of pleasure. "Good luck staying strong, but I promise I will not think the worse of you for your surrender."

He captured her breast with his mouth then, his lips sliding across the tip in a way that inspired liquid heat in her womb. Her toes curled into the bed beneath the voluminous folds of her gown and she bent her head to his. The scent of his clean, dark hair filled her nostrils and she wrapped her arm about his neck to hold him right…there…just a moment longer.

She would give him her body on her wedding night. And she would surely take whatever physical pleasure she could wrest from her husband, since he refused to give her any more of himself than this. That did not make her susceptible to him. It only made her wise to accept her fate with grace and, possibly, a few squeals of delicious discovery.

Tristan could feel the moment his bride gave up at least a portion of her battle. She arched up to meet his mouth, her body every bit as hungry as his.

She tasted so sweet and he vowed that she would drown in the honeyed pleasure of the night. Transferring his kisses to her other breast, he reached beneath her knees to cradle her closer to his chest. The injury in his back still screamed with pain when he moved thus, but Arabella's soft cries of maidenly wonder were a better cure than anything she kept in her herb bag.

He shifted her hip tight against him, allowing her to feel the full extent of what she did to him. Her fingers danced delicately over his shoulder and down his chest, exploring at her own pace while he slipped his hand beneath the night rail.

She possessed the body of a goddess, tall and graceful yet generously curved. He'd seen the shape of her legs through her pale gown when she first arrived in his chamber, and he released her breast to witness the baring of calves now.

"You are—" he searched for the words and could not find them in his overloaded brain "—unspeakably beautiful."

Her hands continued to trace the shape of his arms and his chest while he massaged the delicate hollow beneath her knee.

When her fingers strayed down his side to the muscle at his waist, the need to take her rose up with new ferocity. Did she hasten him purposefully in the hope he would grow greedy and make it easier for her to hold back?

Nay. She was a maiden yet, and unaware of such things. Still, stroking her fingers sweetly down his hip was a cursedly clever ploy, if that had been her intent.

Closing his eyes for a moment to regain control, he slipped his hand up the back of her thigh. She stilled, her panting breath soft and rushed in his ear. The rhythm it set was like a tribal drumbeat, Gypsy music in his blood. He answered it, stretching his hand to its full width and sliding up the rest of her leg, squeezing the plump curve of her bare bottom.

A cry broke from her lips and he was lost to all thought. Her hips arched and he lifted her off him to lie on the bed, wrenching her night rail down her legs to float to the floor. He stretched over her, leaving his braies in place to ward him off at least a few moments more.

Her olive skin glowed with health in the firelight, her breasts dark pink and irresistible. He nipped each in turn while he spread her thighs and settled himself between them. Her hands scraped at his back, restless and needy, while he reached behind her to smooth his way down her spine. Pressing her hips to his, he felt the heat of her through his clothes.

She did not resist. No matter what she had spouted about holding back, she had lost all notion of any ill-aimed reason, her passionate streak as deep and fiery as any man could ever hope for in a wife.

The knowledge might test him sorely out of bed, but the possibilities for the nights... He could scarcely breathe now, when she remained an innocent.

"Bella." He unfastened his braies, unable to wait any longer. "You know that there is some pain at the first—"

"Aye. Please. Do not wait." Her green eyes pinned him as he stood to shed his clothes.

Her avid gaze moved over him like a heated stroke before he covered her again. Not since his earliest encounters with women had he felt such urgency.

"Next time it will be all pleasure," he promised, thinking about her maidenhead as much as what he would do for her when this haze of lust did not ride him so completely.

She might have nodded, but just then she lifted her head to kiss him, her lips finding his with infinite sweetness. He tilted his head for better access, grateful for the distraction that helped him slow down.

At the same moment he strokèd her with his tongue, he penetrated her. She stiffened beneath him, her body going still except for the rapid pounding of her heart.

Rising up on one arm, he eased her legs wider, paying homage to her soft thighs with his hands as he touched her. When she relaxed, he thrust deeper in one quick motion to dispense with the pain all at once.

He caught her cry in his mouth, kissing her deeply as he held his hips perfectly still. The task was a feat as great as any sword battle he had ever waged, sweat popping along his brow while he waited for her pain to ease. Willing back his need, he palmed her breast, cupping the soft weight in his hand.

At last she moaned and wriggled, her passion getting the better of her. He set up a slow rhythm then, as much for his sake as for hers. Releasing her mouth, he smoothed her dark hair from her face and met her eyes in the firelight.

"You are all mine." He had not meant to speak the thought aloud, but the words scratched along his senses, hoarse and guttural.

"Tristan?" She peered up at him through eyelids at half-mast. "It is like I am wound too tightly inside."

She illustrated the notion with a circular wave of her finger and he bit off a grin.

"Aye. 'Tis a state I am familiar with."

Hauling in a few more bracing breaths, he withdrew from her partway and slid his fingers between their bodies. Her eyes widened at his touch. The slick heat of her made it easy to circle the tender nub with his thumb while he thrust inside her again.

Listening for the play of her breath in his ear, he adjusted his touches to her soft moans of pleasure. The effort cost him, the rewards so sweet that he needed to close his eyes at the last to fight off his finish. But soon her body went rigid, arching hard into him, and she cried out his name.

At the soft clench of her body around his, he found

his own fulfillment, spilling his seed deep in her belly. The spasms went on and on, his breathing as rough as a warhorse's after a day on the field.

For that matter, he felt a lot like a victorious warrior riding out of battle, weary but triumphant. He had won tonight's encounter, it seemed. But even as he slid from Arabella's warm body and gathered her sweet nakedness into his arms, he feared he hadn't come close to winning the war.

Chapter Fourteen

A soft rapping on the door called Tristan from his sleep some hours afterward. The fire had burned down to a few glowing logs and a draft blew over the bed, since he had never drawn the curtains. Arabella had curled around a pillow beside him, her hair blanketing his shoulder while her bare rump nestled into his hips.

The knock sounded again, forcing him to set aside the new pleasures of marriage. He stalked across the chamber to don his braies and then wrenched open the door, prepared to take the head off of whatever unfortunate soul lurked on the other side.

"Simon? Sweet Jesus—"

"Sorry, Tris." He put up his hand as if he could halt Tristan's foul outcry. "It's about Ivan and the guy Arabella says stabbed you."

"Hellfire." He glanced out into the corridor and back into his chamber before pulling Simon into his apartments. "We'll talk in here, but you keep your voice down and your eyes on me."

Simon's white teeth showed in the darkness. "Of all the beetle-eyed afflictions, you end up more wounded by lust than a blade. You are far gone on your own wife."

Unwilling to hear his own fears confirmed by the person who knew him best, Tristan scowled.

"You might speak more kindly to me of her, since the king would have likely set you up in marriage if I had not claimed her first. 'Twas your knock-kneed fears that she had done ill by me that set the whole retinue to whispering about her." The idea had moved Tristan to take responsibility for the rumors at court about her without delay. Simon might be the brother of his heart, but Tristan would never have allowed him to touch Arabella.

His wife.

The knowledge still rolled oddly over him.

Simon nodded. "I am sorry. And I will make a better apology to her, as well. But for now, you should know that your spies have returned with reports you will want to hear. Two of them have heard of or seen the foreigners we described. There is a healer outside London who claims she gave ointments to Thadus for a wealth of assorted injuries."

Tristan had remembered that day in Calais more clearly as he had recovered from his fever. And while it gave him some satisfaction to think the milk-livered lout had needed potions to cure wounds Tristan had inflicted, it was not enough to soothe his fury that the man had bested him with a dishonorable cry for mercy.

"I must speak to our men at once and possibly send out scouting parties to track them. I would prefer this problem does not follow us to Ravenmoor, and I am loath to leave the king with an extra concern here when his reign is already burdened with greedy uncles and power-hungry barons."

Simon nodded and moved toward the door. "I will leave so you can tell your wife."

Tristan did not comment, but he had no plans to disturb Arabella's sleep to remind her of their other worries. With any luck, he would be back in bed before the dawn to wake her in an infinitely more pleasurable way.

Dark dreams haunted her.

Arabella knew they were dreams for they didn't make sense. She spoke at length with her grandmother back in Bohemia, except that Tristan stood by her side. He raised his voice to Zaharia for some reason, convinced she was hiding something from him. From Arabella herself.

Understanding danced at the corners of her mind as she remembered odd moments from her childhood. The ways she was hidden from newcomers when strangers arrived at the closest village. Her mother's unusual fears and cautions about men. Whispered conversations that seemed to concern her, which were broken off as soon as she joined her family.

The linens twisted around her in sleep, dragging her back to reality even though she wanted to remain in her dreams to understand what they tried to tell her. Had her family hidden something from her? Perhaps Tristan would understand what the dreams meant. He had seemed so intent on discovering the truth from her grandmother in her visions. Besides, he was her husband now. Her lover.

Remembering their night together, she reached for him, patting the bed where his body should be.

Tristan?

She bolted upright, naked but for the blanket about her waist. The room had turned cold in the pale light of dawn, the place beside her empty.

She slid from the bed to reach for a kirtle before remembering she had not spent the night in her own bed. There were no clothes for her here save the night rail, which would not keep her warm. Searching the chamber, she found one of Tristan's tunics and sniffed the snowy linen to be sure the garb was clean.

The scent of lye soap and something else—apple blossoms, perhaps—was common enough at Windsor. She knew the smell from the garments she had given to the maids for washing since arriving. Tunneling her way into the tunic, she hugged the fabric about her while lacing the tie enough to cover her breasts.

He had left her here to awake alone after their wedding night. The full meaning of his choice only just began to roll over her as she donned her slippers to return to her own room. He had been all too serious about their marriage being a legal matter and not some romantic tale. The knowledge hurt keenly when her thighs still ached from her introduction to womanhood.

Picking up her discarded night rail, a beautiful garment that Anne had gifted her with in the hope of a good marriage, Arabella slipped out the door and into the corridor. If Tristan wanted no more from marriage than a legal union to secure his lands, he had it now. There was no reason for her to lie about his apartments alone when she had friends nearby, a country to explore and new skills to learn as a healer. She would devote her life to serving the sick. That did not have to change just because of a marriage vow to a man who didn't really want her in the first place.

No matter that his kisses had told her something different, something…incredible, the night before.

The worst thing she could do would be to let him know he had hurt her. Better simply to pretend his absence had hardly been noticed. Still, arriving back at her chamber in the early hours of dawn, she couldn't help but wonder what it might have been like if she had spent her wedding night with a man who held her in regard for more than her ability to secure his king's favor.

Tristan might have had better luck chasing ghosts than two Bohemian strangers.

Even villagers on the outskirts of London had learned the value of caginess during the reign of a king who might not have enough power to keep his throne. Tristan received one vague answer after another from people who watched the city walls or worked in fields near the roads to town.

Now, as he charged through the keep toward the great hall, he only wanted to find Arabella. She had not been in his chamber when he returned in the afternoon, nor had her belongings been moved to his rooms the way they should have been. He had not been able to find her with the princess's other women as they prepared for the royal nuptials on the morrow, so he could not ask why she thought she could maintain separate apartments. Once again, he seemed to chase ghosts.

Finally, as he entered the hall, he spied her at a trestle table with Mary and Simon. He might have simply joined them and set aside his frustrations for the day. But the sight of her set his teeth on edge, since she wore her hair wound and plaited within the confines of a wimple like an ancient hag wed for decades instead of hours.

What game did she play today?

"Arabella." He arrived at the table to confront her. His manners vanished in his haste to see her, since they had parted on more awkward terms than he had anticipated.

She nodded a cool greeting while Simon stood.

"Mary has received a message from the emperor that I think you should see." He waved the correspondence at Tristan before taking his seat again. "We have been discussing the significance as we eat."

A server passing a tray full of cheeses bumped into him.

"I have spent half the night and all day seeking the plague that followed us from Bohemia." Tristan's patience had worn thin and he doubted his ability to translate the Latin quickly. "Perhaps you could tell me what it says?"

Mary gestured to the seat beside her for Tristan to join them, while Arabella waved over the wine bearer and filled her cup.

"Of course." Mary took the paper back from him as he seated himself across from Arabella. "He suggests there might be an interloper in our midst, a woman who falsely claimed nobility in an effort to gain our trust and to follow our movements. He doesn't say why or who, but admits the Holy Roman Empire has many enemies."

"What we don't understand is how the empire's

enemies would benefit from knowing more about the princess's activities," Simon added.

Tristan tried to shake off his thoughts of carrying Arabella back to his chamber.

"Perhaps the empire's enemies are interested in more than the princess. Every high-ranking family in the emperor's homeland has a feminine relative here at court now. Perhaps the emperor fears those women could be used for negotiating purposes to undermine his power," Simon continued.

Tristan wished that information could have been shared with him—or with the king—before the Bohemian people had sent such a large group of foreigners abroad. But even more, he wished to be alone with his wife and forget about political turmoil.

"It could be me." Arabella spoke up finally, her fingers passing a bit of cooked pigeon from her plate to one of the cats that kept rats out of the hall.

"We know that you are not the spy," Mary chided, while Tristan weighed the possibility.

"She is an outsider." He hadn't realized he'd spoken the thought aloud until Simon's head whipped in his direction.

"She saved your life, Tris." Simon's brows knit together as he mopped up his trencher with a chunk of bread.

"The interloper would have to ensure she kept her place. And you have to admit, Arabella would have been sent home if anything had happened to me while the rumors flew about her unnatural skills."

Arabella put the cat on the floor in silence while Mary and Simon stared at him as though he had sprouted an extra head. But Tristan would dig through the meaning of the emperor's letter and flush out the men following them soon enough.

He rose from his seat.

"I need to speak with you privately."

Blinking up at him, Arabella didn't appear as surprised as Mary or Simon.

"Now?" She seemed to take renewed interest in her pastry.

Frustration gnawed at his frayed patience.

"Aye." He pulled her to her feet, more certain than ever she meant only to irritate him. Turning to Mary and Simon, he bowed. "My apologies, but I was called prematurely from my bed last night, and I do not wish to begin my marriage under unfortunate circumstances."

Without another word, he tugged Arabella out of the hall and through the long passage. They twined around an old storage tower and climbed to an upper gallery before Arabella's feet slowed.

"You accompany me to my chamber?" She backed against a fading tapestry of a long-ago coronation. The white linen wimple stood out in stark contrast to the bright colors behind her.

"I thought I would assist you in moving your things to my rooms, since you neglected to do so earlier."

"Since we leave for Ravenmoor immediately after the king's wedding, I did not see the need."

"There is a need, if not for all your things, at least for garments to wear tomorrow." He stepped toward her, desiring privacy. Desiring her. "You belong with me now."

He hauled her up in his arms to expedite their trip,

unconcerned about the opinion of two giggling maids they passed on the way.

"I pray you, sir, put me down," Arabella hissed through clenched teeth. "I am capable of walking."

"Not fast enough." He scanned the length of the corridor and tried to guess which chamber was hers, although the temptation to simply press her against the stone wall and kiss her into compliance proved difficult to resist. "Is it this one?"

"Nay. Two down." She wriggled in his arms and he held her tighter as one of his men—Mauberly—passed them in the hall, hiding a grin as he nodded.

Finding her door, Tristan pushed it open with his foot and entered her chamber, unsure that he wanted to let her go even now.

Arabella's flushed cheeks and pursed lips helped make his decision for him. She would never cooperate with him now.

"You simpleminded ox."

"Simpleminded?" Single-minded, perhaps. He had great difficulty thinking of anything save getting her back to his room and peeling off her garments. "Of all the things I have ever been called, I don't believe anyone has accused me of lacking wits."

"You are manhandling me to get your own way, which is incredibly simpleminded. A clever man would speak to a woman, not toss her about like a grain sack."

"Ah. Then I can see where calling me an ox would naturally follow. What would you like to bring with you to my chamber?" He carried his captive to her wardrobe and bent his head to kiss the skin bared above the embroidered neckline of her surcoat.

"Does it not bother you to know I think so poorly of you?"

"First of all, if you truly thought me simpleminded, you would not bother sounding out my thoughts on the subject. Second, it does not bother me, because you make your accusation in anger. Because of that, you don't see that it is extremely clever of me to use the quickest means to exercise my will. Now choose a gown for the morrow or you will attend Anne's wedding in your present garb, which at this rate will be in shreds by then."

She must have seen the wisdom in the words, as she pulled a bundle of blue velvet from her chest full of clothes and dried flowers. This, he realized, was the source of her scent. He spied full blooms of varying colors that had been perfectly preserved and still carried their fragrance. Once she had gathered hose and shoes, some mint leaves and a small bar of soap that she must prefer, they left her room. He gave orders to a maid they met in the hallway to pack Arabella's things for the morning.

They would leave for Ravenmoor directly after the ceremony, but he planned to occupy every second of his wife's time until then.

Arabella hid her face in Tristan's tunic on the way to his chamber, unwilling to meet the eyes of any smiling castle inhabitants who assumed he held her in his arms because he cared for her so tenderly.

No one else knew she had awoken alone after the one night that a husband and wife should remain together. And although he had told Simon and Mary that his sleep had been interrupted the night before, he had not thought to impart any such thing to her. His wife.

Of course, chances were good that he had made up the story to excuse his desire to steal her out of the great hall. If he had needed to leave during the night, why had he not told her? No matter how she turned the story, she came away deciding his behavior on their wedding night only underscored his need to maintain his distance from her. Perhaps that was because she was not the woman he loved—Elizabeth—or perhaps he merely did not believe that the kind of devotion Tristan and Isolde shared really existed.

And for all Arabella knew, mayhap it did not. The realization weighed heavily on her heart as they arrived in Tristan's chamber and he bolted the door behind them.

Setting her on her feet, he took the garments from her room and placed them on a bench near the washbasin. Silently, he moved to the hearth to tend the fire, which was little more than ashes since the sun had not even set yet. No servant would have checked the hearths.

"You might save me the trouble of dispensing with the wimple," he called from the charred patch of stones near the fireplace. "For that matter, I am happy to use it as tinder."

She could not help a small smile at that, since it had not taken her long to realize the restrictive garment did not suit her. Still, it had saved her from having her hair teasing her senses all day, sliding over her skin and reminding her of all the ways Tristan had touched her the night before.

Unwinding the fabric, she freed herself of the linen.

The intimacy of undressing near him sent a shiver through her despite the heat from the blaze he quickly coaxed from the ashes. She pulled at the pins in her plaited coronets, but she was not nearly so skillful as Hilda, dropping pins on the rush mat covering the floor.

"Let me." Tristan rose from his place in front of the fire. "Come here."

She hesitated, knowing that his touch would only hasten her journey to caring too much. He had slid past her every barrier and she feared he could do so all too easily again. Her skin already tightened and heated at the promise of moving closer to him.

Reaching out for her, he reeled her near, situating her in front of the fire. He lifted his hands to her hair and pulled one pin after another from the plaits until he had unwound their entire length from her ears.

"You have unusual skill with women's hairpins." She fought to keep her eyes open as his fingers brushed her scalp. Her temples.

"And a few other skills as well. Like a healer, a knight serves an apprenticeship. We are not as simpleminded as you might think."

"I'm sorry." Her cheeks heated at the memory of words he had not deserved. "My mother swore I maintained a child's temper long after I grew to womanhood."

"Anger is but another side of passion. I thought it had been thoroughly beaten from me as a child, but that day in the forest at Calais—seeing Thadus with you—I realized I must have stored a portion of the dark humors somewhere."

Untying the cords from her long braids, Tristan

started to undo the links of the plaits. As he pulled out each section of braid with his fingers, he shook her hair lightly between his hands to free it.

"I would not wish any child of mine beaten." Arabella had not thought about the babes she would one day bear her husband before now, but the idea of her son being whipped into warrior form sent a wave of illness through her belly.

"I would thrash anyone who touched my child." Tristan's words were clear enough and something about his tone suggested it was a subject he did not wish to elaborate on. She thought back to that day in Cologne when he had refused all talk of himself or his past.

"Was it difficult being a foundling?" She had been raised without a father, but her mother's love had been enough.

She waited for him to speak, surprised he continued to help her unwind her hair, taking care not to pull a single strand unduly. Behind her, she heard the steady rise and fall of his breath as he worked.

"My misery as an orphan made me strong enough to cross the continent at ten summers to pledge my life to the Black Prince—King Richard's father." His fingers slowed their pace as he finished the task and his touch trailed down to the base of her scalp. "Without that determination—a will to live in spite of the beatings and a will to live if only to protect Simon—I would not be the man I am."

He turned her to face him and she found herself inspecting him for signs of his guardian's brutality. Were there marks she had missed in choosing to see him through the eyes of a woman rather than the eyes of a healer? Or were his scars the kinds of wounds that could not be seen?

Hurt for him constricted her chest. She had never created a poisonous potion, but she wondered if a man such as Tristan's guardian might have persuaded her to try.

"I am glad you found that strength, but I am sorry you suffered for the sake of it." She stroked his cheek, which had grown rough with whiskers since their wedding.

"It is in the past." His jaw flexed and clenched. "I do not speak of it often, but I have told you so that you will know me better."

Confused, she wanted to tell him that he had offered her too little, but he was already removing the hauberk covering his chain mail.

"You are well protected for a man still celebrating his wedding." She smoothed a hand across the interlocking rings, surprised they did not pinch her now and hadn't when he'd carried her into the chamber, either.

"Enemies follow us as the emperor suggests."

She wanted to ask him more about the potential dangers of traveling, but he slid his hands around her hips and her thoughts scattered.

"I do not wish to speak of enemies or the past or why you made yourself scarce this afternoon when I scoured the keep for a sight of you." His hands worked the laces of her surcoat, a series of ties up each side from her hip to her arm.

And just like that, her heart kicked into a faster rhythm, her body remembering his touch all too well.

"What would you like to speak of then, Lord Ravenmoor?" Even as her breath caught in her throat, she wondered how it felt for an orphaned boy to have gained the favor of his king in such a tangible, valuable fashion.

"I'd like to know how you fared today in the aftermath of lovemaking." He unfastened more ties at her sleeves, freeing the surcoat to slip to the floor in a pool of velvet and wool.

She felt exposed and unsure how to answer him while he pulled the chain mail off and laid it on the bench.

"I am fine." She would not mention how she had felt to awaken alone in the marriage bed, her thighs flecked with blood and her husband's pillow cold.

Perhaps a man raised without love did not understand how to give it.

"You are not too sore to meet the demands of your lord all over again?" His hands searched for fastenings on her kirtle, a slow journey when he stopped to trace a finger over the mound of her sex and mold her breasts in his hands.

Even if he could not give love, Arabella acknowledged, he could share this tenderness, this heart-racing passion that made her blood simmer.

"Nay." The word was a breathless plea, her skin on fire from teasing brushes of his fingers. "What of you? Are you willing to meet *my* demands, or will you find some other way to fill your time tonight after you leave our bed?"

His hands stilled and he angled back to study her face.

"You have needs left unmet?" A hint of a smile played upon his face.

She shrugged, unsure how to answer. "I do not yet

know my own needs, but I do not think I had time to properly discover them when you spent the night away from me."

She waited for him to argue with her or dismiss her words, but he seemed to be listening intently. When he said nothing, she leaned in to him, testing the power of her touch by skimming her fingers down his broad chest.

"I once overheard a new bride from my village tell my mother that her husband awoke her three times on their wedding night." Arabella had never forgotten the gasps and giggling that had accompanied that whispered conversation, even though she had not understood the full significance at the time.

Tristan's laughter was low and wicked. "It is my guess the new bride was no maid at the start of her wedding night, but I am sorry to disappoint you nevertheless."

She hoped he would explain his whereabouts the night before, but instead he twined a lock of hair about his finger and studied her in the firelight.

"Just when I think you are done surprising me, you knock me flat on my back." He released her breasts to tug her kirtle off one shoulder and then the other. She stood naked before him, her body his for the taking.

She had never been more vulnerable, and yet she experienced a renewed sense of power, too. She might not have been the bride of Tristan's choice, but he was as compelled by her—by this attraction between them—as she was by him. Could she afford to risk her heart by gambling with passion this way? She had not thought it wise last night and she had struggled to hold back. But this might be her only weapon with which to battle her husband's cool distance.

"You have made it clear I cannot expect any depth of undying affection in marriage. But is it wrong to expect a warm bed at least until the dawn?" She did not know where she found her courage to speak to him thus, but the glittering light in his eyes encouraged her.

Without warning, his mouth descended on hers, capturing her lips and coaxing them apart. He gave her no quarter, his tongue exploring her thoroughly while he backed her into a tapestry-covered wall. The stitched wool abraded her skin and her head thumped back against the embroidered falcon sitting on its master's glove, narrowly missing an empty iron torch ring nearby.

With Arabella trapped there, Tristan's fingers went to work on his tunic and braies, his laces melting away under the swift work of his hands. She helped him yank the tunic up and off his shoulders, but she hesitated when her hands fell helplessly at his waist.

She did not dare, so he guided her hands to the hard shaft jutting from the gap in his braies. A soft moan escaped her lips as she remembered the feel of him inside her and she stroked the silky skin stretched over his impossibly hard length.

He shoved off his garments and deepened the kiss while she seemed to melt inside. Her whole world shifted and narrowed to this moment, this man. She seemed to breathe him in, breathe through him, every hitch of air filtered through the warm-wine taste of his lips.

He only broke the kiss for a moment, just long enough to run his finger over her mouth and dip it briefly inside. She nearly came undone when that same finger slid between her thighs. The warm wetness mingled with her own moist heat in a sensation so sweet her knees buckled with it. She might have sunk to the floor if he hadn't planted his leg between hers, his muscular thigh holding hers apart while he stroked a heated response from her.

All around her, his strength dominated her except for that most intimate of places, where he touched her with restraint bordering on maddening. The want in her rose up in her throat like a scream, her spine arching and her hips thrusting forward. Waiting.

Then something constricted inside, a tightening that stole her breath and stilled every movement while liquid bliss flooded through her. He caught her cries as her whole body shuddered with rapturous release.

She hadn't even begun to recover from that exquisite pleasure when he thrust inside her in one smooth motion. Wrapping her legs around his hips, he carried her to his bed and laid her on the down-filled mattress while he stood over her, moving inside her. Their gazes met for a long moment and her breath hitched at the way he looked at her just then, his eyes reflecting churning emotions she wanted to dive into.

Then the look was gone and he pressed deep inside her body, still quavering from the rush of sensations he had made her feel. Now he joined with her so fully, so completely, that she could not exert her own will. His weight on her, over her, inside her provided delicious pressure, chasing away any need to hold back, since she belonged to him.

Her fingers clutched in his hair while her ankles locked around his hips, holding him close. She wanted nothing more than this feeling, this pleasure, this one place where they understood each other completely.

She arched up to run her hands down his chest, feeling his strength and his heat while he stilled. He gripped her hips, steadying her, and then the wave of release must have hit him. His hoarse shout mingled with her cries of pleasure until he fell on top of her, dragging her into his bed and wrapping her in the linens.

Exhaustion stole over her and she remembered that she had been awake since dawn. Smiling and content, she felt the first stirrings of hope since their wedding had been ordered.

Tristan might not have wished to wed her, but he did not feel coldly toward her either. The marriage bed would be her means to know him, her path to the tenderness he would deny possessing. Tonight, she would not consider the emotional danger that method entailed for her own heart. Tonight, she would simply enjoy the murmur of her husband's pulse beneath her ear.

"Sleep well, Bella," he whispered in her ear while his fingers brushed her hair from her cheek. "I will wake you all too soon to fulfill your wifely demands."

Even half-asleep she smiled. And heaven help her, she couldn't wait. She dozed into fitful sleep, wrestling with the notion of the powerful sway this man held over her with the sensual draw of passion.

Chapter Fifteen

The wedding of Princess Anne and King Richard was an historic event all of London wanted to see. It also presented a tactical nightmare for those charged with the duty of protecting the royal procession.

Thankfully, that was no longer Tristan's task. Still, he had reason to believe his wife was even more of a target than the king's new wife, although it bothered him that he didn't know why.

Tristan tucked Arabella near to him after the ceremony, eager to leave the city for quieter terrain where he could control the surroundings a little more. The streets of London were crammed full of guests from every corner of the country and visitors from abroad come to witness the royal marriage, so it was impossible to pick out two particular foreigners.

That did not stop Tristan from making an attempt.

"I have never seen such a display." Arabella squeezed closer as a brightly dressed juggler passed near, his arms full of flaming torches. "Nor so many people."

He recalled her roots in a more rural, wild setting and sought to reassure her.

"The only time I have seen close to this number was on a battlefield. And even then, not quite as many as this."

"I am glad to hear your countrymen would rather celebrate than make war." She stepped around a woman carrying a cage full of blue and yellow birds with a ribbon around it, probably a gift for the newly wed couple.

Tristan watched as the royal procession reached the great hall for the festivities. Richard wore the colors of the Order of the Garter for the occasion, so the majority of his noblemen did, too, including Tristan and Simon. Ornamental garters were embroidered on their mantles. An earl wore about forty more than a knight, while the king wore the greatest number—well over one hundred.

A few moons ago, all of the pageantry would have held great interest for him, but today, he was struck by the need to protect Arabella in a crowd. Would he always feel this sense of obligation to her as a married man? How would he ever go off to battle and leave her behind while plagued by this need to watch over her?

He had thought a loveless marriage full of sizzling nights would be easy, but he was discovering it would not be so simple.

"For myself, I'd rather travel than celebrate today. Have you said your farewells?" Tristan pulled her through the courtyard, where most of the revelers congregated. He needed to get to Ravenmoor to assess the needs of his new keep and put his life back in order after so many years of making war.

The feast would last for the next three days, while the marriage was celebrated with dancing and singing, plays and entertainments. Tristan had no intention of remaining in London for more courtly activities after playing courtier to the Bohemian retinue.

"Yes. And I know the new queen hates to part with Mary, but I am glad she allows her to travel north with us."

"She has no choice, now that the king has acknowledged the possible threat to the Bohemians at his court. He hopes that by dividing the women, he will make them more difficult to target." Tristan did not mention that it would also be cheaper for the royal coffers to disperse noblewomen reliant upon the king's purse. Londoners already complained of the foreigners at court.

In the courtyard there was enough venison, boar, pork, chicken, swan, capon and pigeon to feed all of the guests several times over. Wine flowed freely, and ale was passed among the celebrants. Sweet confections were plentiful, too, including cakes, puddings, tarts and sweetmeats of every conceivable flavor.

Wedding gifts overflowed the heavily guarded display tables filled with heaping piles of gold plate, silver coins and jewels from foreign kings and queens. Other tables groaned with bolts of silk and velvet, tapestries, linens and leather goods from artisans across the country and beyond.

Yet none of the sights and sounds tempted Tristan to delay his trip north. It would take a fortnight to reach Ravenmoor and he needed to take stock of the place before planting season. Since Richard had awarded him the estate, he had learned that the former earl had been executed as a traitor under the order of the king's uncle, John of Gaunt, and the castle had been vacant for nearly a year. The lands of Ravenmoor could very well be stripped and barren by now, or the tenants could have all moved off to seek protection from another lord. Whatever the state of Ravenmoor was, Tristan wanted to see it with his own eyes and begin working to make it a prosperous and peaceful land.

At least Arabella seemed resigned to his haste, and she made quick work of rechecking the contents of her trunks as they reached their horses. Neither Arabella nor Tristan had much in the way of personal possessions. The numerous gifts the king and his new queen had bestowed upon them accounted for most of the baggage they carried. Arabella had seemed touched by the chests full of new linens, silver pieces and tapestries. Of course, he would inherit all of the possessions within the Ravenmoor keep, but it was possible the wealth had already been carted off by looters, despite a small royal contingent sent to guard the lands some moons ago.

The group mounted up without fanfare, since even the stable boys were toasting the royal couple's happiness. One of their company played a tune on a wooden flute, while two maids from the keep took up a dance nearby. Tristan would lead the party with Simon guarding the rear. Arabella, Mary, two maids and ten of the king's men-at-arms rode between them.

Still, all that protection did not prevent Tristan from calling Arabella to his side shortly after they cleared the city gate.

"I hope we are not lost so soon in our journey," she

remarked, smiling, as she drew near. Her skirts fell to one side of her mount, her cloak wrapped tightly about her as a light snow began to fall.

"Nay. I want to make you aware that the men who captured you in Calais may follow us. They have been spotted in London since our arrival and their presence persuaded Richard to lend us extra men for the journey."

"I thought Anne was their target." She frowned and her eyes scanned the horizon. "Why wouldn't they remain in London as long as she is in residence there?"

The music from the city had faded, but even at this distance they could still hear an occasional shout from the crowds.

"Ivan has tried to take you twice." Tristan had pondered the abductions over and over and still he could not understand why she in particular had been targeted. "We must consider the possibility that it is you he is after."

"I do not understand why." She swiped at a snowflake that had landed on her cheek. "My position at court is tenuous and I have no importance or wealth save through our marriage. Although…"

She broke off, frowning.

"What?" He tensed. Was there more to her heritage than she had shared? The politics and hierarchy of Bohemia were unique and he had not taken much time to learn the subtleties of rank while he'd been in Prague. "Might you have some indirect tie to the emperor? Or perhaps your grandmother's notoriety makes you a target?"

She shook her head and gripped the reins tighter as they negotiated a muddy incline along the road.

"No. But I had a dream on our wedding night…."

"A dream?" Frustration rumbled through him. "I speak of life-and-death matters and you wish to share your dreams?"

She straightened in the saddle and he could tell by the stiffness of her shoulders that he had offended her.

But by the saints, what was she thinking?

"I thought the dream would be pertinent as I was thinking about moments from my past and the strangeness of never meeting my father."

"Still, thoughts and dreams are the domain of a mystic, not a warrior. We seek facts to plan our defenses around, not fanciful notions created in your head."

"I have no facts to share regarding my family. My father has never been a part of my life because of his slight to my mother. It seems he took advantage of her innocence while she was at court and then he refused to wed her."

"Yet you are recognized, even though your parents were not wed?" He picked up their pace, hoping to make haste before the sun set, with the snow falling faster. "Is that common in your country?"

"No." She hesitated and he remembered the report from his spies that a commoner lurked within the royal retinue, pretending a heritage she could not rightfully claim.

Would Arabella attempt such a deception?

"It seems we share ignominious beginnings." Perhaps if she knew he would not condemn her for her birth, she would not feel the need to hide it.

"Ravenmoor."

A man's voice shouted to him from the middle of the

riding party and Tristan turned to see one of the men-at-arms escorting a boy on a pony.

"Who are you, boy?" The squire wore Richard's colors over his tunic but no cloak, his face dirty and his shoulders shaking with the cold.

"I bring a note from Windsor." The boy sneered at the man-at-arms, as if the man had not believed his importance.

Tristan remembered the feeling all too well.

"Make haste then, so that you may return to the keep before the snow gets any deeper." He dug a coin out of his pouch and wished he could have given the boy a cloak without embarrassing him. At the boy's age, pride could be far more valuable than comfort.

Taking the note, he passed the boy two coins.

"Volunteer for the king's next dispatch to Ravenmoor if you would like to lift a sword instead of a parchment in the future," Tristan said. He could see now that the dark patch on the boy's face that he had assumed was dirt was really a bruise.

Apparently not too proud to grin over the prospect of wielding a weapon, the boy did not hide his pleasure.

"I will do that, my lord." He nodded and bowed awkwardly from his saddle. "Thank you."

Dismissing the lad, Tristan read the missive, a note the king had forwarded on behalf of one of Tristan's spies. The content was short and to the point.

Ravenmoor, the men you seek belong to a heretical sect committed to overthrowing the Holy Roman Emperor.

"What is it?" Arabella plaited a section of her horse's mane while she waited.

He stared hard at her, this woman seemingly without airs and with the most humble birth of anyone in their company, who still managed to attract attention everywhere she went. A cold wind stirred a few last dry leaves from the branches overhead.

"It seems your admirers Ivan and Thadus aren't interested in any ransom you can bring." He stuffed the parchment in his saddlebag. "They plan to bring down a whole empire. Any idea why they think kidnapping one willful healer will further a heretical cause?"

The whole company went silent, making Tristan realize that even the riders farthest in the back near Simon had caught up to them. They turned as one to gape at Arabella and Tristan instantly regretted his words.

No matter his intentions, by mentioning heresy and his wife in the same utterance, he'd just unwittingly implicated her in yet another dark deed.

A chill fell on her marriage as surely as the winter deepened all around them on their journey northward over the next fortnight. Arabella had never felt such a damp cold in all her life. Winds whipped across the rolling hills from the sea, carrying with them wet snow and misfortunes. One of the men-at-arms took an arrow to the hip from a high cliff and no brigand was ever found. Mary had taken ill two days back and needed the warmth of a dry fire to soothe the rasping breaths that rattled her bones.

Still, Arabella knew she could heal Mary and the unfortunate guard who'd taken an arrow. She doubted her ability to mend her marriage, made in haste and viewed as a mere social convention by her husband. Arabella had hoped the heated nights she shared with Tristan could somehow bring them closer together. But the journey had made such intimacy impossible and the lack made her all too aware how much was missing in her union. How could she hope to find any road leading to love when her lone bond to Tristan involved a meeting of the bodies but never of the minds?

Having grown up in a house full of women, she did not understand men. And she'd been raised knowing that her father had betrayed and abandoned her mother. How would Arabella ever learn to know a man's heart, let alone know when to trust one?

She had to guard her words around him, since he still harbored the idea that her work with herbs involved some sort of magic. His assumption that her dreams were not important had cut her to the quick and underscored a divide she feared no amount of travel would cover.

"Whoa." Ahead of her, he reined in suddenly, his horse stumbling and looking as weary as she felt.

Behind her, everyone else in the party stopped, too, the group as a whole grateful for any break in the difficult journey. Wind grazed her face as they stood at the top of a high cliff looking across a snow-covered valley. On the other side of the shallow glen was an enormous castle perched atop a hill even taller than the one on which they stood.

Ravenmoor.

Foreboding as its new lord, the keep looked as if it

were at the end of the earth. The gray castle loomed high over the sea behind it. Indeed, the walls must have their footing in the rocky cliffs for the water to crash so near the lofty structure. Soaring towers appeared sturdy enough to withstand any siege, were any marauder fool enough to attempt it. Surrounding stone walls curved slightly inward and then out again, which would make them nearly impossible to scale. She counted five turrets from her vantage point, although there could be other smaller peaks hidden among the larger ones.

No doubt this was a knight's dream—a keep that appeared impenetrable. But to Arabella her new home looked more like a prison—inescapable.

Behind her, Simon gave a low whistle.

"You have been well rewarded, my friend."

Tristan said nothing in response, but motioned for the party to continue its progress.

Her horse followed his without her even giving the poor animal a command. Slowly, they trudged toward her new home. Her home with a man who did not understand her. A man who had never denied loving another woman.

Tonight they would be ensconced in the warm comfort of a keep again, a place that would provide the privacy the road had lacked these past days. Would Tristan attempt to visit her bed despite his cool distance since they'd left London?

She didn't know that he even cared to, after he had all but accused her of associating with heretics and after he'd lapsed into days of not speaking to her. The warnings of her grandmother and her mother had come to pass. Once a man got what he wanted from a woman, he did not bother to treat her with the same reverence. She didn't know what the future held, but she knew she needed to find a way to put them on equal footing. And if that meant holding strong against temptation, she would find a way to do so.

Still, she knew Tristan's appeal from experience. If she hoped to resist the man who could reduce her to sighing pleasure with the slightest of touches, she would have to find a way to shore up her defenses as thoroughly as Ravenmoor itself.

Chapter Sixteen

Perhaps if he'd been a philosopher, Tristan thought, he would understand why contentment eluded him even after he had won the prize of a lifetime in Ravenmoor.

He brooded on this during the days he spent training men to guard the keep and he brooded on it during the nights like this one, which he spent searching the walls for an ancient passageway said to link the structure to the outlying hills. The old servants said the story of a tunnel might be a legend with no basis in truth, but since the former lord had turned traitor and the castellan had fled, Tristan had no reliable source to ask. Such a tunnel could pose a tremendous risk to a keep that was otherwise extraordinarily defensible. Especially when a wily castellan might make a fortune selling the secret to anyone wishing to make war on Ravenmoor.

"Do you think we will ever know the comfort of a full night's sleep again?" Simon asked while his hammer tapped lightly at the walls on the western side of the keep. The continual chink of steel against stone was a familiar rhythm, a routine carried out through the waxing and waning of a full moon cycle since their arrival in Northumbria.

"I cannot sleep when I fear my throat might be cut as I slumber."

The threat of an underground corridor had proved so unsettling that he found himself dreaming about the problem, a turn of events that reminded him he had been unfair to Arabella when he had ignored her dreams as fanciful notions. He had wanted to apologize for his words, along with others he had spoken, but his wife often seemed as difficult to find as the passage. After tending Mary's illness and the wound on his man-at-arms from their journey, Arabella had turned her attention to making their home livable, a task that consumed as much of her time as he spent making it safe.

A task, he had noticed, that kept her from his bed as often as possible.

"Why do you think they want Arabella?" Simon did not have to explain whom he meant. The matter of foreigners searching for Arabella was half the reason they devoted so much time to searching for a hidden doorway that might or might not exist.

"I don't know," Tristan replied, though he had spent hours trying to understand it himself. "Her grandmother sounds as if she is widely known and respected in Bohemia. Perhaps this group wishes to control the grandmother through Arabella. Maybe they think the grandmother's blessing will sway followers to their side."

"They are heretics." Simon's words were quiet.

Somber. "Do you really think they are interested in blessings?"

The weight of the words sent a dull echo through the stones all around them.

"Can you think of another reason Arabella would be valuable? Her father is dead. Whether he was a nobleman or not, he did not ever recognize her in any official sense. His possessions went to the throne. This faction cannot think to ransom her for money or power in the traditional sense." His hammer went through a stone, crumbling bits of granite onto his wrist and the floor as it revealed more layers to the thick rock wall behind it.

"What does Arabella say of it?"

Tristan did not respond right away, unwilling to admit that similar walls had grown between him and his wife.

"Tris?" Simon's hammering stopped and beyond the cavernous chamber at the base of the keep they could hear the crashing of the sea.

"We have had little time to speak since our arrival." He didn't remark on the fact that their few talks had led to arguments or that the nights he had visited her bed she had not truly welcomed him, even when he had managed to surmount her initial attempts at resistance.

The difference in her had been so apparent he'd been shaken. Since then, his visits had become less frequent, although on two occasions he had remained all night with her, waking her up in the middle of her sleep to claim her. Only then, when he sneaked past her defenses like a thief, had she given herself completely to him, reminding him of all that had been missing on those other occasions.

"It's because of your wag-tongued foolishness on the

road out of London, isn't it? You all but called her a heretic in front of everyone who now inhabits your keep."

Tristan set aside his hammer.

"I married her to prove her innocence of such crimes." Anger surged through him, as much due to his own fault in the matter as irritation with Simon. "Besides, any dull-witted lout can see she attends chapel more than any of us."

When Arabella wasn't airing out the keep and saving half-ruined furnishings from months of damp neglect, she prostrated herself on the stone floor of the private chapel or the larger church in the village below the keep.

"No doubt she prays for the patience not to poison your trencher, when you plant the very rumors you left London to escape." Across the chamber, Simon lifted his taper to glare at him. "Her foreign looks and accent might make the simpleminded wary without you perpetuating lies."

Tristan had not thought about the possibility of turning the village against her, although even the boy-king Richard had been wise enough to consider what kind of damage that could wreak on a kingdom and he had only fifteen summers. Tristan had been too quick to indulge his fear that Arabella would prove faithless. The way Elizabeth had.

He had accused her of being foolish for taking her dreams seriously, when he had been the one to act without thinking of the consequences.

"Have you heard rumors about this? About her?" Tristan had solved the gossip once with his protection. He might not have anything else to offer her.

"Nay. But I spend my nights scratching the walls in the dark with you and my days are given to helping the mason repair the northern parapets. When would I have time to hear anything save my own thoughts?"

"You are right." He had not been thinking like a noble landowner. He'd approached Ravenmoor like a common knight. "I will host a party for the villagers and servants alike to thank them for their warm welcome and for safeguarding the lands this past year. I will make sure everyone sees the regard I give to Arabella."

Simon's silence did not exactly endorse this approach, but Tristan saw a way to redeem himself from his mistakes. Besides, hosting a celebration would provide him with a tangible goal while helping him forget that he didn't know how to tackle the deeper problem—winning back his wife's favor.

Arabella worked in the empty aviary late one night by the glow of a ring of tapers around her workbench. She couldn't sleep well anymore, her dreams so vivid with thoughts of Tristan that she awoke breathing hard, her whole body on fire for him.

When she did not dream of her coldhearted husband she had dreams of home that made no sense, her mind returning to her childhood, disjointed moments she'd been too young to understand. A man visited their cottage in those dreams. A man with laughing dark eyes and a regal bearing, a man her mother spoke with warmly while Arabella played.

Was that man her father? And if so, why had Luria spoken so lovingly to him when, her whole life, she had warned Arabella about men's false words? Arabella had thought Luria's heartache with men began before her birth, when Charles Vallia would not wed her. If Arabella's dreams were actually real memories, something did not add up.

Here in the quiet of the aviary, Arabella distanced herself from the turmoil of her emotions, her dreams and her marriage. The aviary had been abandoned when the last lord departed, and Tristan did not care about the building for his defenses. Arabella had claimed it for herself, knowing the domed top full of windows would provide a warm place to start a few herbs that needed a longer growing season than this cold end of Britain would allow.

Finding the earth for planting had presented a bigger problem, but Simon had shown up one afternoon with a pick and shovel and had dug beneath the frozen surface for dirt. Arabella had thanked him profusely, still unsure what to think of the knight who had once spoken of enticing unsuspecting maids to his bed. But Simon had assured her that he wished to thank *her* for saving Mary from her illness and Arabella had been struck to the core by the tender look in the powerful knight's eyes. Whatever lustful designs he had once had on the maidens of the Bohemian retinue, she felt certain that he had set them aside for the love and respect of one woman.

The realization only reinforced her fear that her marriage had done a disservice to both Tristan and herself. Tristan deserved a woman who could love him without restraint, something Arabella feared she would never allow herself to do without some reason to hope he could one day love her in return.

"Arabella."

Tristan's voice startled her, making her drop a handful of seeds she had planned to place in a row one at a time.

"Oh!" She cursed her jumpiness, wishing she could be calmer around him. As it was, she had to expend tremendous effort to feign a coolness she did not feel. He had surely noticed that she could only respond to him with aloof distance when she was wide-awake and employing all her wits. In their bed at night, he had sometimes awoken her from dreams of him when she'd been powerless to pretend indifference.

"What are you doing?" His manner was brusque at all times these days, and she knew he harbored suspicions about her herbs.

"I'm planting herbs, as my supplies dwindle." She sifted the seeds carefully out of the dirt to sow them at even intervals.

She could hear his feet on the stones as he came closer, until he leaned into the ring of light around her worktable.

"You plant inside? In the winter?" His voice contained a weariness she had not heard in it before, but then, she did not observe as keenly when she struggled to maintain a certain distance with him.

"It is common enough in colder lands." Her grandmother had taught her well. In Bohemia they had succeeded in growing a few plants native to much warmer climes, although Luria had never appreciated the piles of dirt indoors. "I have brought many seeds for planting, since my grandmother's gardens were extensive and included many flowers I would not find easily otherwise. I need to be careful with them."

He watched her work without speaking for a long moment, and she wondered if he had sought her in order to bring her to bed. Awareness pricked her skin, the way it did so often in his presence. It became more and more difficult to keep the cold wall around her heart each time she let him into her body.

"I have heard you spend much of your time here these days." He lifted a taper and stalked about the aviary, peering up at the roof and into the corners where the floor met the walls.

"I devote my days to work in the hall and kitchens." She had never dreamed the life of a highborn lady would involve so much backbreaking work, but the past weeks had taught her she had—by comparison—led a life of leisure in Bohemia. "'Tis only after sunset that I indulge a pursuit of my pleasure."

She peered at him, silently daring him to hint at even the slightest displeasure over that fact. While she had not spoken against him publicly on the road to Ravenmoor, she considered herself well within her rights to tell him exactly what she thought of his attempts to control her here.

But he did not chastise her and she realized her plants could not hold her interest when Tristan was near.

Covering the row of seeds with earth, she pressed gently against them to promote strong roots. Then, plunging her hands into a pot of half-melted snow she'd brought in earlier for irrigation, she washed her hands and poured some of the water over the seeds.

"I wish to hold a gathering for the villagers as soon as it is warm enough. A feast to celebrate our arrival," Tristan said. Satisfied with his inspection of the aviary, he turned his attention to her and she noticed he was newly bathed, his hair freshly washed and his face shaved clean since she had seen him for the afternoon meal.

The scent of his soap held a sharp note beneath the spiciness. A hint of orange, maybe. She found herself leaning closer, her senses singing with awareness.

"Our food stores are limited since we only just arrived. I did find some wine in a storage area beneath the kitchen, but other than that I have little to work with, unless you can lend some men to a hunt." He resisted sparing his men for domestic chores and twice Arabella had been forced to bribe villagers with the newfound wine to spend some time hunting game for the keep's inhabitants.

"Whatever you need. I want the villagers kindly disposed toward me and I think the rumors of a feast will help flush out our enemies if they lurk nearby." He reached for her, encircling her wrist in his hand. "You must show me this storage area where you found the wine. You say it is underground?"

Her pulse pounded so loudly she could hardly hear his words, but she heard enough to know he thought only of enemies and the infernal escape passage he had been consumed with ever since they arrived.

"You wish to stumble through the kitchens now? In the dark?" She wrenched her hand free.

"It seems we both have our ways of occupying the nights now that you play the game of holding yourself back from me."

Picking up a taper, she blew the other ones out.

"It is your choice not to care for me." She moved toward the door, angry at having her life path laid out for her without her consent, angry that he expected her to smooth the way anyhow.

Pushing through the aviary door into the snowy night, she was struck by the cool beauty spread out before her, the moon imparting a soft white glow and throwing the trees into stark, shadowed relief on the snow. She couldn't deny the appeal of this rugged place she hadn't wanted to like. Ravenmoor belonged to Tristan. It stood for her imprisonment, the walls keeping her from ever returning home. Finding beauty here felt like a betrayal.

"I once said that I would not imbibe a potion brewed to induce love." Tristan's voice was close behind her, the words spoken near her ear. "I do not believe such a libation exists, but if it would bring cheer to your spirit, *chovihani,* I would take a taste."

Spinning on her heel, she faced him. "I never thought there was such a brew, either, Tristan. But I do believe there is a way people can swallow their reservations to seek out the best in each other. Drinking a love potion means believing in the impossible and committing to… passion."

Turning, she hurried up the path toward the kitchens, holding her hand in front of her taper to shield it from the wind.

"Wait." He caught a handful of her cloak and stopped her again. Her candle pitched forward and into the snow, the light going out with a hiss and an acrid flare of smoke.

He reeled her back to him, wrapping her in his arms.

"This I will do." His words were firm and she wished she could see his face more clearly to know if his eyes reflected the intent. "I swear to you, I will."

"What of the other woman who holds your heart?" She had not pressed the matter the last time he had hedged the question, shortly after their wedding. "What of Elizabeth, whom you called out for while you fought the fever brought on by your wound?"

Arabella swayed against him, the temptation to give in to him warming her despite the chill of the air. Something in his expression—a look in his eyes that did not speak of longing for another woman—soothed her.

"I courted her in my youth, in France. Her father was a local baron, a diplomat who met frequently with the Black Prince." He shrugged, as if unsure how to explain the woman's significance. "She made overtures toward me—I can see that now. At the time I thought I was fortunate to attract her notice, but she used me to make another man jealous. Because of my foolishness, she made a lucrative marriage with another when I had already made plans to wed her."

Arabella considered this and how such a slight would affect a man who had fought for some sense of pride and honor all his life. She remembered his regard for the messenger on the way to Ravenmoor, the way Tristan had been protective of the boy's pride while offering the possibility of help. No doubt Elizabeth's rejection had helped forge that fierce streak in Tristan.

"Yet you care for her still?" She drew her cloak more tightly around her, as the wind blew off the sea to the east.

"No. I cannot say why I would have spoken her name while in the throes of fever. It is because of her I had long resisted any possibility of marriage."

Or love.

Arabella did not need him to explain as much.

"Perhaps to a woman raised with many gifts and much wealth, honor is an expendable thing. But I was taught that my family's name is the most important gift I could receive, and I would not diminish that with acts of dishonor." She didn't know if he would understand what she meant, but her time at the Bohemian court had taught her she placed value on things in a much different way than her peers. "I would never abide false behavior."

"I see that more clearly now, but my eyes were clouded by my first vision of you in the oak ring. I could not reconcile that woman with the one you became in the princess's retinue." He plucked her taper from the snow and steered her inside. "But tell me, Arabella, did you never think it peculiar that your family taught you to uphold your family name when you bear your mother's name and not your father's? It is he who hails from a noble line, is he not?"

"Yes, but…" She ducked under his arm as he held the door to the keep for her. She had barely had time to savor the news that he would give their marriage a chance to thrive when he turned their conversation right back around to her and her heritage. "My grandmother swears the Rowans are from ancient stock and that our ancestors belong to the hills, whereas the royal family belongs to the people. I think she may have said this to instill pride in a little girl whose father had abandoned her, but I cannot know for sure."

There was much she wished she had asked Zaharia now that she no longer had the chance. But then Arabella never would have guessed how much the last few moons would change her.

"I think you were fortunate indeed to have the benefit of such a wise counselor." His arm snaked around her waist before she could make her way into the kitchens to show him the storage area he wished to see. "And I think myself fortunate to have you for a wife. Perhaps the storage area in the kitchen can wait until dawn."

He pulled her cloak from her shoulders and tossed it onto a bench in the hall before backing her up the corridor. His hunger communicated itself to her through the folds of her skirts, his strong warrior's body a source of pleasure she had denied herself.

"You are scarcely in my bed and already you make plans to leave it?"

"I would remain longer if I did not place a high price on your safety." His finger traced the neckline of her surcoat, dipping under the fabric enough to make her eyelids flutter. "I want to have you without pretense tonight. Without games that deny both of us pleasure."

She did not think that would be terribly wise, since he had not committed to loving her while her heart was already so full for him that one night of unrestrained passion would surely put her over the brink. No matter how she told herself not to, she would read feelings into his touches, telling herself that no man could incite a woman thus unless he loved her.

"It is not so easy for a woman to separate carnal love from the kind of love you…do not wish." She stood utterly still as he undid the laces on her surcoat even though they were in the middle of an open corridor. A fire burned low in the great hall around the corner, casting them in a dull orange glow.

"Maybe this will be our love potion, Bella." He wrenched her gown down her shoulders, exposing her to the tops of her breasts.

Bending, he brushed a kiss along that bare skin, igniting a flame inside her she feared would never go out. Maybe just this once more, she could take the risk.

"Upstairs." She whispered the word into his hair while his tongue played sweetly across her flesh. "Hurry."

Tristan did not need a second invitation. After all the ways Arabella had sought to put space between them lately, he would not delay when she finally seemed to concede.

Lifting her in his arms, he carried her up to their rooms connected by a shared solar. She felt incredible against him, her whole body given over to him for the night. He squeezed her close, his fingers sifting through the fabric of her gown for hints of skin or even a place where fewer layers covered her. Her arms wound around his neck while she made a keening cry in her throat. He had forgotten how untamed she was, how passionately she gave herself when she did not force herself to hold back.

Now, entering his chamber, he remembered how she acted upon him like one of her herbal remedies, her kisses drugging him into a state of rapt attentiveness and heightened response.

"I have missed this." She looked up at him with intent eyes while her fingers flew over the laces of his tunic. "Those few nights we have been together were not enough. I have missed the feel of you every night, the weight of you covering me."

He dropped her onto the high bed in the middle of his chamber and skimmed off her loosened dress, leaving her clad in a thin chemise. Saints be praised, he was fortunate to have her. Her earthy appreciation for lovemaking would make any man grateful.

Stepping out of his braies and flinging aside his tunic, he watched her body in the firelight as she twisted the chemise up and off her, the linen tangling in her dark hair. She twitched restlessly in the sheets, her thighs brushing together. She reached for him, trailing her hands down his chest until his muscles bunched and flexed.

The need to cover her was fierce, the desire to possess her again more important to him than his next breath, and yet he refused to overlook this chance to make her feel new heights of fire. If he could not sway her to tenderness this night, he might not ever have her in his bed so deliciously willing again.

"Tristan." She gripped his shoulders to draw him down, but he bent his mouth to her belly instead. He tasted her skin, breathing in the scent of her as he ran his tongue from side to side in a path down her hip.

She stilled beneath his kiss and he held her hips steady while he blew a stream of cool air over the damp skin. Her breathing shifted to soft pants that grew louder every time he swept his tongue lower. Lower.

By the time he spread her thighs she trembled violently beneath him, her fingers twisting in the sheets beside her head. The restraint of holding back made him break a sweat, but the reward of her sweet acceptance made his slow approach well worth it. When he placed the most intimate of kisses upon her, her whole body arched in response. Steadying her hips, he continued the kiss, controlling the pace, building the rhythm of soft strokes with his tongue until a shattering cry broke from her lips and he felt the spasms rack her body. Only when the spasms abated did he allow himself to take her, seating himself fully in her heat.

Her legs wound around him, wholly accepting, her hips tilting to give him more of her. She covered his face in kisses, her fingers fastening on his shoulders as if to hold herself steady. But the heat inside him surged so quickly he could not take in all the ways she felt extraordinary in his arms. His muscles tightened and his breathing labored like a warhorse in battle. Arabella gripped him inside and out, her sweet fragrance filling his nostrils until he could not hold back another moment.

His release rocked him like no fulfillment ever had, the force of it bowing his back and taking hold of him for long moments. The pleasure of it made him dizzy, taking his legs out from under him like a squire's first day of sword practice. He fell on her, spent and with his head still spinning, yet he was careful to catch most of his weight with his arms.

He lay there, waiting for his world to right itself, waiting for the weakness to abate. Moments passed, however, and still a sort of tenderness lingered. Blinking into the darkness of the fading fire, he feared his world would not be righted anytime soon. He had laid siege to his wife's heart tonight, but he had not expected to lose his own in the process.

Chapter Seventeen

Arabella awoke after dawn, her limbs aching in a pleasant sort of way. Sunlight spilled into the room from a ring of high windows spanning two walls. Her own bedchamber had those same windows on the two opposite walls since their apartments filled a whole tower.

She knew Tristan was not beside her in the massive bed. But as her fingers trailed over his side of the mattress, she could still feel the warmth of his body. He had not been gone long, and it *was* long after dawn.

Surely she could not feel slighted? She searched her emotions and found she did not, yet she wished he had spoken some words before he left, to give her a sign of where things stood between them now. Was he content merely to end their silent standoff? Or would he try to find some scraps of affection for her now that he had professed a commitment to a deeper connection?

She could not help an uneasy feeling. Lying in the bed a moment longer, she took stock of the chamber in which she'd spent so little time over the last moon. The tapestries depicted scenes of bloody battle, while a wolf skin decorated the floor. Dark, heavy furniture dominated the space.

The bedposts were carved with hideous intertwining monsters. Horned and hoofed creatures engaged in fierce contest all over the wood, while a menacing carved bird perched squarely over the headboard and stared with leering interest toward the mattress. She remembered then that the former lord of Ravenmoor had been a traitor to his king.

Shivering at the thought of sleeping in a traitor's bed, she slid from the mattress and vowed to replace the furniture once she finished planting her seeds. For now, she would return to the aviary and wait to see if Tristan would approach her today. Her heart ached more than her limbs as she weighed the possibility of rejection at his hands. She wanted to honor her family name by fulfilling her duty, but she could not remain captive in a life without hope of having her love returned.

Her love?

Her chest squeezed tight at the notion. She wished she could deny the flood of emotion that surged through her at the mere thought of her husband, but there was no help for it. She had tried to put off the inevitable by avoiding him and defending herself with every weapon she could, but her love for him had started the moment he fought off Thadus to save her from captivity and had swelled even more when he had defended her to his king.

After they made love last night, she had no defenses left to deny what her soul had long been telling her.

Hurrying to dress, she rinsed her teeth and combed

her hair. Her final appearance would not have impressed Tryant Hilda, but as Arabella peered in a looking glass, she thought her attempts at neatness might appease her mother, who had often accused her of being hopelessly wild. Struck by the pang of loneliness that thought wrought, along with the fear that Tristan would not return her tender new feelings for him, she left the chamber and followed the sound of voices down to the corridor.

A familiar woman's voice mingled with a man's in the great hall before Tristan spoke.

"How much farther is your new holding?" Tristan asked the unknown group.

She couldn't hear the man's answer, but her heart already raced from the memory of the woman's voice. A voice she would rather not hear again.

Could it really be? Arabella peered around the corner only to see Rosalyn de Clair seated at a high table near a blazing fire in the great hall. Her husband, Henry Mauberly, stood behind Rosalyn, while Tristan paced near the hearth. His tunic had been fastened haphazardly, the laces loose and fluttering behind him as he stalked.

Had he risen straight from their bed to meet with these visitors?

Arabella felt the presence of someone else nearby and she turned to find a maid scurrying past toward the hall, balancing some sweets on a platter.

"Excuse me." She kept her voice low, not wishing to be seen from the hall until she understood what was going on. Why her husband hadn't awakened her. "How long have they been here?"

"Simon went to retrieve the lord some half an hour ago, I think." She kept her voice low as well. "I need to deliver this."

"Yes." Arabella nodded, confused that Tristan had not woken her to greet their guests. "First, can you tell me where Lady Mary is this morning?"

"I have not seen her, my lady." Bobbing a curtsy, the maid hurried past Arabella with the tray.

"Thank you." Arabella let her move away, but she was not comfortable striding into the conversation in the hall. She had never grown accustomed to crowds and wished that Mary were by her side. Something about Rosalyn made Arabella uneasy. And the fact that Tristan had hidden the woman's arrival made her uneasier still.

Stalling for time, she remembered the new store of wine below the kitchens. She could bring some into the hall as an excuse to enter, and thus discover the purpose of the unexpected visitors. Perhaps Tristan's friend merely wished to pass the night at Ravenmoor on the way to his new holding. That would make the most sense. But since Rosalyn de Clair had once sneaked into Tristan's chamber with the intention of warming his bed, Arabella did not think it wise to assume Rosalyn's intentions were honorable.

Hastening her pace, she entered the kitchens to find two women from the village at work baking bread. The ovens warmed the rooms, the heat making their faces red while they kneaded new batches of dough, their arms flexing with muscle. As they appeared too busy to bother, Arabella passed them without comment and found a young maid sweeping the floor—the daughter of one of the cooks, she thought—and asked the girl to seek out Mary and request her presence in the hall.

Mary's presence would smooth any awkwardness between Arabella and Rosalyn.

Having sent the girl on her way, Arabella opened the door to the storage area concealed behind the wall of ovens. The steps led down beneath the ground where it was cooler and Arabella wondered what else it had once housed. Did the last inhabitants of the keep use this spot to store their ice? She wished she'd brought a taper to guide her steps, but she remembered the wine casks were on the right, along with several jugs that had already been filled from them.

Reaching blindly into the darkness while her eyes struggled to adjust, she thought she heard a sound off to her left. Rats?

She tensed, praying none would run across her shoe. After her trip to the great hall, she would round up every cat she had seen around Ravenmoor and put them to work down here.

After finding one of the jugs, she had turned on her heel to return upstairs when a hand emerged from the black to clamp down around her mouth and drag her backward. She fought the strength of that hand, limbs flailing and wine falling to the dirt floor with a soft thud. But the palm contained something foul smelling she was forced to breathe, a pungent odor that made her dizzy. Sick. Her fingers clawed for purchase against the body behind her while her feet kicked wildly.

But the herb overpowered her faster than the man's

strength and Arabella felt herself being dragged to un-consciousness. Her last thought was for Tristan.

He would never know where to look for her. God help her if he thought she had left of her own accord…

"Tristan."

Rosalyn de Clair's whispered voice in his ear was the last thing Tristan wanted to hear as he finished playing host to Henry Mauberly and his new wife. Rosalyn had behaved herself throughout their short conversation over ale and sweetmeats, but she held him back now while Simon took Henry out into the courtyard to size up the men-at-arms Tristan planned to purchase from the king to help guard Ravenmoor.

"Rosalyn, we have nothing to say to each other in private." He kept walking, wishing now that he'd woken Arabella for this visit. "If you wish to speak further, I suggest you call back your husband."

"It's about your wife's safety, as well as her identity. I don't know that you'll want anyone else to hear me."

He halted his steps. Turned to face her.

"Do you have any idea how unwise it would be to play games with me on the subject of Arabella?" His left eye began to tick, the strain of the last few weeks mingling with uneasiness over Rosalyn's words.

If there was any chance Arabella wasn't safe here…

"What do you know?" His words were gruff, border-ing on mean, but he considered it a credit to his honor that he did not touch her to squeeze the truth out of her lying mouth.

"Her enemies followed you here." Her eyes were

wide as she peered over her shoulder and Tristan realized for the first time that she was nervous.

Was it because she feared her husband's return? Or some larger threat?

"What do you know of her enemies? Hellfire, woman. How do you know she has been followed?" He knew well that Rosalyn had lied in the past, but her words echoed the gut feeling Tristan had harbored ever since they'd arrived in Ravenmoor. He'd scarcely been able to sleep for fear Arabella would be taken from him.

Or, if he were completely honest, that she would dance out of his life on her bare feet as quickly as she had appeared in it. That fear had held him back from loving her as much as any wounds Elizabeth Fortier had left behind.

"I—" Rosalyn appeared stricken, her face going pale as she gasped for breath.

A pang of compassion for her and the babe she carried made him help her to a chair and bring her more ale. Still, his patience was wearing thin.

"Speak to me, Rosalyn, lest I call back your husband and Arabella as well."

"I have been at the mercy of the men who wish to kidnap her. One of them—Ivan—is a very powerful man from the old regime in Bohemia."

"You know Litsen?" The hall remained silent around them, their earlier repast already cleared away by a maid.

"I worked for him as a girl and he…was not kind." She swallowed more ale and peered toward the entrance again. "One day he came to me with a proposition to assume the identity of another girl—a cast-off bastard of a nobleman well-known for his soft heart."

"And you did this?" Tristan began to understand her need to check the door behind her. She obviously did not want Henry to know about her past.

"My mother was a whore and wished to raise me to be the same. I would have taken any way out I could find. It was not difficult to pretend de Clair was my father."

Tristan nodded, accepting this. At least he had been fostered with Simon. Their brotherhood had carried him through hell and given him a purpose.

"Go on." His gut twisted and the hairs on the back of his neck twitched in warning. He wanted to call for Arabella, to check on her safety, yet he knew Rosalyn would not continue if he brought anyone else into the hall.

"It was surprisingly easy. Ivan brought me lavish new clothes and told me to appeal my cause using words of Christian mercy. I merely had to pretend my mother was one of his villagers who had been taken in the last plague." Rosalyn twisted the hem of her sleeve between her thumb and forefinger. "I was so happy when the ploy worked and I had a new life, but—"

"Litsen wanted you to spy for him."

"I did not want to, but he had anticipated how my new life would be so wonderful that I would do what he asked to maintain it."

"What of Arabella?" He did not wish to hear all the ways Rosalyn had most likely been a traitor during her time in Bohemia. He believed her when she said she knew Litsen and all that mattered was finding out what she knew of Arabella.

"Ivan believes her father was not the Bohemian nobleman her mother claims, but a Gypsy king. Arabella might not know because that man—her real father—is a beloved figure among the Gypsies and his support is a political asset to those who wish to topple the empire."

"What?" Tristan stilled. He'd accepted the story until then.

"Litsen has made powerful friends. He has a long-standing rift with the emperor and has made allies with others who also have reason to want the empire to fall. Having Arabella's real father on their side—coerced into supporting the overhaul of the empire to save his daughter—would help the cause."

Tristan could hardly catch his breath. She had to be joking. Yet his need to protect Arabella prodded him to try and sift through her words for any hints of truth.

Calling for a maid, he asked the woman to bring Arabella to him at once. Turning to Rosalyn, he asked, "Do you expect me to believe he shared all this with you?"

"Hardly. But paying attention to what Litsen wants has kept me alive and I am no longer the stupid girl he used so easily when I was naught but a child."

He searched her face for hints that she lied. She had lied to her princess, lied to his king. The woman obviously had no fears for her soul. Yet she met his gaze directly now and he recalled the way she had stared down at her hands in that room in Cologne when Mary had accused him of fathering her child.

Perhaps, this time, she did tell the truth.

"Jesus." He scrubbed a hand through his hair, not sure

he would be able to keep Rosalyn's secret, but damn sure he would take this threat to Arabella seriously.

"Why wouldn't Arabella's mother have told her who her real father is?"

"Perhaps her mother loved her enough to protect her. Her mother might have assumed that the fewer people who knew of Arabella's true parentage, the fewer people who could use it for their own gain." Rosalyn blinked quickly and it took him a minute to realize she fought tears. "I want to be that kind of mother for my babe."

Not sure what to make of this outpouring of emotion, Tristan paced the floor. Hell, he needed every person in his keep aware of these secrets and the dangers they presented in case Rosalyn spoke the truth. And he needed to find Arabella *now*.

Where was that maid?

"What goes on here?" An angry male voice echoed through the hall and Tristan turned to find Henry there with Simon beside him.

Only then did Tristan realize he stood close to Rosalyn as she cried.

Of all the jolt-headed foolishness.

"Henry, your wife may have saved Arabella's life just now, but she has much she needs to tell you."

"No!" Rosalyn looked up at him with desperate eyes.

"Step away from my wife." Mauberly stalked closer and Tristan realized the depth of the other man's misunderstanding, but holy hell, he could not sort through it all now. He released Rosalyn and moved toward Simon.

"We need to talk."

The maid entered the room, her fair hair tangled and her cheeks flushed.

"I can't find my mistress, sir." She curtsied and her nose started to bleed. She pulled off her cap to stanch the bleeding. "But the cook said she was in the kitchen recently and a door to the storeroom is open, but it was dark and I tripped on my way."

Fear opened up a gaping hole in his chest and he felt cold air being sucked into the void. He should have secured the storeroom the moment he'd learned of it.

With a roar of fury, he turned back to Rosalyn.

"If you've led them here, woman, I guarantee you will not know another night's peace."

He barely registered the surprise on Henry's face or the fear in Rosalyn's before he sprinted out of the hall toward the kitchen. Toward the wife he had failed on every conceivable front.

"Arabella?"

The voice seemed far away as Arabella struggled to awaken. Why didn't the caller come closer? She could barely hear her and Arabella's head throbbed.

"Wake up, Arabella, hurry."

The voice pushed her, an urgent edge making Arabella worry. Was that Mary? A rush of memory assailed her. She'd been in the storeroom and someone had grabbed her. Had she remained at Ravenmoor?

"Mary?"

"Yes, Arabella, it's me. Are you all right?" Mary's blue eyes were very close to her, full of concern.

The sight of her friend soothed her. Gingerly, Arabella tried to sit up.

"Where are we?"

"We've been taken captive. Far from the keep, I think. I was stolen out of my bed before dawn and taken through a passageway in the kitchen."

Arabella hurt everywhere as she blinked to clear her vision. "It's the passage Tristan has been searching for. It must be in the storeroom where I found the wine."

"They did not bring you for some hours afterward. Had anyone even realized I was gone?"

"No. Well, I looked for you and no one had seen you, but I didn't think anything of it. I thought you must be working or with Simon." Her stomach pitched with the effort to move.

They looked to be in a spare tower room in an old structure with wooden walls instead of stone ones. The floor sagged in the middle and there was no glass to cover three small windows that were too high to look out.

"By the saints. We could be halfway to London before they even think to look for us." Mary wore a cloak over white linen that must be a kirtle or chemise.

Arabella could not bear to think what her dear friend had been through. And what waited for them next? A deeper fear prickled her skin with goose bumps.

"The last thing I remember is herbane…a foul-smelling tincture." Arabella hated to impart the worst of it. "It can be poisonous."

Mary paled. "One of them is the same man who grabbed you in Prague. Why cross so many countries only to…poison you?"

"Perhaps they don't know the power of their own herbs. The other man with Ivan—is he the pale man I described to you from Calais?"

"It has to be. He frightened me far more than the other."

"Did they…hurt you?" Arabella patted her waist for her herb pouch and found it still there. "I do not have much for remedies with me, but if you are cut I can—"

"No." Mary shook her head. "I am well enough. But these men, they plan to ransom me back to the emperor."

Arabella tried to muddle through the confusion of all that had happened and make some sense of the senseless.

"It must be you they have wanted all along. You must be worth a great fortune for them to have followed you so far."

"The emperor has vast resources and great wealth, but don't they realize I am but his ward? He has cared for me well, but I am not his heir." Mary's voice shook. "I do not think he will pay so handsomely as Ivan and his friend believe."

"Although perhaps they are not as interested in wealth. Remember the note Tristan received that said the men who took me belonged to a heretical sect?" The pieces still didn't fit together to Arabella, but then, she knew little about court intrigue or the politics of the throne. "Although no matter what they want us for, it will take ages to send messages back and forth to Prague. It makes no sense."

"The other man—Thadus—said he will send the ransom demands as we travel. It will be harder to catch him that way. And it is not only me they plan to ransom. They said they have demands for your father as well."

Arabella tensed. "My father is dead."

Mary shrugged. "They called him Marek. You do not know whom they mean?"

Pieces of Arabella's past slid into place at the sound of the name. A name she remembered. Recognized. She had only been a very small child when she had last seen the smiling man she remembered from her dreams, but she knew that man was the one called Marek.

Could he be her real father?

There was a rightness to the claim. Arabella's mind worked quickly, trying to absorb everything at once. She had no notion why her mother would claim a heritage for her that was false, but she trusted there had to be a good reason.

"Where are they right now?" she asked, wondering how much time they had left alone to plot something.

"I'm not sure, but Thadus left about a quarter of an hour before you woke up. I thought I heard a horse trot off afterward. It's awfully quiet."

"How many others were with him? Could you see?"

Mary shook her head ruefully. "He drugged me after we started down the passageway in the keep. I saw nothing more until I woke up here." Before she had finished her sentence, Arabella was already exploring their small cell for possible means of escape. The lone door was bolted firmly on the other side, and the windows were too high up to allow access.

Would Tristan have any idea where to begin searching for them? At least he knew about the storeroom. And with any luck, the door behind the ovens would still be open. But how long before he noticed her missing? He entertained Rosalyn de Clair and her new husband today. Perhaps Arabella's absence would not be greatly noticed.

And—sweet, merciful heaven—could it be any co-incidence that Rosalyn had arrived the day Arabella had been taken captive? She had talked her way out of any responsibility for Arabella's last brush with Thadus, but the timing today looked suspicious.

"He just said he had preparations to make. I assumed he meant for our trip back to Prague, but I'm not certain."

"We need a plan," Arabella mused, wondering how they could possibly battle Thadus and who knows how many of his men on their own.

Hugging her knees close to her body for warmth, Arabella tried not to think about how bitterly cold the room was with no hangings over the windows. She briskly chafed her hands together and then ran them over her body to encourage her thickened blood to flow to her limbs. As she rubbed her legs, her hand met the sack of herbs she carried with her always.

Drawing the pouch from the folds of her skirts, Arabella held up the small bag.

"What is it?" Mary wrapped her cloak around herself.

"My herbs." Arabella undid the knot and began poking through the bag's contents. "If only I had some—oh."

She broke off and pulled out a small twig from an inside pocket of the pouch.

"What is it?"

"Nightshade." She could not help a twinge of satis-faction at finding this tiny branch. "It's poisonous."

Fingers numb from the cold, Arabella stripped the

leaves from the twig and then carefully crushed them in her palm.

"Do you always keep poisons about your person?"

"No." Arabella laughed. "The twigs of the nightshade work well to reduce swelling, or can be mixed with many types of herbs for other healing benefits. But the leaves and berries can be poisonous depending on the amount administered and the strength of the individual plant." She worked quickly to combine the crumbled leaves with a little bit of water from a pitcher Thadus had left them. "This potion won't be lethal. I picked the herb under the full moon, which favors good herbs. And anyway, this particular plant I picked was young, so it would be weaker by nature."

"Ah." Mary sounded worried. But then, maybe she hadn't yet discovered how brutal these men could be.

Arabella didn't plan to let her find out.

"It will make the person who swallows it frightfully ill."

"But how will we administer it? And what about the other men he surely has with him? How will we—"

"I don't know." She couldn't let Mary's fears perpetuate her own. She needed to think. "I wish I did, but I honestly do not. At least we will have some small thing to use for a weapon. Let us pray we can find an opportunity to put it to work."

Mary wrung her hands tightly.

"Simon asked me to marry him last night."

Arabella nearly dropped the leaves.

"Oh! That's wonderful news. And you will have a chance to wed him, Mary, I swear."

She had to believe that. Real love like the kind Mary

and Simon had was all too rare to waste. They deserved to live their happiness the way Tristan and Isolde never had. The way Tristan and Arabella still hadn't discovered.

But, some little voice in the back of Arabella's mind reminded her, if she wasn't going to find happiness with Tristan, it would be because she had tried her best and love simply wasn't there. Because after this ordeal, she *would* return to Ravenmoor to give all of herself to Tristan—give him all the love she possessed—until he had no choice but to see they were meant to be together.

Chapter Eighteen

Tristan pounded down the steps underneath the kitchen into the dank storeroom Arabella had spoken of the night before. Unprepared, he had to call for both a torch and his sword while he searched the storeroom for an opening. He took the cook's cleaver while he was at it, determined that the swine who had stolen Arabella would not walk away from this to threaten her again.

"Tristan!" Simon ran down the steps behind him, a torch in one hand and a shield in the other. His sword remained at his side. "Mary is gone. Her maid says it looks as if she never dressed for the day. Her—"

He broke off and Tristan understood what the woman meant to him. Hell, the fierce look on Simon's face expressed everything Tristan felt.

"Her clothes for the day are laid out on her wardrobe," Simon continued. "Only her shoes are missing."

"We will find them." Tristan could only pray the bastards hadn't gotten much of a jump on them. Although if Mary had been taken from her bed…

His hands found a depression above one of the rocks in the wall and he pulled at the stone. A small door swung open, hidden with clever masonry.

Tristan inserted his torch first and heard the squeals from a chorus of rodents. The little beasts scattered as he entered the narrow tunnel and he hurried down the passageway as fast as the small space would allow. Behind him, Simon cursed quietly. Tristan remembered his friend had had a particular aversion to rats ever since their guardian had punished him with a stay in the dungeon.

"Keep the torch close to your head," Tristan called back to him. "Stepping on one isn't as bad as—"

"Can we just keep moving?"

"Can you tell what direction we're headed?" He couldn't smell the sea and the walls of the passage seemed dry.

"Northwest." Simon didn't speak for a long moment as they followed the corridor. "I'm getting married."

Tristan nearly tripped.

"Bloody hell." He meant it in the kindest possible way, of course. "The emperor's ward? You've always had a talent for turning the heads of the rich ones. Congratulations."

"I was up all night thinking how I ought to word a letter to an emperor. And now I'll just be glad to— We'd better find them, Tris."

"It looks like the passage is widening out again." Thank the saints, too. Spiderwebs coated his tunic. "We'll light a fire under their Bohemian arses the moment we find them."

"As long as they aren't many leagues from here."

Tristan remembered Arabella's flower petals the last time she was captured. She was a clever woman. Smart. Caring. Beautiful. So much better than he deserved.

He didn't know what had taken him so long to see the truth of her goodness, to realize that—pauper or princess, Gypsy healer or wild woman of the forest— he loved Arabella Rowan.

The knowledge rolled over him like the effects of fine wine, bringing with it a warm glow. And holy hell, he could be the most mumble-mouthed of courtiers when it came to his wife.

"Even if they have left, Arabella will leave a trail." Tristan had to believe that, had to believe that she would be all right.

Because God in heaven, he couldn't afford to lose her before he had the chance to tell her he loved her. He would free Arabella today, even if he had to lay down his life to bring her home.

The steady thrum of hoofbeats announced the return of their captors later in the afternoon, but Arabella did not stop stirring the herbs into the water until footsteps sounded just outside the door to their cell.

"Not planning to revolt against your captor already, are you, my fair ones?" Thadus entered the cell with a bow and a flourish, his pale face newly scarred up one side.

She had no doubt who had left that mark upon him.

"You will never make it out of Britain alive." Arabella hadn't meant to begin her confrontation with Thadus so fiercely. The words simply fell from her lips, propelled by her heart. "The English king is fond of his wife and her company."

Seated close to Mary on the floor of their small cell, Arabella set aside the water pitcher so Thadus would not see the concoction that had taken the place of the water he had left. Mary swept remnant twigs under her dress.

"Your king is a boy with enough trouble of his own, but thank you for your tender concern." Thadus appeared preoccupied, peering around the barren cell as if in deep thought. "Besides, there is a much quicker sea route to return home, so we will not have to pass through Richard's domain."

Fear crawled up the back of Arabella's neck.

"You plan to travel by boat?" She knew they were close enough to the water since the waves broke over the foundations of Ravenmoor. Thadus could have them out of the country within the hour.

"Yes." Thadus pried up a board at one end of the tower cell and reached beneath the floor to retrieve a tin box. He opened the weather-beaten box briefly to flash the contents under their noses. A trove of gems and gold glittered within. "It should be enough to book safe passage, don't you think, my Gypsy princess?"

Arabella didn't understand his meaning, but she guessed the jewels had belonged to a royal family. She did understand, however, that he did not mean to linger here for much longer.

"I am thirsty." She cleared her throat to remove the quaver in her voice. The thought of sailing away from Britain, from Tristan, made her determined to act quickly. "Have you no wine to flavor this foul water you left us?"

Thadus stared at her blankly, his pale eyes making her uneasy for a long moment before he emitted a sharp bark of laughter.

"Ivan!" He shouted out the door to the tower. "Bring us some wine and come take away Lady Mary so I might have a private word with the new mistress of Ravenmoor."

Mary squeezed Arabella's hand, a wordless moment of encouragement. Turning, Arabella studied her friend's face and found cold determination there, a fierceness she had never seen in the delicate creature who avoided the Prague court in favor of keeping her own company. Arabella guessed Mary's newfound love for Simon gave her all the more reason to fight, the same way Arabella planned to do.

Seeing that resolution in the tilt of Mary's chin gave Arabella strength as Ivan's heavy steps ascended the stairs.

The older man entered the cell with a filthy cup in one hand and a wineskin in the other. If her plan failed, she might be the one to end up with a small amount of poison in her veins while their captors remained strong and healthy. She prayed at least one of them would drink after she pretended to take a swallow.

"We need to leave," Ivan informed Thadus, passing the cup and the skin without comment.

Thadus tossed both at Arabella.

"I would savor the opportunity to kill the English knight first."

"So you say. But you've had two moons to kill the bastard and still he walks free. We can't risk losing these two for the sake of a grudge."

Arabella only half listened while she hastened to

pour the wine. Mary held the wineskin as Arabella filled the cup half way with water. Then Mary dribbled the wine in a little at a time until Arabella nodded her satisfaction. Too late, she realized that having a large amount of liquid in the cup would make it obvious she hadn't taken much of a drink.

Cursing her fretful mind that hadn't been thinking clearly, she took an actual sip of the mixture, carefully using her teeth to separate the bits of leaves from the watered-down wine so that she would not be taking much of the poison into her system. Mary's eyes grew wide.

"Take Mary out with you and make ready to leave," Thadus said. "Tie her to one of the horses while I speak with our long-sought-after captive."

Arabella held the leaves in one side of her mouth while Ivan yanked Mary to her feet. Unsure how to convince either man to drink from her half-finished cup, she chanced her luck with Ivan—the larger of the two men who looked as if he did not deny himself sustenance often.

"The wine is as rotten as the water," she announced, handing Ivan the cup before she turned to cough into her hand. She coughed the leaves into her palm, hoping no telltale greenery clung to her teeth.

She turned in time to see Ivan down the liquid in one gulp before he pushed Mary out the door. Now Arabella had only to pray he had consumed enough for it to take effect quickly. Mary peered back over her shoulder, the worry in her eyes for Arabella obvious, but Arabella felt more in control. At least one of the men would be down soon.

All she had to do was stay alive long enough for Mary to escape and find Tristan to lead him here. Could she delay Thadus's departure if she kept him talking?

"Mary said you plan to ransom me to my father." Her belly rolled uneasily and she wondered how much of the nightshade she had inadvertently consumed. She had to concentrate on this talk with Thadus. If he went outside before Mary could escape, their potion would have been no use to them and Arabella had no more nightshade.

"Marek, King of the Gypsies," Thadus acknowledged with a twisted smile. "He does not tout the honor as he should. His people adore him, no matter how scattered they are about Bohemia and Moravia. Beyond, even."

"What are you saying?" She blinked through a moment of dizziness. "The Romany have no king."

Arabella did not know much of the people's heritage, but her grandfather—Stefan—had been a traveling Rom, a man Zaharia had loved beyond reason until he died at a young age. Zaharia said she never would have settled in one place as long as Stefan had lived, and it had always made Arabella sad to think how vehemently she meant it. What might Arabella's life have been like if Zaharia had roamed wild and free....

The way Arabella had always longed to.

She had never understood that desire to wander so clearly as she did at that moment.

"Only because they have no lands to claim as their own. But the elders remember the old royal lines and the local tribes all agree Marek is their king. And you, my dear, are their princess."

"My father is dead." Arabella felt sure that Charles

Vallia was not her true father, but she was curious to learn what this man might know of her past. Apparently others understood her heritage far better than she.

She could not help a twinge of resentment that she had been kept in the dark all her life. But it was difficult to feel too angry when a wave of nausea struck.

Why had she felt the need to drink her own potion, no matter how little?

At least—saints be praised—Ivan was probably already falling to his knees with sickness.

"He defiled your mother at court, since it was well-known that she loved a Gypsy prince and Vallia hated the Rom." Thadus laughed. "I am sure it gave your grandmother great pleasure to pass you off as his child after the bastard died. You gained all the rights of the nobility and the blessing of the throne before your grandmother hid you away in the highlands where no one could find you. We might never have located you if you had not answered the call when Anne needed a retinue."

Arabella understood her grandmother's reasoning at once. Zaharia thought she would be safer far away from the unrest in Bohemia.

Tears burned her eyes, both with regret for what she might have learned about her past along with sorrow for the heartache her mother and grandmother had endured. Arabella still had questions, but Thadus seemed to be pulling her to her feet. She blinked, needing her wits.

Had enough time passed to ensure that Mary had left to find help? Just in case it had not, Arabella stumbled to the floor.

"Get up." Thadus's voice was cold but he held out a hand to her.

Arabella took it, taking her time rising until Thadus nearly dropped her.

Surprised, she looked up to see his very pale face had gone a shade whiter still, his glittering eyes no longer fixed upon hers. He stared toward the barred door that led downstairs.

Afraid to take her eyes off him, but curious as to what he saw, Arabella ventured a slight glance backward. She smelled fire at the same time she saw flames lick at the bottom of the wooden door.

A distinctly male voice shouted through the barrier. "Arabella."

Tristan.

Her heart soared to hear his voice. He had come.

"Get the hell out of here, Ravenmoor, or your pretty lady is dead," Thadus shouted as he pulled Arabella's sluggish body to him. "Do you hear me?"

Arabella felt the cold blade of the knife prick at her throat as Thadus locked an arm about her neck. Arabella wanted to call to Tristan—assure him she was safe—but as she took a breath to shout out, Thadus jerked the knife cruelly against her throat, drawing blood from a thin cut across her neck.

"Don't even think about it."

But even as he said the words, the pounding started. The burning door was giving way under the repeated pummeling of the man on the other side. Had the whole structure caught fire? The timber building seemed old. The dry wood would catch in no time.

"I'll kill her," Thadus shouted, eyes glued to the shuddering door that was being burned and pounded off its hinges.

With one last great crack of wood, Tristan crashed through the door, poised for attack. The burning door fell to the floor of the tower cell. They could be trapped up here if they didn't escape quickly.

"Let her go," Tristan ordered, voice full of calm authority despite the burst of flames behind him.

Arabella feared for him, for all of them, as flames ate away the floor.

"Ivan!" Thadus called for his friend, a companion Arabella knew would be unconscious by now.

"Your friend cannot answer you. Give Arabella to me, and I'll see that you do not burn to death in here." Tristan drew his sword and he looked ready to skewer the other man.

Arabella had absolute faith he could do so before Thadus hurt her. She only prayed he did it before the hem of her gown began to burn. The heat in the room made her sweat.

She was so focused on the sword, she barely saw the cleaver whiz past her head and into her captor's throat, but Thadus's hands went limp and he sank away from her.

Relief flooded her, making her knees weak and her hands shake.

"Tristan." She rushed forward to fling herself into the safety of his strong arms, but a flaming wall leaped up to separate them.

She screamed as sparks flew in every direction, burning holes into the sleeve of her surcoat. She caught the skirts before they could catch fire, too, wrapping them tightly around her legs. With her other hand, she clutched the length of her hair to her chest to prevent a flying strand from bursting into flame.

"I'm throwing my mantle down on the count of three," she heard Tristan's voice through the roar of the fire. "Go through the breach fast, do you hear me?"

"Talk loudly," she yelled back, the wall behind her crackling as it, too, burst into blaze.

"One…"

She licked her lips and crouched down to sprint forward.

"Two…"

A long, deep breath.

"Three."

The mantle came flying across the line of fire and landed on the floor to make a narrow escape path. Arabella fairly flew onto it and over it, ducking low the whole time.

She didn't even register what happened next, but Tristan must have caught her somehow, for the next thing she knew she was being rushed down the stairs in the solid protection of his arms. Closing her eyes against the smoke, she clung to him with all her strength.

They burst out into the crisp night air, coughing and gasping. Tears stung her burning eyes and her whole body shook with the knowledge of how close they'd come to not making it out of the building.

Nearby, she spotted Mary, her friend's eyes glued on Simon Percival as the knight tied Ivan Litsen's unconscious form to a horse. Two other men were already tied in similar fashion. Arabella guessed one of them was the missing castellan from Ravenmoor, who had surely sold the secret of the tunnel to Thadus. Clearly, Thadus could afford whatever he wished with the small fortune he had carried in his tin box.

The jewels were still in the burning building and would have to wait to be recovered until another day. For now, Arabella just wanted to breathe fresh air and savor the fact that she yet lived.

Tristan had found her out in the middle of heaven-knows-where and saved her from the plotting of a depraved man. A man who would have let the tower burn to the ground before he would have released her.

"Are you all right, Arabella?" Tristan's dark hair slid forward over his shoulders as he leaned closer to her. Gray eyes full of tender concern, his gaze swept over her.

His broad hand cupped her face gently, forcing her to look at him. What she saw there caused her heart to swell and turn over in her chest. The depth of his emotions was right there for her to see, whether he ever spoke the words she longed to hear or not. She would wait a lifetime for him to see what she already knew.

"Thank you," she whispered, her voice hoarse. "With all my heart I love you, Tristan Carlisle, Earl of Ravenmoor."

She looked up expectantly, hoping her admission would please him even if he did not wish to return the sentiment yet. But she was surprised to see his face twist in pain.

Memories of the past assailed her as she slid from his arms. She half expected to see Thadus behind him, leering cruelly at her the way he had that night in Calais after planting a knife in Tristan.

Instead, she found the tunic singed off Tristan's back. Because he had saved her and protected her from harm, her warrior husband was now covered in burns.

Chapter Nineteen

A scant month after the fire, Tristan waited on the chapel steps with Simon, his mind not on his friend's wedding even though the afternoon served as a feast day for the Ravenmoor villagers as much as a time for nuptials.

"By the rood, Tris, you are more worried than I am and 'tis I who suffers through the wedding attire." Simon tugged at the neck of his new tunic. "You should be celebrating the wealth of your new lands and a village of able farmers who welcome you."

Tristan kept his eye on the hill the women would walk down from the keep for the wedding procession. Villagers lined the path between there and the chapel, a few holding spring flowers to honor the bride. The day had dawned warm and bright, though the sun already slipped low in the sky. Torches ringed the courtyard where tables would soon be laden with the feast.

All of Ravenmoor celebrated—except, perhaps, for him. Tension knotted in his gut as he thought about his hopes for the day. He would not celebrate until later.

"Arabella has received a letter from her mother," he admitted to Simon. "She sends word that Arabella's father is coming to visit and see her new homeland for himself."

"The Gypsy king?" Simon grinned. "And you thought I had done well to wed an emperor's ward. Who knew you'd marry royalty?"

Tristan could not argue his good fortune, since King Richard had sent Arabella a formal letter recognizing her as foreign royalty and pledging peace between them. Arabella had laughed with pleasure and surprise, while Tristan half waited for her family to try and take her back.

Not that he would ever allow it.

He had been waiting for weeks for his burns to heal enough to convince her she belonged back in his bed. Tonight, she had agreed, they would celebrate his health and their marriage.

"At least the emperor is not going to show up in your courtyard to inspect his ward's living conditions." Tristan caught sight of the women coming down the hill and a shout went up from the villagers.

"Sweet Jesus." Simon stared into the distance. Tristan was just as taken by the sight in front of them as was his friend.

Arabella and Mary walked arm in arm, Arabella in silver, her dark hair unbound, and Mary wearing a surcoat of gold that mirrored her fair hair.

They carried small white flowers that Arabella had crowed over finding the day before during a long walk that had Tristan pacing the hall with worry before she returned.

Would he ever be able to let down his guard? He had relived that day she had been taken from him in his dreams, and he planned to pledge his life and his love to her in so many words today after the wedding.

She had been so busy playing healer to him and making plans for a wedding feast, that there had been no time to speak of love. Or if there had, he'd been too racked with pain and—sometimes—sedated by his clever wife's herbs that he wouldn't have remembered even if they had. But he had grown strong again as his skin healed and tonight he would speak of their future. His love for her.

Love.

The word still caught him by surprise as he thought of it, but watching Arabella walk toward him, her smile for him alone, he knew there could be no other way to describe what he felt.

Arabella stepped aside as she reached the chapel steps with Mary, her gaze locked on her husband. He looked so strong. So vital. She had waited weeks for him to be well again, and she almost shook with anticipation of their night together. She was not certain he remembered her declaration in those moments before his burns had sent him to his knees outside the blaze of the crumbled wooden tower.

The night had been too painful to relive, so she had set aside her memories of it while he healed.

Her cheeks warmed when he smiled at her and

nodded approval at her surcoat. His eyes swept over her appreciatively, lingering in the most untoward places. How brazen he was, she thought, feeling the familiar tremors at his intimate look.

Arabella hardly heard the priest's solemn words due to her keen awareness of Tristan's stolen glances. Her pulse thrummed wildly in anticipation of the moment they could be alone.

"I now pronounce you man and wife."

As the priest completed the sacrament, Simon wrapped Mary in a heated embrace to the great enjoyment of the celebrants. Arabella was so happy for them both. The emperor would send gifts, and until then, King Richard had rewarded Simon with a keep some hundred leagues distant. The king had been most appreciative to receive Ivan as a prisoner along with the former castellan of Ravenmoor, who had been as traitorous as the former lord. Simon had escorted the prisoners to London personally and had returned to Northumbria with a royal holding. The properties were close enough that Arabella would see Mary again and stand at her side to deliver her babes.

A cheer went up for the new couple as the party danced off toward the castle for the huge feast that would follow.

Seeming to read each other's thoughts, Tristan and Arabella lingered behind the boisterous crowd until the chapel cleared out.

"Come outside with me," Tristan ordered, taking her hand in his own.

She followed him out the door and into the twilight.

Torchlight danced merrily around the courtyard, where the tables would be full of food by now. Arabella could look at a torch again without shuddering, but it had taken a few days for her nightmares to cease. Apparently Ivan had knocked Simon's torch onto the wooden tower before he had passed out. The old structure had caught immediately.

"Can you conjure up a full moon whenever you fancy one, sweet *chovihani?* Or do I need to call you princess now?"

"I have no power over the moon, but I will confess I convinced Mary that to wed underneath it would bring her good luck." She followed him to a clearing on the hillside near the chapel, the dew clinging to her hem.

"I think you knew what your silver dress would look like in moonlight. You capture the moonlight and radiate it back tenfold." He spun her into his arms, reminding her of the dance he had once taught her.

Arabella smiled. "You would deny it always, my proud warrior, but you have a courtier's tongue."

"I think it cannot hurt to give my warrior ways a rest now and then." He lifted her up in his arms. "Permit me."

She wasn't sure what he meant until he slid his finger into her silver slipper.

"I made a solemn promise that you would not have to wear these when you danced with me." He slipped off each thin shoe in turn before setting her back on her feet.

From the courtyard, they could hear the stringed instruments begin a lilting tune in honor of the newly married couple. Arabella could not hide her smile as the soft strains drifted toward them on a light breeze.

"Do you feel at home here, Arabella?" Tristan asked, turning serious as he guided her body back into the swirling dance they had begun. "My country is not as horrible as you thought it might be, is it?"

"No." She had learned to love the rugged beauty of the coast and the fierce winds that swept the hills clean after a storm. "I never would have guessed how much I could love a foreign place. I can hardly wait for summer—there is so much woodland. I also have a horse of my own, I have people to take care of, and—"

"What of me?" He halted his step and pulled her even closer to his body. "You were forced into this marriage, Arabella, and I would know how you fare under that particular condition."

His gray eyes shone in the moonlight, probing her for an answer. Arabella lost her breath at his intense look.

"I... You did not hear me the night you rescued me from the fire, did you?" She touched his shoulders gently even through his tunic, since her healer's hands understood exactly how much torment he had endured for her sake.

"Hear what?"

"I told you that I love you," she admitted softly, hoping the time was right to repeat it. Would it please him? She waited for what seemed like an eternity while he scrutinized her. "With all my heart I love you. I want to make you happy and plant a garden here and dance with you under the stars."

She smiled up at him tentatively, reaching out her hand to stroke the sharp angle of his jaw with her fingertips.

With no warning, he crushed her against him and kissed her hungrily.

"You have bewitched me, I am sure of it," he whispered into her hair. "I have lain awake at night thinking how to tell you what I feel for you, and yet you beat me to it. I think I fell in love the day I beheld a woodland nymph in the Bohemian forest."

"As Tristan loved Isolde?" Tenderness welled like a pool inside her.

"Even more, my lady fair. For I would not allow any other man to touch you or take you from me."

His words wrapped around her in a loving embrace as he kissed her lips tenderly.

"Tonight we will celebrate our own wedding night all over again," he informed her as he gathered her in his arms and carried her swiftly up the hill.

"Will you stay in my bed for days on end this time?" she asked archly as she allowed her fingers to run lightly over his chest through the brocaded houppelande.

"You will have to beg me to leave it."

* * * * *

Enjoy a sneak preview of
MATCHMAKING WITH A MISSION
by B.J. Daniels,
part of the
WHITEHORSE, MONTANA *miniseries.*
Available from Harlequin Intrigue
in April 2008.

Nate Dempsey has returned to Whitehorse to uncover the truth about his past…

Nate sensed someone watching the house and looked out in surprise to see a woman astride a paint horse just on the other side of the fence. He quickly stepped back from the filthy second-floor window, although he doubted she could have seen him. Only a little of the June sun pierced the dirty glass to glow on the dust-coated floor at his feet as he waited a few heartbeats before he looked out again.

The place was so isolated he hadn't expected to see another soul. Like the front yard, the dirt road was waist-high with weeds. When he'd broken the lock on the back door, he'd had to kick aside a pile of rotten leaves that had blown in from last fall.

As he sneaked a look, he saw that she was still there, staring at the house in a way that unnerved him. He shielded his eyes from the glare of the sun off the dirty window and studied her, taking in her head of long blond hair that feathered out in the breeze from under her Western straw hat.

She wore a tan canvas jacket, jeans and boots. But it was the way she sat astride the brown-and-white horse that nudged the memory.

He felt a chill as he realized he'd seen her before. In that very spot. She'd been just a kid then. A kid on a pretty paint horse. Not this one—the markings were different. Anyway, it couldn't have been the same horse, considering the last time he had seen her was more than twenty years ago. That horse would be dead by now.

His mind argued it probably wasn't even the same girl. But he knew better. It was the way she sat the horse, so at home in a saddle and secure in her world on the other side of that fence.

To the boy he'd been, she and her horse had represented freedom, a freedom he'd known he would never have—even after he escaped this house.

Nate saw her shift in the saddle, and for a moment he feared she planned to dismount and come toward the house. With Ellis Harper in his grave, there would be little to keep her away.

To his relief, she reined her horse around and rode back the way she'd come.

As he watched her ride away, he thought about the way she'd stared at the house—today and years ago. While the smartest thing she could do was to stay clear of this house, he had a feeling she'd be back.

Finding out her name should prove easy, since he figured she must live close by. As for her interest in Harper House… He would just have to make sure it didn't become a problem.

* * * * *

Be sure to look for
MATCHMAKING WITH A MISSION
and other suspenseful Harlequin Intrigue stories,
available in April
wherever books are sold.

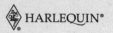

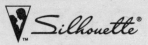

Romantic
SUSPENSE

Sparked by Danger, Fueled by Passion.

The Taken

Tierney Doyle is used to being criticized for
her psychic abilities, yet the tough-as-nails—
and drop-dead-gorgeous—detective has no doubt
about what she has uncovered in the case of a
string of unsolved murders. And Tierney is slowly
discovering that working so close to her partner,
detective Wade Callahan, could be lethal.

Look for

Danger Signals
by Kathleen Creighton

Available in April wherever books are sold.

REQUEST YOUR FREE BOOKS!

Harlequin® Historical
Historical Romantic Adventure!

2 FREE NOVELS PLUS 2 FREE GIFTS!

YES! Please send me 2 FREE Harlequin® Historical novels and my 2 FREE gifts (gifts are worth about $10). After receiving them, if I don't wish to receive any more books, I can return the shipping statement marked "cancel". If I don't cancel, I will receive 6 brand-new novels every month and be billed just $4.94 per book in the U.S. or $5.49 per book in Canada, plus 25¢ shipping and handling per book and applicable taxes, if any*. That's a savings of 20% off the cover price! I understand that accepting the 2 free books and gifts places me under no obligation to buy anything. I can always return a shipment and cancel at any time. Even if I never buy another book, the two free books and gifts are mine to keep forever.

246 HDN ERUM   349 HDN ERUA

Name	(PLEASE PRINT)
Address	Apt. #
City	State/Prov. Zip/Postal Code

Signature (if under 18, a parent or guardian must sign)

Mail to the **Harlequin Reader Service:**
IN U.S.A.: P.O. Box 1867, Buffalo, NY 14240-1867
IN CANADA: P.O. Box 609, Fort Erie, Ontario L2A 5X3

Not valid to current subscribers of Harlequin Historical books.

Want to try two free books from another line?
Call 1-800-873-8635 or visit www.morefreebooks.com.

* Terms and prices subject to change without notice. N.Y. residents add applicable sales tax. Canadian residents will be charged applicable provincial taxes and GST. This offer is limited to one order per household. All orders subject to approval. Credit or debit balances in a customer's account(s) may be offset by any other outstanding balance owed by or to the customer. Please allow 4 to 6 weeks for delivery. Offer available while quantities last.

Your Privacy: Harlequin Books is committed to protecting your privacy. Our Privacy Policy is available online at www.eHarlequin.com or upon request from the Reader Service. From time to time we make our lists of customers available to reputable third parties who may have a product or service of interest to you. If you would prefer we not share your name and address, please check here. ☐

COMING NEXT MONTH FROM

HARLEQUIN®
HISTORICAL

- **KLONDIKE FEVER**
by **Kate Bridges**
(Western)
Robbed at gunpoint, chained to a drifter, Lily thinks life can't get any
worse—until she realizes that she's shackled to the one man she's never
been able to forget!
Don't miss the continuation of Kate Bridges's thrilling Klondike series!

- **NO PLACE FOR A LADY**
by **Louise Allen**
(Regency)
Miss Bree Mallory has no time for the pampered aristocracy! She's
too busy running the best coaching company on the roads. But an
accidental meeting with an earl changes everything.
Join Louise Allen's unconventional heroine as she shocks Society!

- **A SINFUL ALLIANCE**
by **Amanda McCabe**
(Tudor)
Marguerite is exceptionally beautiful—and entirely deadly! Sent by a
king to assassinate the gorgeous Nicolai, she finds herself torn between
royal duty and ardent desire....
*Award-winning Amanda McCabe brings us scandal and seduction at
the Tudor court!*

- **THE WANTON BRIDE**
by **Mary Brendan**
(Regency)
With disgrace just a breath away, Emily ached for Mark's strong arms
to comfort her. Yet she held a secret—one that would surely prevent *any*
gentleman from considering her as a suitable bride....
*Can his passion overcome her fears? Find out in Mary Brendan's
Regency tale.*